WHAT THE CLUCK? IT'S MURDER

A FRANKIE CHANDLER MYSTERY

JACQUELINE VICK

Copyright © 2024 by Jacqueline Vick

All rights reserved.

No part of this book may be reproduced in any form or by any electronic or mechanical means, including information storage and retrieval systems, without written permission from the author, except for the use of brief quotations in a book review.

ISBN: 978-1-945403-37-8 (Paperback)

ISBN: 978-1-945403—30-9 (ebook)

ONE

"You can't make me."

I took a hurried step back from the source of my fear, stumbling over my own feet in the rush. The solid chest of Detective Martin Bowers broke my fall. He hooked his arms under mine to help me catch my balance.

Normally, I'd enjoy physical contact with the handsome police officer, currently off-duty. However, my attention remained on the black eyes that locked onto me in an unblinking stare. It didn't take a pet psychic, which I was, to tell those eyes held more than contempt. They held murder.

The eyes belonged to the snow-white face of a Leghorn hen, and she showed no signs of the happy, *aw shucks* attitude of Foghorn Leghorn, one of my childhood cartoon heroes.

Why on this beautiful early afternoon in March was I, Frankie Chandler, reluctant communicator with all things furry or feathered, facing off with a vicious hen?

It goes back to my best friend Penny's wedding cruise last fall. There had been laughter, tears, and a few murders.

Not that the murders were part of the agenda. They just happened, and I discovered the first body below my stateroom balcony.

Penny tattled to Detective Bowers in Wolf Creek, Arizona, and she made it sound as if I was a damsel in distress. That irritated me to no end, as Martin Bowers had made it clear he wanted nothing to do with me. It wasn't so much that he couldn't handle the embarrassment of dating a pet psychic. The clincher came when he, while holding my hand, got caught up in one of my psychic experiences with an angry feline, and he didn't like it.

Baby.

Anyway, he responded to Penny's request for a White Knight and joined the cruise a few days later, and in between finding corpses and searching for the kitty who held the key to solving the murders, Bowers and I had a few friendly moments. At the end of the cruise, the normally stoic detective approached me in an unusual state of nervousness to ask for another chance at romance. Or maybe it was a first chance since we had never made it to an actual date.

That was the good news. For balance, there had to be bad news. Bowers also wanted me to meet his sisters. All seven of them.

Yes, seven. After the death of his mother, Bowers had been raised by a week's worth of sisters who doted on him as if he were the pearl without price. The invitation to meet his guardians, the guardians who would hate me for stealing their

little brother away, was as enticing as a naked run through a minefield. I expected disapproval in the form of tight-lipped silence and sarcastic comments. Maybe a voodoo doll. Still, it was important to him, so after a few months of dating—I mean honest-to-goodness dating with dinners and goodnight kisses and things normal couples do—I finally gave in.

Now I was paying for my moment of weakness. Here I stood on June's ten-acre farm in Cave Bear, Arizona, almost paralyzed with fear. Maybe not a farm. More of a homestead. It was a lot of land with some cows, horses, several sheep, a few goats, and these damn chickens.

Bowers' eldest sister, June, was the only sibling I'd met so far, and though she intimidated me the way Sister Ellen did in high school English class, she seemed nice. So far. Maybe she was waiting for her six backups to arrive.

In response to my reaction to the angry chicken, Bowers rested his hands on my shoulders and chuckled. "It's a hen, Frankie. Not a pit bull."

Craning my neck sideways to address him without losing site of the bird, I said, "Bully breeds are snuggly, friendly pups unless someone's abused them. This—this *hen* wants me dead."

He sighed at what he considered unnecessary drama. "June said there's a gap in the western fence. I'm going to take a look. I'll be back in fifteen minutes. Maybe twenty. You'll be done by then. You should be done by then." He sighed again. "There's no earthly reason you won't be done by then. You're only collecting eggs."

I was momentarily distracted by the thought of Bowers, wearing a white t-shirt, blue jeans, and brown leather work boots, doing physical labor. Normally he's performing sedate activities like interviewing suspects or writing reports, but here in the wilds of the Arizona desert, his tall, lean body would be lifting heavy bags of feed, or shoveling hay to the horses. Maybe working up a sweat that would make his dark, wavy hair curl. Perhaps, while chopping wood, he might get hot and need to remove his shirt. I sucked in my breath. Outdoors-man Bowers might be the only highlight of this weekend.

"Tell you what." I picked up the basket and shoved it toward him. "Why don't *you* steal their young and *I'll* go look at the hole in the fence?"

"No can do."

The violent image of what the wannabe mother intended to do to me had left an impression. I stamped my foot, which was a prissy move, but I was one notch below terrified. "Why not?"

"First, how much experience do you have fixing fences? Second, and more important, there aren't any young to steal. The eggs haven't been fertilized. Animal husbandry 101. No rooster, no chick."

The beady eyes glaring at me sent out a powerful wave of longing that started in my belly and moved to my chest. As the ache intensified, tears filled my eyes. This was followed by a ferocious desire to hurt anyone who might hurt mine. My heart raced as my entire body tensed up in fight-or-flight mode.

Still riding the wave of emotions sent by the chicken, I twisted around, grabbed Bowers' shirt in my fists and shook him. "She doesn't agree with you."

Bowers and I have been through a lot, much of it involving my reactions—and occasional overreactions—to what animals tell me. Even after his first-hand experience with psychic phenomenon, he stubbornly refuses to discuss, acknowledge, or endorse what he refers to, vaguely, as *my thing*. Naturally, he ignored me.

He kissed my forehead, and with mock solemnity said, "Good luck. When I get back, I hope you'll have gathered your courage...and the eggs."

WHAT THE CLUCK? IT'S MURDER

And then he left me alone with the murderous chicken.

I sized up my surroundings in case I had to make a quick escape. The coop was a rectangular wooden building with a cement floor covered in earthy-smelling mulch. This was where the chickens slept and laid eggs and ate from PCV piping that released their food. They even had a water bottle with nipples they pecked at when they were thirsty and a round thingy that held little pebbles to help them break up their food. I shoved this last item aside with my foot to give me a clear escape path.

Several wooden clothes-drying racks leaned against one wall under a high wooden shelf, both providing places for the chickens to roost. Along the opposite wall, half a dozen nesting boxes sat atop a pine box about three-feet tall and ten feet long. It reminded me of the caskets they used in the Wild West.

The nesting boxes consisted of milk crates set on their sides and stuffed with hay. Bowers' sister had put up little privacy curtains, something I found hysterically funny until I opened one and found the angry chicken inside.

Most of the birds had abandoned the coop and moved to the run outside to scratch for bugs or do whatever chickens did to amuse themselves. Maybe Bowers was right. They didn't care, so why should I?

I moved down the row of nesting boxes and felt around each one. As I picked up the warm eggs and added them to my cache, the few birds remaining in the coop watched my progress with soft clucks. Too soon, I was back to old beady eyes.

Even though the window shutters kept the warm, spring sun out, and the temperature inside was a cool seventy degrees, sweat trickled down my back.

When June had asked me to perform this chore, I'd

foolishly thought, *"What an easy way to get into her good graces."* Stupid, stupid, stupid. If I blew this, she would think I was an idiot or, even worse, an incompetent female who'd spent her pampered life avoiding hard work.

That would not happen. Counting today, Friday, I had three days to win over those seven women, and I would not waste this opportunity because of a moody hen.

"Here chick-chick," I said in a sing-song voice as I stretched out my hand. "Be a nice girl."

Her body stiffened, and she hissed at me. I pulled back my fingers just in time to avoid a peck.

I gritted my teeth. "Look. That egg is just an egg. It's not a chick, so hand it over." Then I sent her an image of an egg cracking and no chick inside. I sensed her stiffen.

Reaching out my hand, slowly, I continued to hold eye contact. She stared back without blinking, though she trembled a little. My fingertips touched her feathers, and still she didn't move. They crept under her, and I splayed my fingers so they could surround the first egg. Gently, gently, I pulled.

"See? That didn't hurt."

And then the chicken from hell attacked.

TWO

"What in blazes happened to you?"

I had made my way up the hill from the coop to the back door leading into June's farmhouse, and I slumped against the door frame of the small cloakroom leading into the kitchen and stared, dazed.

At her question, I looked down at my hands and saw bloody scratches. The sleeves of my favorite blue sweatshirt hung in shreds. "Nothing. I mean, no big deal." I kept my tone casual, as if I fought chickens every day, because I didn't want to be labeled a problem on my first full day here. "I just need to wash up, that's all."

June pried the basket of eggs from my fingers and shooed me to the closest of the plain wooden chairs that surrounded a long oak table in the center of the room. The table was large enough to seat a dozen farm hands—or Bowers' sisters. As I sat and waited, she rummaged through the upper shelf of one of the white cabinets over the countertop.

While she conducted her search, I considered the first of my seven hurdles. She stood about five-feet-five and had a plump, sturdy body and short, curly hair that showed more gray than black. Her wide, expressive mouth made it possible to gauge her mood. Right now, the corners dipped in a frown.

"Was it Lola? I was afraid she was broody."

"Broody?"

"It means she wants to be a mom. She'll fight to hold on to her eggs."

She pulled down a first aid kit and beamed at it as if it had found her.

Paranoid Frankie wondered why Bowers' sister hadn't warned me about the broody hen before she sent me to collect the eggs. Did she want to see me fail?

She set the kit on the table. "Why didn't Marty help you?"

Though the question *sounded* innocent, I wondered if it were a test to see if I would blame her baby brother for my catastrophe. Did Marty ever take the blame for anything?

"He was busy," I murmured. That sounded neutral, unlike *he ignored my warnings and then abandoned me.*

Even as Paranoid Frankie chatted nonstop in my head, June bent her gray curls over me and gently checked my wounds with her warm hands. No one with such motherly instincts could wish another person harm. I was foolish to think she might want me to fail.

The methodical tick-tick of the egg timer had a calming effect, and my shoulders relaxed. Only then did I notice the scents of ginger and cinnamon wafting from the oven. Maybe if I sat still, she would reward me with a cookie.

Now that she had assessed the damage, June rooted through the kit. She had her back to the door, so she didn't see the grim expression on Bowers' face when he walked in the back door.

"The gap in the fence is—"

At the sound of his voice, she straightened up, and he caught sight of me and gaped.

"What happened?"

My hands flew to my face. "Am I maimed?"

He crossed the room. "Your face is fine." He gently took my hands and turned them over, assessing the damage while he pressed his lips together in a thin line. June selected a bottle of iodine and some bandages. "Lola's broody. You should have noticed. Aren't you supposed to be a detective?"

Bowers spread his arms wide. "What? The hen didn't do anything. How could I have known?"

His voice had a tinge of whine in it, as if he were reverting to his teenage self. I understood. The same thing happens to me when I'm in my mother's presence.

June gestured toward the basket. "There aren't nearly enough eggs for a morning collection. The darn bird's probably stealing from the other hens. Do I wait her out and see if she's serious? Or should I take the eggs and give her some golf balls to lie on?"

She was talking out loud, not asking for our input, but if she expected me to make the exchange, I fervently hoped for the former. She finished her handiwork and gave my shoulder a pat.

"You'll be fine."

I held up my tightly wrapped hands. Red splotches of iodine leaked through the white bandages. "I look like Frankenstein."

For such a stout, no-nonsense farm woman, June's laughter reminded me of bubbles. She gurgled.

"Your girlfriend's a card, Marty. And tough. She managed to hold on to the basket. Not one broken egg."

Maybe I wouldn't tell her I'd been holding it up as a shield.

As she packed up the kit and returned it to the cupboard, she asked, "Now, what were you saying about the fence?"

Bowers got the grim look again. "Someone cut the wire. Only the bottom two wires."

June turned around, and I got a peek at the expression I'd see if she decided I wasn't good enough for her baby brother. "None of my livestock has opposable thumbs, Marty."

"Exactly. You've had intruders."

"Is anyone missing?"

By anyone, I assumed she was talking about her chickens, since horses and cows are hard to miss.

She answered her own question. "We'll have to count the chickens tonight after they've roosted." Her glance rested on me and my Frankenstein hands. "I'm sorry to mess up your vacation like this. You shouldn't have had to collect the eggs, but after Duane didn't show up again this morning.... When that man gets off his bender, we're going to have words."

June had made the same complaint last night when we arrived, so I was up-to-speed on the family drama. Duane Stoddard was the hired help, and his absence was the reason I'd been doing his chores.

According to June, he was the nicest man whose only fault was to disappear occasionally and drink himself silly. I'd never even met the man, but a glance at my hands made me certain he would never be one of my favorite people.

Before I could tell her again that it was no big deal, she glanced at the apple pie-shaped clock over the kitchen sink.

"The first wave is due to arrive soon. I've got to get dinner on." She transferred her gaze to me. "I think you said you wanted to freshen up?"

Son-of-a-hen! My shredded shirt and Frankenstein hands might give Bowers' sisters the impression he had met me on a violent crime scene playing the corpse. The timer went off, and June's attention turned to removing the cookies from the oven.

Bowers took hold of my elbow and helped me to my feet. "Come on. I'll help you upstairs."

"And can you bring me down the laundry basket? I think it's on the chair in my room." June gave her little brother a sweet smile that didn't fool me. She had specifically given Bowers his old room at one end of the upstairs hallway and sent me to the room at the far end. I swear she patrolled at night to make sure we weren't up to any shenanigans. I had heard footsteps creaking the floorboards outside my bedroom last night.

"Will do," he said, and then he steered me to the staircase behind a door in the short hallway off the kitchen.

The stairwell was a narrow passage between two walls, almost claustrophobic, especially after you closed the downstairs door behind you. There wasn't room to walk side-by-side, so I took the lead, and Bowers followed.

The door at the bottom of the stairs opened, and June popped her head in. "I want to get a load started before company gets here, so don't be long, Marty."

"No problem."

She left the door open, so I stifled my giggle until I reached the top of the stairs. When Bowers heard me laugh, his eyes reflected relief, and he pulled me in for a hug.

"You doing okay?"

I stepped back and held my hands in front of his face.

"Your sister thinks these are an aphrodisiac. I mean, what does she think I could do with these?"

He cracked a smile, but his eyes got a smoldering look that gave me goosebumps. "I'm sure I could work around them."

He kissed my palms one at a time, and then he leaned into me. At the last minute, he pulled away and stepped back. "Frankie..."

"No need to explain. I can smell myself."

When we got to my door, he frowned down at me. "Are you going to be able to..." He motioned toward my hands. "I could help you...you know."

"I'm sure I'll manage."

June called from downstairs. "Marty! Where's my basket?"

Bowers rolled his eyes and called out. "I'm just helping Frankie get undressed!"

"Don't say that," I hissed, even as I heard thumping from the stairwell.

June rounded the corner, dish towel in hand. She stopped when she saw us standing in the hallway, fully clothed. "Oh, you!" She flicked the towel at his rear end. "He always was a joker, Frankie. You remember that."

She dragged him down the stairs, and as I went into my room, I heard him say, "What about your clothes basket?"

THREE

I sighed as I closed my bedroom door and wondered why I couldn't have fallen for an only child. On a scale of one-to-ten, my personal skills rated a three, probably because I could count on one hand the number of folks I liked, including my parents. I preferred animals.

The dresser against the wall came with a large, square mirror, and when I stood in front of it, I sucked in my breath at the crazy lady staring back at me. My shoulder-length auburn curls resembled a bird's nest, and I had a smudge of something green on my cheek. I sniffed the air. Add the smell of fright sweat and chicken poop and I made quite the catch. Bowers' sisters would be impressed.

I shook myself to chase off the Negative Nellies and tried to channel Positive Frankie. All I needed was a quick cleaning and a change of clothes.

I gingerly pulled my sweatshirt over my head, tossed it on the floor, and assessed the damage. The scratches on my arms only marked the surface and weren't bleeding. Nothing permanent.

June's voice called out to her husband from the

backyard under my bedroom window. If I hurried, I'd be in and out of the bathroom before Carl came upstairs. After establishing the coast was clear, I skittered across the hall in my bra and jeans.

The upstairs bathroom had a claw-footed bathtub but no shower, so I settled for a basin bath. My arms stung a little as I held them under the running water, and then I splashed my face a few times and scrubbed at the green smear with soap.

The bathroom faced the drive that ran along the side of the house. The crunch of gravel announced a vehicle's arrival, so I kicked into high. After locating a washcloth in the top drawer of a slim white dresser next to the sink, I gave myself a quick going over with the citrus-scented soap, rinsed, and then dropped the washcloth into the hamper.

I cracked the door open, ready to make a dash to my room, but the upturned face of a young boy reaching for the knob greeted me. My appearance startled him into taking a step back. Brown eyes studied the portion of my face peering through the crack, while his wide mouth drooped in a frown of curiosity.

"Who are you? I have to pee."

I tossed his question back at him.

"Who are you?"

"Marc."

"Well, Marc. You need to leave."

He pushed on the door. "I told you. I have to pee."

"Why don't you use the downstairs bathroom?"

"My dad's in there, and Mom said I'd better come up here."

"Well, I have to get to my room. In private."

His mouth spread into a grin that revealed a tiny gap between his front teeth. "Are you naked?"

Kids are not my specialty. I'm never sure what to say to them, but I was certain that my nakedness, even partial, was not an appropriate topic.

"One of the chickens scratched me and I had to wash the cuts."

He pushed on the door again. "Are you bloody? Let me see."

I shoved back. "I had to take my top off to assess the damage. So, you need to clear out. Just for a minute, okay? Then you can urinate to your heart's content. And Marc? Let's keep this between ourselves."

After reluctantly agreeing, he moved to the stairwell and disappeared down the steps. Just in case, I grabbed the embroidered hand towel off the rack and covered my front with it. I waited a beat and then fled across the hall. Just before I closed my door, I caught sight of his little head peering around the corner. Darn, darn, and double darn.

I opened the door to the small closet and looked over my limited selection. We were only staying for a long weekend, so I'd packed accordingly, not that I had a lot to choose from in my closet back home. Most often, I wore a sweatshirt and jeans.

Animals don't care what you look like.

Was it too early in the day for a formal dinner? Or would it be casual, since all the siblings knew each other? Would they dress up to meet me and expect me to do the same? If they didn't dress up, what did that say about their opinion of me? I huffed at this imaginary slight. If they were planning to diss me, maybe I should throw on sweatpants and a t-shirt.

I took a steadying breath and smiled, remembering my mother's words of wisdom to a teenage Frankie. *"Don't be the slob in the room. It puts you on uneven footing because, even if no one else cares, you will."*

I wiggled into a pair of black slacks and slipped on an emerald-green blouse. After using my fingers on my hair because the comb wouldn't get through the tangles, I swiped on some lip blush, smacked my lips together and studied my reflection in the mirror. Auburn shoulder-length curls under control. Check. All buttons buttoned. Check. Black pants wrinkle-free. Check. As much makeup as I could stand. Check. I decided I wouldn't embarrass Bowers. Actually, I looked good.

After a few minutes of debate, I tore off the bandages and dropped them in the wastebasket on my way out of the room. I didn't need anyone to make a clever connection between Frankie and Frankenstein.

FOUR

The first time I saw little Marc's mother, I figured I should call it a day and return to Wolf Creek a single woman. I freely admit she intimidated me.

After I stepped out of the stairway and into the downstairs hallway, I followed the voices outside. June and Bowers stood next to a blue Honda parked on the gravel patch behind the house.

Facing Bowers with her back to me, a tall woman with glossy black hair cut into a fashionable bob waved her hands as she talked. She wore a stylish white blouse, blue jeans, and high-heeled leather boots. Slightly plump, enough to have curves, she could have been a magazine model, if magazines reflected real women.

I ran my hands over my hips to wipe the sweat from my palms and stepped off the back stoop just as she punched Bowers on the arm. I must have made a noise because his gaze moved to me and she spun around and shrieked.

"You *are* real! I thought Marty made you up to hide the fact he's gay."

Now I understood where Bowers had perfected his

neutral cop expression. He wore it now. "Aggy, Aggy. You're just jealous because vampires don't have beating hearts. Tom only married you out of pity."

Tom, almost as tall as Bowers, slim, and with blond hair graying at his sideburns, held up his hands. "Keep me out of this."

Agatha snorted, and June, leaning against the car, wore the tolerant smile of a parent who was secretly enjoying the banter.

Bowers motioned and grimaced. "This *person* is my sister, Agatha. Agatha, this is Frankie."

When Agatha swept across the gravel, gathering speed as she closed in, I took a step back. She wrapped her arms around me and shook me from side-to-side.

"Let the girl breath," June's husband, Carl, called out as he approached us from the direction of the barn. His gray mustache twitched as he smiled. "You don't want to scare her away."

"I'm just happy to meet the figment of Marty's imagination." Agatha gripped my arms in strong fingers and pushed me back for inspection. "Tell us about yourself. Are you from Arizona? Does your family live around here? Do you work with the Wolf Creek Police Department, too?" As she pulled me through the back door, she grinned over her shoulder at Bowers. "Or is she a criminal you rehabilitated?"

Following close behind, Bowers refused to make eye contact, and at the mention of my work, his bland expression returned. I straightened my shoulders, sucked in a deep breath, and prepared for the first interrogation.

As soon as we were all inside the kitchen, I tried to remember Agatha's questions.

"Well, um, I'm from Loon Lake, Wisconsin," I began,

but the loud rumble of a truck engine drowned me out. I raised my voice. "My family lives there."

Distracted, June wandered to the kitchen sink and looked out the window. "The Texas contingent has arrived."

A heavy slam of vehicle doors marked the couple's progress, and then the back door swung open so hard it hit the wall. A short woman walked in holding a pan.

"You can all relax, now. I'm here!"

Though I knew June was the eldest sibling, this sister looked older. She had soft white curls and the skin on her narrow face had weathered to the point of leather, but her crystal-blue eyes were sharp.

The man who followed her in looked just as old with his bald head and stooped posture.

The woman held up the pan as if presenting the Bowers family with an award. Apparently, it was, because everyone exclaimed and oohed. Even Bowers wore a look of reverence as he stepped forward, pulled by an invisible force.

"Is that strawberry-rhubarb crunch?" Bowers held his face inches from the pan.

Up to that point, I felt—erroneously—I was prepared to meet whatever questions Bowers' sisters sent my way. And then the latest arrival opened her mouth.

Her face crinkled into a deceptively sweet smile. "We want to make a good impression on your girlfriend." She turned her cheek and accepted a kiss from Bowers. "Silly term. You're too old for a girlfriend."

"Until she's his fiancée, girlfriend is good enough for me," June said as she took the pan and placed it on a wicker trivet on the counter. "It's better than lover."

"We're not . . .we haven't...." I desperately looked to Bowers, but he had the cop-face on again. Just kill me now.

"Where are my manners?" June put her arm around the woman. "This is my sister, Cecelia, and that's her husband, Joe. They came all the way from Texas to meet you."

Cecelia folded her hands in front of her chest and said, "Well. Let's have a look at you."

Bowers recovered his manners and escorted me forward for my introduction. "This is Frankie."

She looked me over. "Frankie, huh?"

"After St. Francis," Bowers said.

That brought on more exclamations of approval than the crunch did.

"You were just about to tell us what you did for a living," Agatha said.

I held back a glare. "Was I? I, um, specialize in animal behavior."

"Except chicken behavior," June offered. "Lola had a go at her."

Agatha noticed my hands and gasped. "Broody?"

"As a teenage girl."

"Why wasn't Duane feeding the hens?" she demanded.

June sighed. "He's off doing goodness knows what. Haven't seen him since yesterday afternoon."

Carl and Tom passed through the room with the luggage and headed upstairs.

"You should just get rid of him." Agatha brushed the air with her hand, clearing Duane off the slate. "You don't need someone like that hanging around here. I'm surprised he hasn't stolen all the silverware by now. And I don't want him around Marc."

"Now, Aggie, everybody makes mistakes. Duane has paid for his."

Cecelia frowned. "Are you talking about Duane Stoddard?"

WHAT THE CLUCK? IT'S MURDER

Agatha crossed her arms. "He's missing in action. I still think you should take an inventory of the silver."

Cecelia nodded. "I agree that he's not a good influence."

As the sisters berated the absent Duane, my mind wandered to important things, like what they were wearing. They all had on blue jean. Would they think I was a prima donna in my dress pants and blouse?

In a self-conscious move, I ran a hand over my black dress pants, pausing mid-buttock. Casually, I rubbed my finger back over the spot where I thought—yes. There was a small tear. My cat, Emily, who delights in hanging from the clothes in my closet, had ripped a small hole in the seat of my slacks.

Was it noticeable? How big was it? I poked at it with my fingertip and felt the loose threads snap. Well, now the hole was bigger.

Casually, I stepped backwards toward the outside of the group, grateful that I preferred briefs to bikinis. I wasn't following the conversation, so I jumped when I heard my name.

"Isn't it funny that Frankie works with animals," Agatha said with an impish grin in my direction. "Just like St. Francis, right?"

"That is a coincidence." Cecelia didn't seem to trust coincidences. She pulled back her head and looked down her nose. "Frances is the name you were born with?"

"Yes, ma'am."

"Oh, Cissy!" Agatha laughed. "You're a ma'am."

I hadn't meant it as an insult, but with Agatha's help, Cecelia would sure see it that way.

"I didn't mean that you look old. Because you don't look old. I mean, as a society, we usually equate white hair with the elderly, but that's not fair." I finished lamely with, "I don't subscribe to agism."

It just came out. Bowers pinched my side, and I backpedaled.

"I was brought up to call women over twenty ma'am."

"You didn't call me ma'am." That came from Agatha, who I was starting to dislike, but then she burst out laughing and punched me in the arm. "Just having fun with you."

Carl and Tom returned, and Cecelia lost interest in me. "So, are we going to eat, or what?"

I perked up at the thought of sitting down before anyone noticed my exposed underwear. White, of course. I planned to invest in black underwear the minute I got back to Wolf Creek.

Savory smells of garlic and rosemary had replaced the sweet odor of cookies. My stomach growled. "Don't we need to wait for everyone to get here?" I asked Bowers.

June opened the oven door. "We are all here. Dym called and said she had plans she couldn't cancel. She isn't coming until tomorrow."

I leaned close to Bowers and kept my voice low. "Dim?"

He put his mouth next to my ear. "Dymphna. Patron saint of nervous disorders. Irish, if that helps."

When I giggled, Cecelia's sharp eyes locked onto us. "Would you care to share the joke?"

They had to notice my face flush. Cecelia had it in for me, because Agatha and Tom were in the corner whispering and giggling like schoolgirls, but they hadn't received a reprimand. Operation Defend Baby Brother from the Trollop had begun.

"It's nothing," I muttered. "Just, Dymphna is an unusual name."

To my surprise, her features softened into a smile. "Our

mother named us after her favorite saints in the hopes we would follow their examples. Dymphna was named after the patron saint of mental illnesses. Mother hoped she'd be a psychiatrist. I owe my name to the patron saint of music."

June pulled one of those huge pans they use at restaurants out of the stove and peeled back the foil, releasing a burst of steam. "Cissy plays a mean organ."

Cecelia nodded to accept the praise and then pointed at Agatha. "Patron saint of nurses."

Agatha grinned. "I'm a computer programmer. Still, Mom hoped one of us would work in the medical field."

Holding up her hand, Cecelia bent a finger as she named off the remaining sisters. "Edith's name saint is Edith Stein, naturally, because of her high intelligence and love of learning. Mary and Martha are kind of obvious." She glanced at Bowers. "I wonder why she didn't name you Lazarus. Seems kind of mean to leave their brother out of it."

I glanced up at Bowers. "So, who are you named after?"

"Martin de Porres."

Cecelia barked out a laugh. "Mom botched that one. Saint Martin was a lay Dominican. She thought he was a priest. She had hopes for Marty."

Great. Not only was I stealing Bowers from his sisters but also from God Himself.

"But, what about June?"

Cecelia's brow furrowed. "That's the month in which she was born. Mother got the idea about the saints later. Are you Catholic?"

Before I could answer, a loud clattering descended the stairs, the door flew open, and out popped the kid I'd run into upstairs. Agatha placed a hand on his shoulder and moved him forward.

"This is our son, Marc."

Foolish me believed the kid would keep our bargain and pretend he'd never met me before. I half bent and said, "Marc, I'm Frankie."

The kid smirked. "We met already." He pointed at me. "That's the naked lady."

Silence. Complete and utter silence. And every pair of eyes in the room fixed on me, waiting to give me the benefit of the doubt but wanting an answer. Except Bowers. His raised brows gave him a wistful look, as if, having never seen me naked, he regretted that the kid had gotten the jump on him.

Marc shifted his shoulders, pleased at the reaction his news had earned him, and he grinned at me to thank me for my role in it.

Still bending to his level, I said, "How old are you, Marc?"

Agatha squeezed his shoulders and glared at me. "He's only ten!"

I nodded. "Then you know the difference between a lie and, well, let's say exaggerating for fun."

His grin got wider, and I noticed the doubt creeping into Agatha's eyes.

"Did you see me naked?"

"Ugh! That would have been gross!"

Bowers let loose a relieved chuckle.

Agatha twisted her son to face her. "Why would you say something like that?"

The kid wasn't fazed. "I saw her bra."

"What color was it?" I asked, sweetly.

He scrunched up his face in a frown. "Purple."

I shook my head.

"Oh, yeah. It was pink."

"Wrong again."

"I couldn't see it under the towel."

Everyone breathed a sigh of relief.

"Marc's purity is unstained," Carl said with a laugh. "Now, let's eat."

First, I excused myself and slipped into the downstairs bathroom at the end of the hallway. Turning my back to the mirror over the sink, looking over my shoulder, and then standing on tiptoe gave me the view I needed. It's possible paranoia had taken hold, but the glare of white underwear peeking out from my black pants seemed as obvious as a neon sign.

I untucked my blouse and tugged at the hem. From my waist to the hemline, the fabric was wrinkled—the result of being tucked in for almost an hour.

Since both options were unacceptable, I flipped a mental coin and then stuffed my shirt back into my pants. I'd have to keep my backside pointed away from Bowers' family the rest of the night. Or, I could walk around with my hands on my butt.

I should have thrown the towel in.

FIVE

As Bowers escorted me to the dining room, he explained that only four sisters would be here this time around. He squeezed my hand as if to stave off disappointment, so I gave him a smile that said I understood and would bear through it. Inside, I was thrilled. I wanted to burst into song. Four sisters were challenge enough for me.

Bowers and I took our seats on the window side of the dining room table with the afternoon sun on our backs. Since June had already set the table, we only had to watch and admire as the food processed in.

June carried a large tray of crispy fried chicken that promised leftovers. Carl followed with mashed potatoes and rolls, while Agatha carried the gravy and fresh, steamed green beans. I was happy to note they approved of butter and had put two dishes on the table.

I looked forward to eating, and not just because of the wonderful odors filling my nostrils. With their own mouths full, Bowers' sisters would have to give their questions a rest. And then I got my first hint that wishes were for fishes.

Agatha shoved Bowers out of his chair and Cecelia took

the chair on my other side, surrounding me. Since Marc slid onto the seat next Agatha—and who was going to chase the young away from its mother?—Bowers was forced to the opposite side of the table.

Carl led grace, adding thanks for the safe arrival of everyone present, and then we all served ourselves family style. I had my food groups segregated on my plate so as not to mix flavors and was ready to dig in when Agatha passed me the butter from my right the same time Cecilia held out the gravy boat from my left.

Were they fussing to make sure the guest had everything she needed? Or was this a subtle game to see which sister I preferred? Perhaps they wanted the expose me as a glutton, heaping tasty fats on my food with abandon. Feeling clever, I took both their offerings at the same time.

Holding the butter plate in my right hand, I poured a little gravy next to my mashed potatoes with my left, since I prefer to dip as necessary. Then I crossed my left hand to Agatha to hand off the gravy so I could apply butter to everything but the chicken. Since Cecelia declined the butter, I set the dish down and prepared to tuck in.

Cecilia stared at my plate. "Did you get enough? That's not enough gravy to cover a French fry."

I frowned at my plate, which was perfect. "I can always add more."

"Here."

Agatha reached over me with the gravy boat. I held my hand over my plate in the manner of a diner refusing the waiter's offer to pour more wine, but she poured anyway. Gravy rolled off the back of my hand and between my fingers to drench my veggies and roll in brown sauce until it spilled over the edge of my plate.

Now I had soup. I didn't want soup. I cautiously shook my hand over my food and wiped off the rest with the blue cotton napkin resting under my silverware.

"Um, thanks."

"Is there any left for me?" Marc cried. He sent a withering glare in my direction.

June had to go back to the kitchen for a refill. When she returned and started on her own dinner, she nodded to Carl. "Did Marty tell you someone cut the fence in the front pasture?"

Her husband looked at Bowers, who also nodded. "That's a bugger." He chewed thoughtfully. "And odd that they would bother with us." He explained for my benefit. "Livestock thieves usually pick places with more animals, so it's not as noticeable when a few go missing."

"What else would they be after?" I asked.

"That's the question."

"Maybe it was teens messing around," Tom offered, helping himself to more chicken.

June announced that Marty planned to count the chickens when he put them away tonight, and that seemed to satisfy Carl.

I'd rescued most of my mashed potatoes from under the blanket of gravy, and I discovered that smothered green beans weren't bad. I had to use a knife and fork to eat my soggy roll. Fortunately, my chicken had been spared.

As I took a bite of drumstick, savoring the crunchy skin and moist meat, Agatha leaned in wearing a wicked grin.

"What do you call a chicken that stops laying eggs?"

I stopped chewing. "Old?"

She swept a hand toward the serving plate. "Dinner!"

Dropping the leg, I covered my mouth to stem the instinct to spit out my food, something I haven't had to worry about since I was ten months old. Marc laughed so hard milk came out his nose.

My voice came out a choked whisper. "Lola?"

The sisters reacted with loud laughter. Even Bowers pressed his lips together to hold back his grin.

Cecelia pointed her fork at the pan. "Math's not your strong suit, unless you've met a chicken with four legs."

I wasn't about to take guff from a woman who ate fried chicken with a fork, but this was, after all, Bowers' sister, so I tempered my answer. "I hadn't gotten around to counting them."

"Don't worry," June assured me. "It's nobody you know."

Marc shook his drumstick at me. "Grampa says never name the food."

"That's right," Carl said. "So Lola's safe."

My throat constricted as I swallowed, so I washed it down with the glass of water provided with my table setting.

"What's the matter?" Agatha's gaze held a challenge. "Fried chicken's my sister's specialty. She made it just for you."

Everyone stopped eating. It's possible they each were calculating how many extra pieces they could have if I skipped dinner, but it was more likely they had never heard anything more offensive than a guest refusing to eat June's famous chicken.

June waved her hand. "Don't nag the girl. If she doesn't like chicken, I can scrounge up something else for her to eat."

I considered how wise it would be to insult the family matriarch just as I was feeling comfortable around her. The smell of chicken and spices wafting up my nose decided me. I didn't know these chickens any more than I knew the chickens I ate at Dina's Diner. I couldn't make this personal.

With the determination of a pious martyr, I picked up my drumstick and returned to enjoying the best fried chicken I'd ever tasted.

"This is delicious."

Take that, Agatha.

As I helped myself to a second piece, earning a pleased smile from June and a relieved grin from Bowers, I hoped fervently that Dymphna would be the nice sister.

SIX

Dinner finally ended. I excused myself and cleaned my hands in the downstairs bathroom. When I came out, the others had cleared the dishes, and coffee and rhubarb crunch were being handed around. I followed the procession into the living room.

Agatha dropped into one corner of a large sectional couch as if it were her rightful place. Tom, Joe, and Cecelia joined her there. June took the beige recliner opposite Carl near the fireplace.

As I looked for a spot to sit, Cecelia said, "You never answered. Are you Catholic?"

My smile lacked enthusiasm, probably because Penny's wedding was the last time I had been in a church. "Born and baptized." Which was true.

"How do you like Our Lady of Fatima?" Agatha asked.

Was this a test? As I had nothing against the woman who foretold civilization's doom in the early 1900s—she was just the messenger—I said, "I like her fine."

"The statue," Agatha said, smirking.

"Which statue?"

Bowers walked over to a picture of the Sacred Heart. Under it was a statue or Our Lady in a white robe with a blue mantel.

"Oh, that statue," I said, trying to cover my ignorance. "I thought you meant the one at the shrine." There had to be a shrine, right? And what shrine would be complete without a statue?

"Lovely," I murmured, touching the smooth base. What was I, British? No American says lovely without sounding pompous, but the sisters agreed with me.

"It was Mother's," June offered.

I pulled my hand away. "Then it must mean a lot to you."

June smiled. "It does."

I made a note to look up images of Marian apparitions before I went to bed in case there were any other statues lurking. And Catholicism. If I didn't bone up on my faith, they'd probably banish me to the netherworld or force me to wear a scarlet letter—H for Heathen. If they wanted a battle, I'd bring it to them with a plethora of insightful, theological remarks.

There were two spots left on the couch, but Marc, who had been toying with the ceramic frogs on an end table, plopped down and sprawled out, taking up both places. After stealing his gravy, I wasn't about to ask the kid to give up his spot, so I took the remaining rocking chair and let Bowers nudge his nephew aside to make room.

When I finally sat, I rejected the natural impulse to rock, intending to remain invisible in case Agatha and Cecelia got any more playful ideas. I was afraid I might react with something other than meek chuckles.

My first taste of strawberry-rhubarb crunch foiled my

plan. The sweet strawberries and sugary crunch topping balanced perfectly with the face-puckering tart rhubarb. I'm sure I made a noise because Cecelia glanced over and smiled. I should have seen it coming.

"Do you bake?"

I stopped chewing and swallowed. "You mean cakes and pies and cookies?"

"Cookies don't count," Agatha said. "Anyone can bake a cookie."

"Cake's my favorite," Marc said.

"We had an apple pie for Thanksgiving," Bowers offered. He had brought that to my house, along with appetizers so my guests wouldn't starve.

"Was the crust latticed?" Agatha asked, sweetly.

I looked her in the eye. "It sure was." Then I took another bite of the crunch and ended the conversation by asking Cecelia for the recipe, knowing that particular question was every celebrated home-cook's nightmare. A few months ago, the police come close to accusing my aunt of murdering a woman over a fifty-year-old recipe.

Cecelia frowned and turned to Agatha. She brought up someone they both knew, and the other siblings joined in and caught up on the latest news. Their funny stories made little sense to me since I hadn't a clue who they were talking about. They had their own jargon, which made it more confusing. After Agatha railed against an undermining co-worker, Cecelia said, "Drum roll!", and the sisters broke into fits of laughter.

Bowers had shifted to join Tom and Joe, but I couldn't hear enough of their conversation to follow. Carl fell asleep, and I closed my eyes in imitation and hoped everyone would ignore me.

Around eight-thirty, June stifled a yawn. "I'm usually in

bed by now." She sat up straight with a jerk. "The chickens! Darn that Duane! It's his job to lock them up."

Bowers stood and stretched. "Frankie and I will take care of them. Besides, you wanted me to take a headcount, remember?"

Holding onto the chair arms, June pulled herself to her feet and patted his arm. "Thanks, Marty. You too, Frankie. Let me know if we're missing anyone in the morning. I'm going to bed."

Bowers headed to the kitchen, and I followed. He handed me Carl's jacket off a hook on the wall by the back door and grabbed a vest for himself. After taking a flashlight from the corner shelf, Bowers led the way outside.

And that's when the *actual* nightmare began.

"That went well," I said, closing the door behind me.

Bowers turned, wrapped his arms around me, and pulled me in for a hard kiss. When he let me go, I had to recover my breath. He grinned.

"So, is your bra purple or pink?"

Taking my cue from Agatha, I punched his chest, though I'm sure he didn't feel it through his quilted vest. "Neither."

"I guess I'll have to lurk outside the bathroom if I want to find out."

I moved to punch him again, but he pulled me in for another kiss, this one gentler and lasting a full minute. Then he took my hand, and we headed for the coop.

An enormous shadow loomed in front of us. Cecelia and Joe had arrived in a huge Suburban pulling a camper. I stopped and stared.

"That is so cool."

"You don't see many Suburbans these days."

I nudged Bowers. "Not the truck. The camper. When I

was a kid, I thought the ultimate would be to spend the night in a camper. Sleeping in a nook sounded as much fun as bunk beds."

"Note to self. Frankie likes to sleep in strange places. Do you like to camp?"

Leaning my head back, I admired the night sky. Since downtown Cave Bear was about five miles away, the sky over June's farm seemed black and was blanketed with stars. Typical of the desert, the temperature had dropped along with the sun, and I pulled the heavy jacket closed and wrapped my arms around my middle. The only sound was an occasional snort from the horses in the back field. It was both creepy and cool.

"I enjoyed camping on Penny's farm. I don't know that I want to be in the wilderness with only a sheet of canvas between me and a bear."

Bowers chuckled and slung his arm around my shoulder. "I'd protect you."

With a full tummy and Bowers to myself on a romantic, starry night, I relaxed. And then I remembered *the incident* and wondered if I could recover my reputation.

"I hope that wasn't too awkward for your family back there. Me and my nakedness."

Bowers smiled down at me. "They're probably laughing about it right now."

"Because I sent the kid away before I ran to my room."

"You should have known better. But I forgot. You didn't have brothers. Boys' hormones are constantly warping their brains and causing them to do things like lurk around corners, all for a peek at a strange lady's bra."

"I'll bring my bathrobe with me next time." If there was a next time.

"Good call. I hope you realize that my sisters were just

teasing you at dinner. And in the kitchen before dinner. And after dinner."

"Oh, sure." I lied because I needed at least one person on my side. If I told him I thought they were banshees on the attack, he might feel the need to defend his guardians.

He unlatched the gate to the large, fenced-in run that surrounded the coop. There weren't any stragglers scratching around for bugs, so we headed inside. It only took a glance to tell there were chickens missing. Half the roosts were empty.

"Aw, hell." Bowers pulled back the curtains on the nesting boxes, but they were all empty except Lola's. "I fixed the break in the fence while you were getting dressed, and with all the activity as people arrived, I didn't expect the thieves to try again tonight."

While he ranted, an excitement built in my chest. It was weird. Frenetic. My breathing became short and shallow, and I put a hand over my heart, hoping to slow it down. My shoulders shook.

"What are you doing? Trying to find the chickens with your mind?" Bowers tried to make it sound funny, but he had enough belief in my gift to make him nervous.

I sniffed the air a few times and finally took a deep breath, trying to take in more of the heavenly aroma scenting the air. I'd smelled it before. At dinner? No. It wasn't fried chicken or mashed potatoes. And how could I be hungry? I'd stuffed myself and still managed to fit in rhubarb crunch for desert, but it was as if someone had set down the most irresistible plate of food in front of me, and I wanted it. I wanted it bad. That smell. A vague memory. I should recognize it. I'd been around it before. Not often, but often enough to recognize it.

And then I knew.

WHAT THE CLUCK? IT'S MURDER

"Son-of-a-cave-bear!"

I grabbed the flashlight from Bowers and moved outside, swinging the beam around the run. Light reflected off the chicken wire and into the darkness beyond. He stepped out the door and watched me.

"What is it?"

I froze and held up my hand. "Quiet."

I heard a soft noise. A satisfied purring, and it was coming from around the corner of the coop. Steeling myself for what might be lurking, I rounded the corner.

"There they are," Bowers said when we saw a cluster of feathered butts surrounding something on the ground. He took a step forward and then blocked me with his arm. "Stay put."

It was too late. I'd seen the shoe. I clutched at his outstretched arm. "I-I—-"

He pried the flashlight from my fingers and his arm from my hands and moved forward, nudging the birds out of the way with the toe of his boot. They responded with angry squawks. He crouched down and reached out his hand but then changed his mind and pulled it back.

I crept closer. "Is he—?"

Stupid question. No one alive would let a gang of chickens peck at his face. And his arms. And everything else.

Bowers stood and took me by the shoulders. "Listen to me. I want you to go back and call the police."

"Look at all that blood." That was the smell. Blood. I swayed.

"Look at me."

I did and found comfort in the quick flash of concern in his dark blue eyes.

"Go to the house. Call the police. Keep everyone inside."

Turning away from the gruesome sight, I walked with stiff shoulders until I reached the gate. And then I ran.

SEVEN

All friendly chatter stopped the minute I walked into the room. Cecelia, who had commandeered the rocking chair in my absence, stopped rocking. It must have been my expression because Agatha paled, jumped up and said, "Where is Marty?"

I cleared my throat, but my voice still cracked when I said, "Telephone?"

Me and my cell phone don't hang out a lot.

Agatha pulled hers from her back pocket and held it out. "You need to call someone? Is everything okay?"

Everyone knows the bearer of bad news gets blamed. Eventually, they would learn the details, but I didn't want those details to come from me. I chose my words carefully.

"Um, no. Definitely...no."

"What is it? What's the matter?" Agatha demanded.

My brain, trying to reign in words that might panic my audience, was having the same luck as a crossing guard trying to hold back stampeding fourth graders on the last day of school. Valiantly I scanned my choices: bloody corpse, mutilation, desecration, and the oversized giant trying to push his way past my lips—murder. But was it murder?

The strain proved too much for me, and the words gushed out in an unintelligible stream.

"I'd call, but you better. I don't know the address here and I don't want to wake June . . . ." Carl sat up in his chair, awakened by the commotion. "Maybe Carl would be better, and since I don't live here and the police won't know who I am—they might even think I'm a crank—it should probably be a familiar voice, familiar to them, and I—"

Agatha slapped me, harder than necessary, I thought. *"Where is Marty?"*

I shook my head and let the marbles fall back in place.

"We need to call the police. Bowers and I found Duane, and—" I hauled in a deep breath, "he isn't doing too well."

The color returned to Agatha's face, and she punched some numbers into her smartphone. "Then we need an ambulance."

My gaze went to Marc who to me looked like one gigantic set of ears. I tried to soften the news. "Worse than that."

Cecelia thought the young one needed toughening up. "You mean he's dead?"

Marc shot off the couch and hurried to the door. The thought of the kid seeing Duane's mangled face reduced me to barking out orders as if he were one of my animal clients.

"Stop! Come touch!" I automatically held out my hand, realizing too late that I didn't have a treat.

It worked. The kid skid to a halt and turned around.

"Bowers said no one should leave the house."

Going off my reaction, Tom sprang to his feet and matched my volume. "Marc! Stay here."

The youngster looked at us in turn, and he obviously

thought we had lost our minds. "But Uncle Marty might need my help."

"Wait until he asks for it," Tom said in a more reasonable tone.

I didn't think the rule applied to Carl, who headed for the kitchen.

"Wait." I slipped off his jacket and handed it to him, and a few seconds later, the back door closed behind him.

Agatha held up a finger to quiet us. "Yes, this is Agatha Petrie calling from the Baxter place off The Old Road. Yes. June Baxter is my sister. I'd like to report . . ." She covered the phone. "What am I reporting?"

Killer hens? I didn't know how Duane died. He might have had a heart attack. Would the charge be rude behavior with a corpse? Could you charge a chicken? Would law enforcement put them down now that they'd tasted blood? I didn't want to be responsible for the extermination of June's entire flock. "Tell them there is a dead man by the chicken coop and Bowers told me to call."

The operator must have heard me, because Agatha explained who Bowers was and identified him as a cop. She said some more, but I couldn't hear her over the ringing in my ears. As soon as she disconnected the call, I started to tremble.

Agatha put her mom skills to work and retrieved a handwoven blanket from the back of the couch. She wrapped it around my shoulders and led me to the kitchen. As if by consensus, everyone gathered around the table while Cecelia made coffee, the American version of tea for shock. Marc was the first to instigate conversation.

"What did the dead guy look like?" he demanded.

I sipped my coffee and made a face. Without the addition of cream, it tasted bitter, as if it had percolated for a hundred hours for the benefit of sleep-deprived cowboys driving cattle. "I don't want to think about it."

"Was he blue? Because dead people turn blue. At least they do in *Zombie World*."

My expression must have gone blank because Agatha explained. "It's a magazine." She narrowed her eyes at Marc. "A magazine he probably shouldn't be reading."

The boy clapped his hands together, and I jumped.

"Is he going to turn into a zombie?" He leaned his head over to look at his mom. "Maybe we should burn the body."

"Definitely shouldn't be reading," Tom mumbled.

I cringed. Hadn't the poor man's corpse suffered enough indignities? Agatha ruffled her son's hair and murmured a response I didn't catch. It didn't have any impact on Marc because he swung back to me.

"Did he have a sword sticking out of his chest? Maybe he was the victim of a ninja attack. Was his face like this?"

He cocked his head, rolled his eyes back, and twisted his features into a horrible grimace. I scooted my chair around to face him.

"Look, kiddo. Why don't I tell your mom and dad about it later, and then they can decide what they want to tell you?"

That earned me an approving nod from Agatha. Maybe not enough approval to make up for flashing her son, but it was a start.

Cecelia placed a glass of milk in front of the boy and asked if anyone wanted a refill. The coffee continued to percolate because she wanted to have enough for the police.

When the law finally arrived, they weren't announced by sirens or flashing lights. Only the crunch of gravel let us know they were here. Agatha and Tom exchanged glances, and Tom put a protective-or possibly restraining—hand on their son's shoulder.

After a knock on the door, Cecelia let in a tall blond man in a black uniform and his shorter, huskier sidekick. The tall man spoke.

"I'm Marshal Kipper. This is Deputy Macoritto."

Did he say marshal? As in Marshal Wyatt Earp? I'd never seen a real marshal before. He looked like an ordinary cop. No Stetson hat. No handkerchief tied around his throat in case he ran into a wind storm. No drooping mustache.

Cecelia pointed at me. "This is Miss Frances Chandler. She'll be able to tell you more."

He strolled up to me, his thumbs hooked over his belt. He had a wide, thin mouth and crinkles around his eyes. When he spoke, his voice was soft, with no hint of a drawl.

"You found the body?"

"Me and Bowers. Detective Martin Bowers of the Wolf Creek Police Department."

He turned his head toward Cecelia.

"My baby brother."

I put on my big-girl pants and stood, pushing the blanket off my shoulders. Marc snatched it up, and it reminded me how young he was when he snuggled into it, losing the fight to stay awake.

"I'll take you to the—er—place."

"I'd appreciate that, ma'am."

And so we went off to view the corpse of June's handyman, who was suffering the aftereffects of his last bender ever.

EIGHT

As I escorted the marshal and his deputy to Duane Stoddard's body, I wondered if Bowers' sisters were sprinkling holy water and blessed salt around the doorways to keep me from getting back inside. I couldn't blame them if they considered me bad luck.

"What time did you and Mr. Bowers come down here?"

I roused myself out of my brooding to answer Marshal Kipper's question. "We left the house around eight-thirty. June noticed how late it was and said she was ready for bed. She and her husband own the place."

"And the two of you felt like a last stroll before turning in? The chicken run isn't very romantic."

"We needed to put the chickens away. And count them. You know. Since the help wasn't around to do it."

The silent Deputy Macoritto finally spoke up. "Count them?"

"There was a gap in the fence—I think someone cut it—and June wanted to make sure she hadn't lost any birds."

The two men exchanged a glance, and I gasped.

"That's right! Maybe Duane surprised chicken thieves."

The marshal stopped walking. "Duane Stoddard?"

"I think that was his last name. He worked for June. Did you know him?"

"I know many people," he said, which didn't answer the question.

We had reached the run, and I hesitated long enough to sniff the air. All I smelled was the usual farm scents, mostly fresh outdoor air mixed with a hint of manure. I unhitched the closure and led them inside.

"It's right around the back of the coop."

"Not inside the coop?" Kipper asked. "I thought you were counting chickens. How did you discover the body?"

Bowers stepped out of the shadows and interrupted my coughing fit. When he saw me, he got bossy, just like he did when he was in charge of a case.

"Frankie, go back to the house."

I ignored him. "Marshal Kipper, Deputy Macoritto, this is Detective Martin Bowers."

Bowers reached forward to shake their hands. "Off duty. Around here, I'm Marty."

"Call me Sam," the marshal said. The deputy made no such offer.

"The body is around the corner with my brother-in-law," Bowers said, leading them to where Carl stood guard with his hands shoved in his jacket pockets and his body angled slightly away from the scene. "We haven't touched anything. It wasn't necessary to check for a pulse."

Bowers or Carl had rounded up the chickens and put them back in the coop, so we had an unobstructed view of the body.

"Holy moly!" Deputy Macoritto leaned in for a closer look.

"The chickens got to him before we found him," Bowers

explained. He looked at Carl with concern. "The marshal is here now, and I can answer his questions. Why don't you go back in and break the news to June?"

The older man nodded. "It's going to be a shock."

And not just for June. I could see how Duane's death affected him by his stooping shoulders and drooping mustache. He glanced once more at the body on the ground and sighed. "You men let me know if you need anything."

As he walked away, he looked ten years older.

Marshal Kipper angled his head to get a better look at Duane's face. "When was the last time you saw Mr. Stoddard?"

"When Frankie and I got here last night, he was already gone."

The marshal glanced up. "You mean dead? How would you know that?"

"Gone as in missing. My sister assumed he was on a bender."

"How well did you know him?"

"Not at all. I haven't been up here in a few months. He was a new hire. The last guy didn't work out. Paul Jones. You'll have to ask my sister, June, about it."

I'd been slowly backing away from the trio until I reached the doorway into the coop. When they weren't looking, I ducked inside. I had some chickens to talk to, and I didn't want an audience.

A forty-watt bulb hung from the center of the ceiling, which left the edges of the room in shadow. Bright light wasn't necessary, as I didn't see a benefit in watching the hens' expressions as I communicated with them but considering what happened last time I was in the coop, the gloom gave me the creeps.

I took a deep breath and tried to rid myself of the images

I'd seen outside, making myself a blank page. I conjured up a highway leading from their tiny brains and my superior noggin, and then I prepared to receive any information the chickens were willing to send me.

A few clucks broke into the quiet, and finally, I picked up a signal. It was a low, steady hum, like a guitar string that had just been plucked and was now reverberating through an empty room, but there was an underlying tension. The wire might snap at any moment.

I followed the sound, and it led to Lola's nesting box. Pulling back the curtain confirmed the humming came from the wannabe mother. Her intensity made my back molars vibrate. I let the curtain drop and gazed around the room at the rest of the calm, sleepy faces. Silence.

Maybe the animals had to be wide awake before they could communicate with me. How did one tell if a chicken was sleeping? Did they snore like Chauncey? Wiggle their toes while they dreamed?

Maybe they weren't really dozing but only resting while they had a think. Reimagining the highway between their little brains and mine, I took several deep breaths, squeezed my eyes shut, and pictured Duane's face. Several clucks followed, then nothing.

I blew out a breath. I'd try again tomorrow. June would never forgive me for waking up her chickens. It might throw off their egg production. And the cops—

I sniffed the air. The metallic scent of blood filled the room, growing stronger. At first, I had a craving for a rare steak, but as it worked its way up my nostrils and down my throat, I choked. Putting a hand over my mouth, I reached out to pull myself through the door and into fresh air.

I didn't make it.

Suddenly, I was jostling my feathered family aside to

get a taste of the good stuff. Someone pecked my face, and a spike of rage swelled in my chest. I squawked. Warm, tasty —I couldn't contain my excitement and squawked again.

My tiny bird brain recognized Duane's clothing, and I associated it with eggs. No. Nests. More specifically, nesting material being tossed around the coop. And then the thought skittered away, and I went back to feasting.

My unconscious *human* brain screamed GET ME OUT OF HERE! I had enough control to bring the imagined highway to mind. I staged a spectacular explosion, and my body jerked with the release. When the room came back into focus, I was sitting on the floor, leaning back on my hands, and panting hard. The chickens hadn't moved. They were still on their roosts, only they were watching me with interest.

After struggling to my feet, I stepped up to the closest bird and studied its face. Then I noticed traces of blood on its beak and claws. At least I thought I did.

Hunching over and wrapping my arms around my middle, I teetered on the brink of hysteria. And then I toppled right over the edge.

"There you are."

I spun around. Bowers and his new friends were standing outside the door to the coop. I still had my arms wrapped around my middle, and my boyfriend gave me an understanding smile.

"Trying to keep warm?"

"Um, yep." I rubbed my hands together to emphasize how cold I allegedly was, even as sweat trickled down my back. "Yep, yep, yeppity, yep." I clapped a hand over my mouth. The excitement I felt via the chickens still coursed through me. I wanted to cluck. I wanted to fight.

My emotions ran a roller coaster of peaks and valleys. A

WHAT THE CLUCK? IT'S MURDER

need to burst into tears. A yearning to scream as loud and for as long as possible. An overwhelming desire to laugh. I didn't know how long I could hold back on all those urges in my current fragile state.

"You don't have a piece of chocolate on you, do you?" I shouldn't have blurted that out, but my vision had also left me really, really hungry.

Bowers glanced in the direction of the mutilated corpse and back at me. "You're hungry? Must be the shock."

"We'll take it from here," Marshal Kipper said, his voice full of understanding. "Thank you both."

I found an old mint in my pocket. I couldn't remember the last time I'd worn these slacks, but what the heck. After picking off the lint, I popped it into my mouth. Seconds later, I hacked and pulled a hair off my tongue.

"The light is on a timer," Bowers said, talking to Kipper but keeping his gaze fixed on me. "Do you want me to leave it on for you?"

Kipper glanced at the single puny bulb. "I'm sure our crew will want to use their own lights."

"Of course," Bowers muttered. He turned a knob, and the room went dark. Outside, he hesitated. "Will you want to talk to the family tonight? I don't think June is asleep yet."

"June." I giggled, feeling the uninhibited emotions of a drunken college student. "Cheer up, Sleepy June," I belted out to the tune of *Daydream Believer*. "Oh, what can it mean to a daydream believer and a homecoming queen." I dissolved into a cascade of giggles that I strained to control.

Bowers frowned at me, concerned. When I snorted on my inhale, the other two men turned away, disappointed in what they considered a girly reaction to finding a corpse. Men.

"We'll leave the interviews until morning," Marshal Kipper said. "I imagine we'll be busy until then."

Bowers pulled his wallet from his back pocket and handed the marshal his business card. "In case you need to contact me."

The sweat had cooled on my back, and I started shivering in earnest. Bowers put an arm around me, and after an exchange of manly farewells that consisted of curt nods, we left the law to get on with their job.

"Why do men do that?" I asked. "Hello." I bobbed my head in an exaggerated nod. "Goodbye." I bobbed again. "Hello-hello-hello-hello-goodbyeee, goodbyeee." I nodded in time and snapped my fingers to keep the beat.

As Bowers closed the gate behind us, he said, "Maybe I should go back and warn them not to leave this open."

I snorted rudely, threw my arms out to my sides, and let them drop. It felt good, so I did it again. "Seriously? They work in Cave Bear. Everyone has animals of some sort. Don't you think they already know?"

As soon as the snippy comment came out, I knew it wasn't justified. I'd never felt such a loss of control over my mouth and my actions, at least not after I'd put distance between me and my animal subject. Or, in this case, subjects.

We walked a few yards, and then he turned back. "Wait here. I forgot to count the chickens."

His backside disappeared around the corner of the coop, and I was alone in the cold. And the dark. June's friendly homestead suddenly seemed ominous. A dark stretch of desert loomed outside the glow of the security lights. A dark stretch where a killer could lurk. A killer who might still crave blood. No way did I want to be pecked at by chickens, not even after I was dead and most likely wouldn't care.

A rush of air created by beating wings passed overhead, and I twisted and looked to the sky, wary of hawks and owls. Were there bats in the desert? Or was it a myth that they got tangled in your hair? I pulled my hair back and twisted into a knot, just to be safe.

A sudden chorus of high-pitched yipping broke the silence. Coyotes had made a kill. Instead of being horrified, I thought, "*Hurrah! Listen to them yip. Yippity yip.*" I leaned my head back and howled. When I realized what had come out of me, my body tensed in an effort at self-control, and I held that pose until the yipping ceased and silence surrounded me silence again.

I sighed with relief. I hadn't closed my mental doorway after talking to the chickens. Once I shut it, I'd be fine. Maybe. Taking a deep breath, I imagined the heavy slab of wood I used to keep out messages from animals. Before I could slam it shut, Bowers returned. He put his arm around me, and we continued our walk to the house.

The mental door swung back open, and I saw the leering faces of hordes of chickens.

I cleared my throat. "So, everyone accounted for? No chickens on the lam?"

"Seven birds are gone."

I gulped. Maybe the coyotes were feasting on chicken tonight, just as I had. My mouth watered, and I swiped the drool from the corner of my lower lip.

He looked over his shoulder. "Maybe I should—"

It's not that I could read his mind, but my senses were on high and I could feel his longing.

"It just kills you not to be part of it, doesn't it?"

He laughed, softly. "You read my mind." As soon as the

words were out, Bowers tightened his grip on my shoulder. "You didn't, did you?"

I shrugged him off and wiggled my shoulder a few extra times for good measure. "For the last time, that only happened once, and I didn't need to. You were so obvious." I pranced a circle around him. *"Here's my card. Call me. Anytime. Day or night."* I jumped up and down with my hand raised. *"Pick me! Pick me!"*

"It's not nice to tease." With one swift move, Bowers threw me over his shoulder, and he slapped by bottom for good measure. He carried me that way back to the house.

A shriek or two came out, along with some laughter. Apparently, we were heard. Cecelia opened the door when we reached the stoop, and Bowers set me down.

"I guess you're used to the uglier side of life, Marty." I classified her tone as censorious. "Death doesn't affect you the way it does most people."

Spoil sport. If she wanted repentance, I'd give her an apology she'd have to accept. Pulling a long face, I lowered my body to get on my knees and crawl into the house, but Bowers grabbed my elbow, jerked me to standing, and pushed past his sister and into the dimly lit kitchen. "That's right, Cissy. I am immune."

"And you?" She dipped her head at me.

"Well, I—" A chuckle gurgled in my throat.

"Frankie just witnessed something horrible." His glance moved to me. "She's not herself right now. None of us are." He put a hand on her arm. "We're all on edge. You might as well get some sleep. The marshal doesn't think they'll get to the family until tomorrow morning."

"I'll just make sure everything is locked up. You two go to bed."

She blushed, and I threw back my head and laughed.

Even in my crazed state, I realized this wasn't the right response. I lowered my voice.

"We know what you meant."

On impulse, I gave her a quick hug and kissed her cheek. Both Bowers and his sister gaped at me with surprise, and then Cecelia said a hurried good night and left the room.

Bowers opened the stairway door. "What possessed you to do that?"

I shrugged because I didn't trust myself to speak.

"My family isn't really hands-on. Except Aggie, but she prefers punching to hugs. But it was a nice gesture."

I dropped my voice to a loud whisper. "It wasn't a gesture. It was an impulse. Maybe she needed a hug."

Bowers walked me to my room against my protests. "I don't want June thinking we're up to any funny business."

He raised his brows. "Funny business? You mean like breaking out in song and howling at the moon?"

I giggled. "You heard that?"

"As did Deputy Macoritto and Marshal Kipper. If they decide it's the work of a maniac, I'm going to have a hard time convincing them you're innocent." He stopped and put his hands on my shoulders. "Now, tell me what's going on."

My giggles turned into silent laughter, shaking my entire body. Tears streamed down my face, and finding it difficult to breathe, I doubled over.

"Frankie."

My energy level took a nosedive, and a desire to cry replaced the snicker fit. I gave into the sobs, and Bowers pulled me close and stroked my back. His body relaxed, finding tears the proper response to the evening.

"I'm sorry," I mumbled into his shoulder. "It's just—" I paused.

"Sh. It's okay. I'm so sorry you were with me when we found Duane."

Bowers' apology gave me the guilts because the reason I'd cut off mid-sentence was I had decided not to tell him about my experience with the chickens. He would freak out and tell me not to do it again, and I had to get back into that coop and find out if their beady little eyes had witnessed anything. If only I could steer them away from the tastiness of Duane Stoddard.

Bowers brushed the wetness from my face, and the knot in my hair came loose. He tucked my bangs behind my ears and leaned his forehead against mine. "This trip isn't going the way I planned."

Now that I'd made a decision, a calm filled me, and I realized this was the first time we'd been alone since our arrival yesterday afternoon. I mean really alone. No chance of June calling up the stairwell or Marc spying on us from around corners. Or dead bodies popping up.

"How did you see it playing out?" I stepped closer and wrapped my arms around his middle. "Like this?"

I got on tiptoe and gently kissed his mouth.

Pulling me close, he lowered his head and returned my little peck with a solid kiss.

I broke away and grinned up at him. "Oh, Marty!"

His throaty chuckle was cut short when June's door opened, and she peered out. "Marty? Is that you?"

He released me. "You go to bed. I'm going to check on my sister."

That sobered me up, and as I dressed for bed in an old pair of sweats and a t-shirt, I wondered if this was a house in mourning. How well did they know Duane?

I snuggled under the quilt and tried to get comfortable, but the handyman's face kept popping into my head. Maybe

I'd feel better once I knew how he had died. Or not. What if he'd been shot? Or stabbed? Or strangled? Then I'd worry that I was sharing a house with a killer.

A question niggled at the back of my head, but I couldn't put it into words. It had come to me when I was leading Kipper and his sidekick to the run . . . Nope. It was gone.

A bright light burst through my window, reflecting off the white ceiling and obliterating any shadows in the room. I slid out of bed and peered down at the barnyard. The backup cavalry had arrived from Phoenix, and they'd set up spotlights to help them examine the body and potential crime scene. Or did it have to be a crime scene before they showed up? I'd have to ask Bowers.

As I snuggled back under the covers, I had to admit that sleeping in a strange house was less intimidating with my gigantic night light.

Before I drifted off, I imagined that immense door in my head. The chickens were still peering out from behind it, along with a squirrel and two coyotes. I gave it a good shove and turned the lock.

Before the door had blocked out the faces wanting to chat with me, I'd noticed Lola staring at me with those black eyes. It felt as if she had something important to tell me.

NINE

The next morning, I was dressed in jeans and a sweatshirt and had my face washed by seven o'clock. Thank goodness I'd been wearing my black flats last night, because the police had taken them instead of my tennis shoes.

I descended the step, feeling impressed with myself . . .until I opened the door. The rest of the household sat around the kitchen table eating breakfast, even Marc.

Bowers stood. "I thought you needed to sleep in after yesterday."

"Sleep in?" I repeated, unable to understand how anyone could consider seven am sleeping in. "I'm fine."

"Of course she's fine," June said as she served Marc a second helping of pancakes. "It's not as if she knew Duane."

Her tone had a tight cheeriness that warned of an emotional storm ready to burst. Bowers narrowed his eyes in a way that hinted he was aching to point out that discovering the corpse came with its own reasons for not being fine but didn't think it would be appropriate to argue. Instead, he pulled back a chair for me. As soon as I sat down, June placed a plate of pancakes, eggs, bacon, toast, and a glass of juice in front of me.

"All the food groups," I said with a bright smile.

Halfway back to the stove, she turned and jammed a hand on her generous hip. "You're not slimming, are you?"

Assuming that slimming meant dieting, I said no, and June turned back to the stove.

I vowed to clean my plate just to keep her happy. In fact, I intended to make serious headway into all the Bowers Girls' good graces today to make up for any fumbles made yesterday. It wasn't difficult to keep my promise to June, not with all the butter mingling with the maple syrup and salty bacon.

"I don't know what all of you had planned for the day," Bowers said to everyone, "but the marshal should be here soon. It would be a good idea to stick around until he's had a chance to talk to you."

Agatha set her fork down with a clank. "Did they put you in charge of the household?"

Bowers' eyelids lowered to half-mast as he looked down on his sister. "No. But they told me their plans last night while I was standing in the cold next to the dead body. While you were snuggled up in bed. And I am familiar with the routine. I thought you might want to be polite and helpful, but do what you want, Aggie. You always do."

They were about to have a sibling fight, and if it got nasty, I might be tempted to defend Bowers. The siblings would eventually make up, but I'd be labeled *Marty's interfering girlfriend*. I got to my feet. "I'm going to let out the chickens."

Bowers looked up. "I already did."

"Then I'll feed them."

He glanced in the direction of the coop and then back at me, narrowing his eyes. "It's done."

I clenched my jaw and spoke through my teeth. "Then I'll go *look* at them while they eat."

June handed me the egg gathering basket. "Good idea. There may be some early layers today or late ones from yesterday. I imagine with the trouble you didn't have time to look last night."

Reluctantly, I took the basket. "Sure. I'd be happy to."

Bowers placed a hand firmly on my arm. "I'll go with you."

"That's not necessary."

"But it is."

He herded me out the back door without stopping for jackets. That was okay, as the temperature was already around sixty.

The high, clear call of a Gambel's quail carried over from the scattered scrub bushes and a lone tree that looked as if an outlaw should be hanging from the branches. Wildflowers had bloomed early this year, and purple and gold clumps dotted the landscape.

I couldn't believe that last night a man's life had ended—if it ended last night, and he hadn't been dead for a while before we found him.

I glanced at Bowers' profile. He'd never been with me when I'd found a body. A refreshing new aspect. I didn't need to explain myself to the cop because he was there. Just like he was now. Drat.

With Bowers sticking to me, I wouldn't be able to bond mentally with the chickens. And I so wanted to, especially when we arrived and they were wide awake, clucking and pecking and jerking their tiny heads back and forth. To my eyes, they looked like they were full of gossip and ready to share. Maybe I could listen to them without Bowers' knowledge. Of course I couldn't. Bowers had mentioned more than once that I made faces whenever I focused on hearing with my mind. Embarrassing.

My interest in the case wasn't limited to good citizenship. The sooner this investigation wrapped up, the sooner Bowers and I could leave. And if I could prove Duane had an accident? All the better for the Bowers clan.

We entered the coop and went to work, and that's when I realized I had a bigger problem.

I can't claim to know *how* my ability works, but I know what's worked in the past. By building an imaginary highway and sending images back and forth. However, I didn't know what Duane Stoddard looked like when he wasn't hen-pecked. Literally.

"Bowers," I said, reaching for an egg. "Does June have a picture of Duane?"

"Why?"

Smart man.

Shuddering, I adjusted my voice to sound vulnerable—high and slightly whiny. "I couldn't sleep last night because I kept seeing the same image of Duane's face, over and over. I thought, maybe, if I saw his face at a happier time, I could replace that image." I peered at him through my lashes. "It would really help."

Ah, the male dilemma. He knew I was full of poop because he'd seen and heard me at vulnerable moments. Usually, I upped my volume to a yell, hoping to chase fear away. However, gallantry wouldn't allow him to call me a liar just in case I was serious. I watched the struggle taking place. The corner of his left eye twitched.

"I'll ask her."

"That would be great. Thank you."

I gave Lola's eggs a pass, and after gathering the deposits left in the rest of the nesting boxes, we walked back to the house. There wasn't much conversation. I had won that round, and Bowers knew it, which ticked him off.

When we returned to the kitchen, I was reminded again of chickens. The women were in a circle, clucking over something. They parted, and a tall, slim woman with long, straight, dark-brown hair glided forward. Or maybe she floated. Anyway, she moved like she was unencumbered by corporal limitations. Like a ghost.

Her dress might have been responsible for the effect. It was made from layers of feather-light fabric in a mossy green. She wore two necklaces. The longer was made of leather knots and seashells, and the other was a fine, gold chain that held a large, gold heart.

"Marty. How lovely."

Her words whispered out of her, and I leaned forward, straining to hear. She looked into my eyes.

"Mumble mumble mumble."

"Excuse me?"

"Mumble mumble mumble."

"I'm sorry. I didn't catch that."

"She says she's happy to meet you. Frankie, this is my sister, Dymphna."

I shook her hand, which was like flinging around a spaghetti noodle. This was the sister I'd been counting on to like me, but I couldn't even have a conversation with her.

"We're all here," June said, as if they'd been holding off the fun until this moment.

"And we can use all the support we can get," Agatha added.

Dymphna raised a thin brow, inquiring. She probably didn't have the strength to speak again.

"Haven't you heard? Duane's dead."

There wasn't anything ethereal about the thump the ghost-woman made when she hit the floor.

TEN

Right about the time we got Dymphna laid out on the couch with a cold compress on the back of her neck, the law showed up.

June invited the marshal and his deputy into the kitchen but blocked the entrance to the living room.

"My sister is feeling poorly, so if we could keep our voices down, it would be kind."

When invited, Marshal Kipper hooked his hat on the corner of one chair and sat. Deputy Macoritto remained standing in a corner of the room at the ready should any of us make a break for it.

"I'll need to speak to you one at a time. I'd like to start with you."

His khaki-green eyes focused on me.

"Okey-doke," I said, keeping it cool, and I took a seat across from him.

Bowers thought he should stay. "After all, we were together when we found Duane."

Marshal Kipper kept his eyes on me dismissing Bowers. "I'd prefer to speak with the lady alone first."

June pulled her brother out of the room before he could protest further, but he got in one last worried look before the swinging door closed behind him.

I hadn't realized he was so needy. Wanting to be at the center of things. This was a first for him, being on the sidelines of a murder investigation. I thought his ego needed the respite Marshal Kipper had provided, and it made me smile.

Remembering Bowers warning about the law looking for a crazy person, I decided that the smile needed an explanation, since most people frown when being questioned about a suspicious death.

"Bowers is used to being the lead investigator."

"Do you work together?"

I hadn't expected that. How to answer. "We have. Sort of. I've been a consultant of sorts."

One corner of his mouth curled up. "Of sorts? On what?"

"Pets."

He squinted. "You're an animal wrangler? Did you hear that Mac?"

Deputy Macoritto nodded. "An animal wrangler. Takes skill."

"Animal behavior is my specialty." I said this before he could ask me to wrangle something.

Kipper pulled his head back. "I thought I knew most folks around here, at least by name, and I'm sure I'd remember you. Are you a local gal, ma'am?"

Ma'am. There's something about that word. It made me feel respected. Like a lady. I sat taller in my chair. All men should have to call women ma'am. Maybe then we'd behave ourselves. To be fair, all women would have to call men sir, but I'm not sure the guys would get as big a charge out of it.

He leaned his head forward to catch my eye. I was grinning again. "Ma'am?"

I shook myself and put on my serious face. "Wolf Creek. It's about an hour-and-a-quarter from here. Maybe longer. Is that considered local?"

When he smiled, the corner of his eyes crinkled, which made him look boyishly handsome. "I guess it's all relative, ain't it?"

He sounded just like one of those rugged cowboys from the movies. I grinned back.

"Are you and Marty an item?"

I might have blushed. "Yes." It amazed me that, after almost two years of *maybe-we-will—maybe-we-won't*, I could say that with confidence.

"So, is this your first time meeting Marty's family?"

"It is."

He lowered his voice. "Must be intimidating."

"It *is*. I've only just met Dymphna, but I was introduced to the others yesterday. And I've talked to June before on the phone." I squished up my face. "She's a little intimidating." I thought about Agatha's punches and rubbed my arm. "But not as intimidating as Agatha, though with Agatha there's good reason."

He laughed. "How so?"

Warning bells sounded. This man made it too easy to share with him. I chose my next words carefully. Truthful without being critical.

"Agatha seems very enthusiastic."

He seemed to sense the change in me, so he moved to another topic. "Now, when you got here the day before yesterday, Duane wasn't around?"

"No." I couldn't hurt anyone with a brief answer. However, in my head, I replayed the conversation that we'd had with June about the missing handyman, and it must have made it to my face.

"You seem to be a perceptive lady. When we ask questions, most of what we hear we can discard because it has nothing to do with the crime. But we need to make that decision for ourselves."

"Yes, sir."

He smiled. "Now, do you want to expand on that answer? How did you know Duane wasn't around?"

"June told us," I answered, still reluctant to expand.

"What did she say?"

I saw an upside to giving Kipper the details, stressing that Bowers and I were innocent bystanders to the drama. Also, I reasoned, if June thought Duane was out drinking, she was ignorant of his death.

"Well, one of the first things June did was complain to Bowers that her farmhand was missing. She thought he was probably out drinking. I guess he's done that before."

"I bet she was madder than a wet hen."

The mention of hens made me queasy. I cleared my throat. "She wasn't happy."

I take full responsibility for what happened next. The conversation unraveled because I live alone with two animals. I'd gotten into the habit of muttering to myself out loud, and I did so now.

"She said she could just kill him."

As soon as I realized the implications of that innocently uttered phrase, I panicked. "Don't misunderstand me. That's just what people say, right? They don't mean it literally."

"But she was mad."

While trying to make amends to June, my backpedaling dropped me right into a ditch. "Well, yeah, but she wasn't half as mad as Agatha. *She* thought June should get rid of him. Oh, Criminy. Not get rid of as in kill. Fire him." Now Agatha sounded like a suspect, so I adjusted my course. "But it wasn't just Agatha. Cecelia didn't like him either. Or maybe I should say that neither of them trusted him. That's it. They just didn't trust him. Agatha warned June to count the silverware. But she could have been joking, too. Some people use a lot of sarcasm, but they mean to be funny. Agatha could have been sharing a joke with Cecelia."

"Did you get the impression they were joking around?"

Since I'd tied myself into a knot, I simply shrugged. "Don't listen to me. I'm new around here, remember? I don't know these people from Adam. You shouldn't look to me for an opinion about anyone."

"You said June mentioned his disappearance to everyone. Did anyone react oddly?"

I relaxed back in my chair. I couldn't see how I could mess up this answer. "Like I said, they were mad that he had pulled a disappearing act on their sister. Irritated is probably a better word. All the extra work would be hard on Carl, so I can see why they would be *mildly* irritated. And they were. All except Dymphna."

"How did Dymphna take it?"

"She fainted, but my first impression is that she isn't a strong person." I wanted him to understand I wasn't being judgmental. "She whispers a lot, and her handshake is like grasping air."

"You've mentioned the women. What about the men in the group? Did they have an opinion?"

"Not that I noticed. Then again, men usually wait until there aren't any female witnesses before they gossip, don't they?"

He ignored my jab at his fellow men.

"So, if you only live ninety miles or so away, why come for a long stay? Especially your first time around."

I fidgeted in my chair. "I tried to talk Bowers into making it a day trip, but he insisted that he wanted me to get to know his sisters, not just meet them. There are a lot of them. They're not even all here. Cecelia and her husband drove all the way from Texas, if you can believe it. I'm not sure where the others live."

"They must have really wanted to meet you. But I'm sure they'll love you. You seem like a nice lady."

That made me blush.

He smiled at me again. "You've been very helpful. If I have any more questions, I'll let you know."

I stood. "Seriously. These people are very nice. Just hard-working folks. They wouldn't hurt a fly."

He looked down at his pad of paper and made a note. "I thought you said you didn't know them well?" Without looking up, he added, "Could you please send in Agatha?"

There went my hopes that he would forget everything I'd said.

"Of course I will." And I did.

ELEVEN

Half an hour later, the kitchen door opened, and Bowers came out. His expression was difficult to read, mostly because he didn't have one. Just his blank cop face.

Kipper and Bowers had probably spent the last twenty minutes staring at each other across the table and practicing their neutral gazes. I wondered who won? Was Macoritto the judge? Hardly fair.

He motioned to June, and she set down her coffee cup and went in with the attitude of a woman prepared to humor some uninvited guests. Then he stood over me, lips pursed in thought until he abruptly said:

"Come on. Let's look at the chickens."

We left out a side door off the living room to avoid the interviews in the kitchen and walked around to the back of the house. Once again, Bowers didn't have much to say. In fact, he was ominously silent, so it was up to me to start the conversation.

"How did it feel to be on the other side of the interview?"

"An interesting experience. I picked up a few techniques."

I nudged him. "Really? Did Kipper grill you? Now you know how it feels."

"Mostly he asked me to confirm things." He hesitated. "Things you said."

I nodded, nervous. "Like what time we found Duane, and the fact that we didn't know him? That was really all he asked me about."

"Maybe he couldn't get a word in," he mumbled.

Shoot. Kipper had squealed.

"It's not my fault," I cried. "I'm used to speaking my thoughts out loud to Chauncey and Emily at home. It slipped out."

"Which part? You said a lot."

I growled with frustration. "I was very careful in how I answered his questions. He asked how we found out Duane was missing, and I said that June told us when we arrived. And . . .you know how scenarios play out in your head? I remembered that June said she could just kill Duane, and without meaning to, I said it out loud. But I immediately pointed out that was just something people say all the time without meaning it." I lowered my gaze. "And I kept trying to make it better, but I might have made it worse."

He nodded. "You noticed a lot. You're very observant."

It sounded like a compliment, but his voice had an edge.

"I like to think so. It's my job."

"You mean your job helping the police with pets?"

The skin on my face warmed. "I didn't want to go into details with him. That seemed like the easiest answer."

"Thank God for small favors. Too bad you didn't feel the same way about my sisters."

Pulling down my upper lip with my bottom teeth, I silently acknowledged that I had been a tad talkative, but I'd been nervous. "But he already knows you guys. You're friends with him."

"What makes you think we're friends?"

I thought about it. "Cave Bear isn't that big, and your sister lives here, so he probably runs into her all the time at the supermarket. In fact, he mentioned that he knew everyone in the area except me. And he referred to you as Marty. That's what you family calls you."

"He played you. I met Kipper for the first time last night. Didn't you notice when we shook hands? You introduced us yourself."

"I thought it was just a formality. You know. An official greeting between cops."

He sighed. "It's not your fault. You're naïve and he took advantage of you." He opened his arms for a hug. "Come here."

I stayed where I was. "Are you sure you want to get that close? My stupidity might be contagious."

His arms dropped. "That's not what I said. You got bested by an expert. That's all. I just wish you hadn't been so...chatty."

"So, I'm chatty *and* stupid? Gee. I can see why you like me."

We were interrupted by the exuberant arrival of two dogs. I'd brought my ginger mutt, Chauncey, along for the weekend because I thought he would like the wide, open space. His new best friend was June's German shepherd, Hero.

I had to admit surprise at their bonding. I'd always seen Chauncey as a loner, but he'd jumped out of the car, given a bark of joy, and after sniffing Hero's butt, run off with him.

This was the first time I'd seen my dog since we arrived. I picked a burr off his coat.

"Hello, boy. How ya doing?"

His large mouth split into a grin and his butt wagged with delight. Chauncey was a rescue, so I didn't know his history, though I suspected he'd been abused. I'd never seen this side of him.

At home he was pleasant, ignored my cat, Emily, and enjoyed his walks, but he'd always had a guarded response to my attempts to bond with him. And he was the only animal I couldn't read. It was as if he blocked me from seeing inside his head. But here, he radiated joy. Just looking at him made my heart burst. Now I understood how mothers felt about their young when they made a new friend.

After Hero greeted Bowers with nudges and snorts, he politely allowed me to pet him before he took off toward the back pasture. Chauncey gave me a last tail wag and bounded after his new friend.

"Why can't people be simple, like dogs?"

"You're not going to get a collar on me," Bowers joked. So, he was still talking to me.

"I'm sorry if I said something I shouldn't have."

"Just keep your opinions to yourself. If you want to talk to someone, talk to me. Not Kipper. I know. He's got the *aw shucks* cowboy routine down, and he's not bad looking, but that doesn't mean he's on your side."

I didn't need to read Bowers' mind to see that he was offended, as if I'd picked the lawmen over him in a contest. He even sounded a little jealous, which shocked me.

There was one problem with sharing my thoughts with Bowers. I considered this weekend a test. If I didn't get along with his sisters, it was bye-bye Frankie. Not that

Bowers would break up with me over it, but the knowledge that I didn't like the people most important to him would create a wedge we wouldn't make it past.

And I didn't want to lose him.

As we'd been walking and talking, we had come to the run, and Bowers pulled the gate open and motioned me inside. I looked around, uncertain. Why were we here? The chickens were out and fed. We didn't have a basket to collect eggs. I thought he had used the chickens as an excuse to get me alone so he could chastise me over my poor skills as an interviewee.

It was kind of cruel to bring me here. I'm positive he knew I wanted to communicate with our feathered friends, and since he knew I wouldn't try anything with him around, coming here seemed like a taunt.

And then he surprised me.

He meandered around the edge of the fence, his hands shoved into the back pockets of his jeans and his feet kicking at the dirt. Every time he did so, a few hens would run over and check for unearthed bugs. He seemed fascinated by the clouds of dust he generated. So fascinated that he kept his gaze focused on his feet. Finally, he stood still.

"Well?"

"Well what?"

He waved a hand toward the chickens happily scratching and pecking at tufts of grass.

"Aren't you going to try your *thing*? That's why you've been trying to sneak down here, isn't it?"

If my father had seen the way my bottom jaw dropped, he would have said, "*Put a hook in it!*" followed by his second favorite, "*That's a good way to catch flies.*"

"Oh." Bowers patted his shirt pocket and pulled

something out. "I got this from June." He leaned forward and stretched out his arm to avoid coming closer because he thought my psychic abilities were contagious. Like cooties.

I took the photograph and studied a group shot of Carl, a wiry older man with gray hair and a nose like a beak, and a slightly overweight man with a light fringe of brown hair. The picture must have been taken in the summer because they were all wearing short sleeves, and a pot of lavender sitting on the back steps behind them was in full bloom.

"Which one is Duane?"

"The one with the brown hair."

I frowned. "I thought he didn't work here until a few months ago. That would have been late fall or winter. And who's the other guy?"

"Paul Jones. June's old handyman. Duane helped out a few times last year when Paul worked for them full time, so when June and Carl let Paul go, she asked Duane to take over, since he was already familiar with the routine."

"Why'd they let Paul go?"

"He left June's Guinea hens out overnight. None of them survived." Bowers paused, as if an idea had just occurred to him, which it had. "Paul swore he had locked them up and tried to blame Duane for their escape. That's probably why he got fired. June can accept a mistake, but not a lie, and definitely not finger-pointing." He didn't sound satisfied with that explanation.

"Does June pay her help a lot? Offer benefits? Paid vacation?"

"Are you serious?"

I made a face. "Then it doesn't sound like the dream job. The kind that someone would fight dirty to get."

Holding the picture close, I studied the details of Duane's face. He had a slight dimple in his left cheek when he smiled. His hair was more sandy than brown, and the beginnings of a double-chin bulged out above his shirt collar.

Self-conscious, I turned my back on Bowers for privacy.

After closing my eyes, I opened the mental door. Then I imagined a series of dirt roads running from my mind to the feathered skulls of the flock. I conjured up a movie of Duane doing tasks that would be familiar to my audience. Tossing feed onto the ground. Shooing the hens back into the coop at night. Carrying the dreaded egg basket and collecting the day's offerings. And then I waited.

The steady clucks continued uninterrupted except for few squawks when two birds went after the same worm.

I broke off my connection and turned back to Bowers.

"How did Duane die?"

"I'm not a mind reader."

I'd hit a sore spot. The police weren't about to share their thoughts with Bowers, and to say he was annoyed would have been an understatement.

He rubbed his hands over his eyes. "Sorry about that. They took the tools with them. I'm assuming he was struck on the head with one of them. Maybe the shovel."

Ew.

Going back to the chickens, I conjured the dirt roads, replayed my movie, and then showed a shadowy figure whack Duane on the back of the head.

Nothing.

"What's happening?" Bowers asked.

"I don't think Duane was killed in front of them. Either that, or he wasn't hit on the head."

"They told you that?" he demanded, his tone turning snippy because of his discomfort over the whole idea of talking to animals.

"No-o-o. They didn't *say* anything. Nothing I've presented them with has provoked a response."

"This was a bad idea. I can't believe I—" He ran a hand over his forehead.

There was something more here than manly embarrassment. I stood in front of him.

"You're really worried about your sisters. I mean, you think Marshal Kipper actually suspects one of them?"

He put his hands on his hips and pressed his lips together, and I had a flashback of the overworked, overtired, serious cop who showed up at my door two years ago to interview me about the disappearance of Margarita Morales.

"If I were Kipper, I would."

I set my teeth on my lower lip and glared at the hens. "I can't make them talk." I held up a hand. "Wait. Let me try something."

Back we went to the dirt roads and Duane's day on the farm. This time, instead of showing the killer in action, I had Duane walk around the yard with a shadowy sidekick. Since I'd never heard him speak, I gave him a drawl and threw in some argumentative language followed by Duane shouting for help.

Nothing.

I threw my hands out to my sides. "It's *not* me. You know what the problem is? These stupid chickens don't care." Frustration increased my volume. "Or maybe they're too dumb to think things out. How big is a chicken's brain, anyway? The size of a peanut? I'm surprised they find their way into the coop at night! No wonder they're on everyone's dinner menu. That's all they're good for. Stupid birds! Stupid, stupid—"

I froze. Little pricks of pain, like tiny darts, peppered

my skin. Was I having a heart attack? Or a stroke? Maybe a panic attack? Driven to my death by fiendish fowl. Then I remembered I hadn't closed off the dirt roads.

Spinning back to the birds, I couldn't see any signs they were talking to me. Not by their postures. They continued to scratch and peck like before.

I yanked on Bowers' shirt. "What did I just say?"

"You were ranting about a chicken's lack of intelligence."

"That can't be it. Before that."

He shook his head. "Nope. That was it. You insulted their brain size, called them dumb, and said they were only good for eating."

Gee. That wasn't nice of me. Were the hens thinking bad thoughts in response? Is that why I felt the pricks on my skin? I squeezed my hands into fists. "Argh!"

As another wave of pin pricks assaulted me, I dropped my hands to my sides and blinked. "Argh?" I said it in a normal tone, and the chickens didn't respond.

"I've got it!"

"You don't need to yell."

"Yes, I do! Don't you see? They're responding to the yelling." I wiggled and twitched at the annoying pain. "That's it!"

The barrage of twinges and needle-like pain continued, and I had an idea. One that Bowers would hate.

"I need you to do something for me."

He eyed me, wary. "What?"

"I need you to take my hand—whoa! Hear me out. Take my hand and yell."

He stood preternaturally still, as if he faced an armed criminal and the slightest movement might send a bullet flying at him.

"You've faced dangerous situations in your career, right?"

"Of course." I noted the tinge of pride.

"This is a tiny inconvenience, and it will help a lot."

He reached out and took my hand. "What am I supposed to say?"

"Doesn't matter. Just say it loud."

"It's warm out here!"

Nothing.

"Try it again."

Confident now that nothing freakish had happened, he squeezed my hand. "Duane is dead!"

No response.

I let him go. "Thanks, anyway."

"What was supposed to happen?"

"I thought you would feel tiny prickles of pain!"

Which I did. A whole wave of them. I panicked. What if the hens kept it up all day? If they were as dumb as I thought, they might be single-minded and just antagonize me because it didn't occur to them to stop. I'd go mad. I swept a broom over the imaginary dirt roads, and as an extra measure, slammed shut the gigantic mental doorway.

The stinging stopped, and I shuddered and ran my hands up and down my arms to rid myself of the remaining tingles on my skin.

Bowers watched with interest. "So, what happened to Duane?"

"I'm not sure." I looked into his tired blue eyes, sorry I would have to add to his worries. "But I do know, at least I'm pretty sure, before he died, Duane was arguing with a woman."

He let out a long breath. "Oh, hell."

As we were climbing the stoop to the back door, June stepped out with Marshal Kipper and his silent sidekick.

"Is everything alright, June?" Bowers voice sounded flat, which meant he was covering powerful emotion.

"The marshal wants me to look over Duane's living quarters and see if anything's missing."

Without being asked, Bowers and I tagged along.

TWELVE

Duane's shed, which is how I thought of it, was a wood building about five hundred square feet. An added overhang covered a small area outside the door where Duane had set out a lawn chair and a small folding table on which rested an overflowing ashtray, a weightlifting magazine, and an empty glass—the kind you might use for lemonade or ice tea.

Kipper unlocked the door and allowed June to pass him inside. Bowers and I stayed outside, Bowers because he didn't want to contaminate the scene, and me because I didn't want to crowd the woman in what must be an emotional moment. Also, by standing next to Bowers, I looked like the supportive girlfriend ready to face any unpleasantness for the sake of his family. An easy point in my favor.

And it gave me an excellent view. Bowers looked depressed, especially after what I'd told him about Duane arguing with a woman. If I could see something that would help him free his sisters of suspicion, I'd be a happy lady. And a heroine in their eyes.

June's first reaction after gazing around the room was surprise. "Good heavens!"

"What is it, ma'am?"

She put her fists on her hips. "Well, look at the place."

From the doorway, I glanced at what I thought a typical male apartment might look like. Clothes strewn across the unmade bed with a pile of dirties in the corner. The drawers on the small dresser partially open, and one of the few knickknacks on top of the dresser, a replica of the Eiffel Tower, resting on its side.

She looked up at Kipper, her eyes worried. "Duane was one of the neatest men I know. This isn't like him at all."

As if to prove June a liar, the smell of bar-b-que beans drifted over from the dirty dishes piled in the small sink.

She moved to pick the clothes up, but Kipper stopped her.

"If you could stay back here, ma'am."

"Oh. I suppose you don't want me messing anything up."

"The crime scene team has already been through, but it's better if you don't wander. Can you tell me if anything obvious is missing?"

So, Kipper thought the mess resulted from a search. Before or after Duane's death, I wondered.

June sent a glance around the room. "It's hard to tell in this mess."

"Fair enough. Did he keep any valuables in here?"

"He banked at the savings & loan, so I don't imagine he kept all his cash in here. We paid him a fair wage, but not enough to get rich on. I can't imagine he had anything worth stealing."

"You don't think it was an accident." They both looked

at me when I spoke. Since Kipper didn't answer, I assumed we were talking murder.

June struggled to process the information. "Do you think that's why he was killed? He interrupted a robbery?"

That didn't make sense. He died near the coop, not here, and I said so. Bowers' ears pricked up, and I could tell he was happy that I'd brought up the point.

Kipper stared at me long enough to make me wish I had said nothing, especially with the way June stared at me, too. She seemed to think Marty's girlfriend wasn't such a nice girl after all.

"We haven't nailed down exactly where he was killed."

I nodded knowingly. "All those chicken footprints probably messed up any drag marks."

Bowers snorted to cover a laugh.

"And—" Could I actually ask the question? Why not? I'd never see Kipper again after this weekend, and depending on how it went, June either. I adjusted my tone to reflect someone who had experience assisting the police, since that's what I'd told the marshal I did with my spare time. "Dead bodies don't bleed, right? So, no matter what the chickens did to the, um, corpse, if he didn't die on that spot, there wouldn't be a lot of blood. At least not under his head where he was hit, right? Or was it more of a concussion and internal bleeding?"

My word, I hadn't realized how much horrible information I'd picked up since moving to Wolf Creek.

"My word," June murmured, echoing my sentiment.

The marshal's gaze flitted in Bowers' direction, probably wondering if my boyfriend had coached me. Finally, he shrugged. "I don't see the harm in telling you the cause of death was blunt force trauma. We suspect the killer used the shovel from—" He noticed June pale. "From things the scientists can tell us. We also believe he was killed in the run and hidden behind the coop, though most of the footprints in the run belonged to you two. We matched them to your shoes."

He looked at Bowers and me. To be fair, if he was disappointed, he hid it. "The killer covered his or her tracks pretty well, but it was dark and he—or she—was in a hurry. We could still see where the body probably fell and was dragged.

"Do you know what time he died? It would make me feel better to know that we weren't too late to save him by minutes." Which wasn't a bright thing to say, as we hadn't witnessed anyone running away. Kipper didn't appear to expect more from me.

"Not minutes. You came out at 8:30. He'd most likely been dead an hour. Maybe two."

Kipper herded June outside and locked the door again. "I must ask you to stay out of here until we're finished."

She nodded, and Bowers put an arm around her shoulder and led her back to the house. She glanced over her shoulder at me, as if wondering what other surprises Marty's girlfriend had in store.

THIRTEEN

The lawmen left after that, and we returned to the house to find Dymphna sitting up on the couch and sipping from a glass of water. June took a seat on one side of her. Cecelia had already claimed the cushion on the other side. Agatha shared the love seat with Marc, who, restrained by his mother's loving arm, seemed desperate to escape the sickroom atmosphere brought about by whispering voices and a general air of solicitude.

The boy looked up and grinned when we entered the room, though I'm sure he meant the smile for Uncle Marty.

"Mom says I can't go outside alone. Will you go with me?"

"In a minute, kiddo."

Bowers nudged his sister June over and took the spot on Dymphna's left. Once she assured him she was feeling much better, he began the interrogation. I moved in close so I wouldn't miss anything the mumbler said.

"Dym, why did you faint when you heard Duane was dead?"

Dym, which rhymed with dim, stared at her hands and shrugged. "It's not every day you hear about a body."

"Look at me." Bowers used a much gentler voice than he'd ever used to question me during previous murder investigations.

She did, though with the reluctance of Chauncey when I tell him to drop whatever he's snatched up on our walk.

"Why did you faint?"

The way she squirmed in her seat reminded me of, well, me. There were many times I'd struggled to reword my answer to Bowers so I'd give him get just enough information to be satisfied without telling him the entire truth. Now I understood why he always caught me.

His sister went on the attack, a move of which I approved. I'd used it myself.

She straightened her shoulders and spoke with enough volume that I could hear her clearly from five feet away. "Not everyone is used to dead bodies, Marty. I knew Duane. Not well," she added in a hurry. "Still, when someone you know—or know of—dies unexpectedly . . .." She shrugged again. "You never know how you're going to react until you do."

He narrowed his eyes. "That's it?"

June put an arm around her sister's shoulders. "You stop bullying her, Martin."

She shot me a look that said questioning Dymphna was off limit to me as well, a look that Agatha caught. She raised her brows. I stared ahead and put on my innocent expression.

"Your sister is upset," June continued, "and the last thing she needs is you throwing your weight around. You may be a police officer in Wolf Creek, but around here, you're just one of the Bowers' children."

WHAT THE CLUCK? IT'S MURDER

As much as I enjoyed seeing Bowers taken down a notch by his sister, I was distracted by something tickling my right ear. I rubbed it gently, then scratched it harder, but the tickling continued until a small, white, curly-haired dog trotted into the room and jumped into Dymphna's lap. She gave it a hug, and it leaned back its head and licked her nose.

"Keep her on your lap," June said. "I don't want dog hair on the couch."

Dymphna kissed the top of her dog's fluffy head. "Windy doesn't shed. Do you, precious girl?"

Bowers cleared his throat. "As I was saying, I'm trying to help. Lying will only get you in trouble."

Dymphna looked up from her love fest. "I would never lie."

Cecelia tapped him on the knee with a bony finger. "Don't be rude, Martin."

Bowers kept his tone reasonable, though I noticed the twitch next to his left eye. "Marshal Kipper is going to interview Dym sooner or later. She might as well get her story straight."

Cecelia brightened. "You're going to coach her? That's very thoughtful of you, Marty."

The sisters gave approving nods.

"There's no question of coaching. I'm simply going over her statement so it will be easier to repeat *the truth* when Dym talks to Kipper. Now, how well did you know Duane?"

"Not well," she murmured.

I jerked my head back as a series of images played out. Dymphna and Duane involved in heavy-duty snogging. Heavy on the passion, light on the clothing. I frowned at the dog. Windy was staring at me, tail wagging. Then she opened her mouth wide and hacked, as if she had a furball, giving me her opinion of Duane Stoddard's relationship with her mistress.

"Okay," Bowers said. "If you say so."

I stared at him, willing him to turn his head. When he finally did, I glanced at the dog and back and gave my head a small shake. It was comical the way Bowers' eyes moved from his sister to the dog to me to the dog and back to Dymphna. His jaw muscles clenched because he couldn't use his new knowledge. Because telling your sisters that your girlfriend communicates with animals and has information that one particular sister is a big, fat liar is not the way to win their approval of the aforementioned girlfriend.

His shoulders sagged and he leaned back into the couch.

June stood. "Honey, you must be starving. I know shock does that to me. Let's fix you up a snack. Anyone else hungry?"

Marc sprang off the couch and whizzed past in a blur.

June giggled. "Boys are always hungry."

As the rest of the adults headed for the kitchen, Bowers remained behind and herded me into a corner. He didn't need to ask.

I gave a delicate cough. "Your sister, Dymphna, is a surprisingly passionate woman."

He grimaced. "Duane?"

"In the flesh. Literally."

He shuddered. "I'm glad I don't have a pet. I'd never be comfortable getting out of the shower."

I pursed my lips. "Maybe I could let you have Emily for the weekend."

Pulling me close, he grinned down at me. "Maybe you can see for yourself sometime."

"See what?" Marc stood next to Bowers holding a chicken leg. Remnants of crunchy coating and grease encircled his mouth, and I noticed that cold, leftover chicken smelled as good as the original. "Are you going outside? 'Cause I want to, but I need adult supervision."

Bowers released me. "What about our lunch?"

Marc held out the half-eaten chicken leg, but Bowers politely declined and asked if I was hungry.

I shuddered. "Not after what I just saw."

Bowers reached for the side door. "Let's go out this way."

Marc beat him to it, leaving the doorknob covered in grease. Bowers held the door open for me and then wiped his hand on his jeans.

The kid jumped down the steps of the small side porch and took off toward the back of the house.

"Don't run and eat at the same time," Bowers called out, but the kid was already halfway across the backyard. He waited at the gate of the chicken run until we got there and then flipped up the latch and ran inside.

"Where was the body? Is there still blood on the ground? Show me the blood. Oh! Maybe there's a clue!"

I let Bowers escort him to the scene of the crime while I waited. They were back in a few minutes, and Bowers said he and I were going for a ride.

"Can I come? I call shotgun!"

Bowers considered his nephew. "All right. Ask your mom."

The kid must have tossed out the question as he raced through the room, because he was back outside and climbing into the front seat of Bowers' sedan in under a minute.

I stretched out my legs on the back seat as Bowers drove down the mile-long dirt road that led to the main thoroughfare through downtown Cave Bear, which was called, no kidding, Cave Bear Road. Then again, according to Agatha's call to the police, June's driveway had a name. The Old Road.

Bowers clicked on what looked like a garage door opener and the wooden gate swung open to let us out. Our mission was to fill up the gas tank so we'd be ready to leave once Kipper gave us permission. We were supposed to go home tomorrow. That didn't leave much time for Bowers' sisters to discover my winning personality, so I took the vicarious approach, at least with Agatha, by impressing her son.

"Did you solve the mystery?" I asked Marc.

"Nah. There weren't any clues. Just a lot of dirt."

I smirked. "No blood?"

He turned and leaned over the edge of his seat. "Well, there *was* this one spot on the ground. It looked a little darker than the rest. I think it was blood." He pulled a zippered bag out of his pocket and shook it at me. "I gathered the dirt up like they do on television." He sat back in his seat and contemplated his prize. "I think Marshal Kipper might need to see this."

I couldn't help smiling, and when I noticed the way Bowers was grinning down at him, my heart flip-flopped. We hadn't reached the point where we talked about permanent things, like kids, and I wasn't sure how Bowers felt about it. From his expression, I thought he was in favor. Me? I hadn't given the subject much thought since, like Lola the hen, no husband, no chick.

WHAT THE CLUCK? IT'S MURDER

His sideways gaze caught my eye, and the grin turned into something more serious. Jeepers.

After two miles of driving past nothing but open space, Bowers pulled into a gas station with a mini mart.

"Can I have a candy bar?" Marc asked. He was already out the car door and halfway to the store before Bowers answered.

I climbed out, stretched, and closed my door and the front passenger door that Marc had left standing open. "I'll handle the chocolate situation while you gas up."

Inside, the store was clean but crowded. Their stock included the usual food items, fountain sodas, coffee, and beer, but they also carried brake fluid, windshield fluid, tire chains, fishing tackle, and gun lubricating oil. Next to the bagged ice in the freezer sat a cooler marked "bait".

The stocky, blond woman behind the counter looked middle fifties. She had a friendly smile and wore a yellow polo shirt and gray polyester pants. I greeted her and went over to wait while Marc perused the candy on offer.

"You're new around here," she said, though she didn't seem to hold it against me.

"I'm visiting the Baxters."

"How is June? She wasn't in for her newspaper today."

As I grabbed a copy of *The Arizona Republic* for my hostess and contemplated how much I should say, she mentioned she had seen the marshal's car drive by last night. And an ambulance. In fact, traffic had been heavy until late.

"There was an accident, of sorts."

She put her hand over her heart. "Is everyone okay?"

By her panicked look, I suspected she thought the victim might be June or her husband, Carl.

"A workman died."

She gasped, and her eyes bugged out. "Duane?"

"Did you know him well? I'm sorry."

"I used to babysit him and his sister. He was such a nice man. Helped me fix my generator last winter. What happened?"

I shrugged.

She peered out the window in the direction of the gas pumps where Bowers was replacing the nozzle. "Makes me nervous being so far from help sometimes. What with gangs and drugs and smugglers. You never know who's going to walk in that door. Even if it were just a heart attack . . . I've got an emergency button under the counter, but by the time Sam Kipper or an ambulance made it out here I'd be dead."

"Who's dead?"

Marc dumped seven assorted candy bars on the counter.

I patted his shoulder and grinned one of those happy, adult smiles that every kid can see through. "No one's dead."

"Duane is. Unless he comes back as a zombie. Or a vampire. That would make him undead. Maybe I should keep watch tonight."

The bell jangled as Bowers walked in. He headed for the counter, but the woman waved him over, just in case.

"Marty, I just heard about Duane. What happened?"

She obviously wasn't satisfied with my shrug.

"I'm really not sure yet," he lied. "It appears he hit his head on something."

She nodded as if the world were filled with dangerous objects intent on smashing into skulls.

"You tell that sister of yours that if she needs anything to let me know."

"Thanks, Susi. I will." He glanced down at Marc's candy stash. "Put four of those back."

Marc didn't argue, and I suspected he had grabbed a few extras just to see if he could get away with it. I swiped an extra chocolate bar for us, since we hadn't eaten lunch. Bowers paid, and we headed back to the Baxter house.

"I hope I didn't worry that woman too much," I said as I leaned forward and handed Bowers half the chocolate. "She asked how June was doing, and—" I glanced at Marc, who was focused on unwrapping his candy bar, "Duane's death kind of slipped out."

"Susi's a tough woman. She'll be fine."

"Really? She seemed nervous to me."

"Nervous? About what?"

"Drug smugglers and gangs, mostly. Also heart attacks."

"I'd be more worried about ninjas," Marc declared.

Bowers grinned. "She was being dramatic. If anyone like that showed up, which I doubt would happen around here, I'd put my money on Susi. Even against ninjas."

Marc abandoned us the minute Bowers parked the car. I suspected he wanted to stash his candy before his mom spotted him.

Without the kid around, I was free to say what had been on my mind since we had been in Duane's cabin.

"You realize that someone walked onto June's property and killed a man while we were all inside the house eating chicken."

"It had occurred to me."

"Do you think Duane's death had anything to do with the fence being cut? Maybe someone wanted to steal chickens, and Duane tried to stop them."

"It's possible."

"It must have been chickens because you couldn't get a

cow through the space you described. And there are chicken's missing."

"Maybe."

His reaction disappointed me. "You think it's too obvious?"

"I think I'd like to believe it, so I'm trying not to count on it being the answer."

That wasn't what I'd hoped to hear.

FOURTEEN

As we stepped into the kitchen, my worries were lifted by the smells of both sweet and savory floating through the room.

A pan of fresh cinnamon rolls rested on the stovetop, and June was pulling a foil-covered pan from the oven. She peeled back the covering and both Bowers and I peered over her shoulders.

"You're just in time to take me to Phyllis's house."

"Should I know Phyllis?" Bowers reached for a roll and she swatted his hand.

"Duane's mother." She made a noise of disbelief. "Phyllis Stoddard. She was widowed six years ago, and Duane and his sister were all she had left. Now there's only Nancy to comfort her, poor woman."

"Duane was several years older than me," Bowers pointed out. "We weren't in school at the same time, so there's no reason I should know his mother. I didn't even know *him*."

"She's in my knitting group at Holy Redeemer parish, Marty, and she's practically a neighbor. I can't believe you don't know her. Maybe if you visited more often, these people wouldn't be strangers."

He kissed her on the cheek. "Does that mean you miss me?"

She snorted. "Hardly. "

He snatched a cinnamon roll before she covered the plate.

"I'll meet her when we take you to her home." He took a bite. "Are you bringing all of this?"

"Of course."

I understood. There's a reason they call it comfort food. Back in Wisconsin, people met tragedy with serving dishes filled with casseroles, fruit salad, brownies, and more casseroles. It was a way of showing you cared, and though people often joked about the onslaught of food, when someone was numb from the loss of a loved one, or even temporarily incapacitated because of a surgery or the birth of a child, homemade dinner ready to pop in the oven or microwave made a difference.

"That's nice," I said without thinking.

June looked surprised. "I suppose is it. I wouldn't consider *not* doing it, so I hadn't thought of it that way."

I recognized the crusty topping of buttered crackers. "Is that a cheesy hash brown breakfast casserole?"

She nodded. "With cinnamon rolls for a quick fix." She placed the hot pan in a quilted carrier and secured the top. "Ready?"

The back seat was all mine again. Well, I shared it with the food. We went back down The Old Road, but this time we turned left when we hit Cave Bear Road. Bowers drove until we reached a small housing development Following June's instructions, he turned in at a large, stone sign that welcomed us to the Indian Creek community.

"Is there a creek?" I asked.

"Used to be," June said, happy for the distraction. "It makes a showing during monsoon season and then disappears again until the next year."

When I'd moved to Wolf Creek from Wisconsin, Arizona's monsoon season took me by surprise. Monsoons sounded like something that happened in India, not the desert, but every summer, from June to September, residents prepared for high winds, dust storms, and flash floods.

My first year here, a woman's car had been swept away when she tried to cross a road clearly marked as dangerous. Firefighters rescued her from the top of her vehicle. I hope they charged her for the call.

Unlike my neighborhood in Wolf Creek, the Indian Creek development was built on flat land. After a few turns, Bowers pulled up in front of an older ranch house. He and I carried the food for June and followed her to the front door.

The white-haired woman who answered was dressed for company in a black pantsuit and heels. She looked us over, vaguely, as if she weren't sure we were there, and then she turned and walked away. June followed her inside and pointed us toward the kitchen.

As we stepped into that room, we were overpowered by a combination of conflicting smells. Sugar and spices battled it out with savory meats; the biting odors of sour cream and vinegar mingled with the cloying sweetness of mixed-fruit bowls. Every food group was accounted for. We made room on the counter for our gifts and fled back into the living room.

Since this was a house in mourning, Bowers and I remained silent, stood off to the side, and tried to blend in with the periwinkle-blue wallpaper.

June sat next to Phyllis Stoddard on a comfy-looking gold couch and held her hands, speaking to her in a gentle murmur. I'm not sure if the bereaved mother took in the consoling words. She stared straight ahead.

"And I know what a comfort he was to you. I can't tell you how sorry I am this happened."

Phyllis came to life and looked at June. "What is *this*? The police won't say. All I know is my boy is dead. I'm never going to hear him walk in that door and call *Mom* ever again, and I don't know why. I want to know why."

"The marshal is trying to figure it out. Give him time."

Phyllis nodded. "I got all the time in the world."

"How's Nancy?" June asked.

"She's flying back from Chicago tonight. She's hiring an Uber driver, so I don't have to pick her up at the airport. My night vision isn't great."

June rested a hand on her friend's shoulder. "She'll be a comfort to you."

Phyllis' laugh startled me. "Don't kid yourself. We'll be fighting within ten minutes."

"Surely not."

"I want to bury him. She'll want to save the environment by cremating him. Probably want the urn to be some recyclable tin can."

"Well," June said, ever practical, "it will keep your mind off Duane."

Though we had both been quiet, respectful, and, I hoped, invisible, the mourning mother shifted her position and looked directly at Bowers. "You're Marty, aren't you?"

June raised her eyebrows and dipped her chin at him to let little brother know that not everyone was vague about their neighbors.

He stepped forward. "Yes, ma'am. I'm sorry for your loss."

"Me too," I murmured to be polite.

"You're with the police, aren't you?"

"Yes, ma'am, but not around here."

"You could find out what's happening, couldn't you?"

She'd just named Bowers' fondest wish.

"I'm sure Marshal Kipper will keep you informed."

"I don't want to be informed. I want answers." She struggled to stand, but June gently pulled her back down. "Do you freelance? I can pay you. Vincent had insurance."

I assumed Vincent was her late husband. She would have written Bowers a check right then if June hadn't kept a firm grip on her.

"I'm afraid I can't work outside of my jurisdiction." And then, since he couldn't help himself, he asked, "Did Duane have any enemies?"

Phyllis looked pleased, as if by asking the question Bowers had capitulated to her wishes. "Not my Duane. He was a good boy."

June and Bowers exchanged a glance, and Phyllis flushed. "I know what you're thinking. Some of his friends were a little frisky, that's all. Duane just went along with them because, to be frank, he was a follower. One of his only faults. But he hasn't seen any of them for ages."

"Who were they?" Bowers asked.

She lifted her chin. "Duane never introduced the entire group to me. I know Tommy Kincaid was one of them. He went to grade school with Tommy. He's the one that introduced Duane to the others."

Bowers forced his expression into neutral. "What about women?"

June gasped. "Marty!"

Phyllis held up her hand. "It's alright, June. He needs to know these things. There wasn't anyone steady." She pursed her lips together. "But there must have been someone. I was washing his clothes for him." She sniffed. "He didn't have a washing machine in his place."

"He knew he was welcome to use mine," June said.

"Maybe he just liked the way I did it. A mother's touch, you know. Anyway, around Valentine's Day, I found a present in one of his jacket pockets. A gold charm shaped like a heart. It was thick. Three-dimensional, so it must have been a locket."

Suspiciously like the locket Dymphna wore.

Bowers tensed. "Was there a picture in it?"

"Duane walked in just then and he said something like *there it is,* like maybe he'd lost it, and he took it from me."

The doorbell rang. Since I was closest, I opened the door, and another neighbor stepped inside with a casserole.

June rose and hugged Phyllis. "Don't become a recluse. We're always available for you."

The new visitor nudged June aside and took her turn hugging Phyllis, but the bereaved mother watched Bowers over the woman's shoulder.

"You'll let me know if you hear anything?"

"Yes, ma'am. I will."

What other answer could he give?

We took a detour to the mini mart on the drive home because June said she needed laundry detergent. Apparently, the mini-mart was the go-to place for everything other than serious grocery shopping. After smelling all the food at the Stoddard house, I wanted a snack, so I offered to go inside with her. Bowers said he'd wait in the car.

Susi was still behind the counter and hailed June before she could get to the household items.

"What is going on at your place?" And then she answered her own question. "Duane's dead."

"Yes, he is."

"Well?"

The cashier leaned her arms on the glass counter and settled in for a chat, and June sighed and approached her for privacy. There were several other shoppers in the store, and they had all looked up at Susi's announcement.

"I've seen Marshal Kipper's car drive by umpteen times," the cashier said, jerking her head sideways toward the front window. "And I also saw several sheriff's cars pass by late last night. And an ambulance, though they didn't have the lights on."

I wondered if Susi lived at the mini-mart, and then I noticed the cot in the small office behind the counter. At first the thought of her living in this small store made me sad. Then I realized, if I were in her position, I'd have everything I needed to make me happy—including that chocolate I'd come in for—right at my fingertips, twenty-four hours a day. Not too shabby.

"You and I both know they only send for the sheriff when it's too big for our local law to handle, like when they need crime scene people." Susi shook her head. "Not for an accident. So, what gives? Should we be worried?"

I looked over my shoulder and saw that *we* included the other four customers, who had gathered close to hear the news. I excused myself to retrieve the laundry detergent and my chocolate.

There was only one brand of detergent, Desert Sun, and it came in super-size. I grabbed it by the handle and almost lost my balance from the weight of it. By the time I had decided on something both chocolate and crunchy, the conversation up front had moved on to Bowers. Now I understood why he remained in the car.

June folded her hands, almost in prayer, and nodded. "If anyone can figure out what happened, Marty will."

"Isn't he a patrolman?" Susi's wide eyes and smirk said that she knew he wasn't.

"Keep up with the news, honey. He's a detective. The brightest they have in Wolf Creek. Isn't that so, Frankie?"

I returned their impressed stares. "Um, yes. Definitely the brightest." I thought about the highly competent Detective Gutierrez's reaction to that declaration and smiled. "No one else comes close."

Susi snorted. "You'd say that. You're his girlfriend." She looked me up and down. "At least, I assume you are."

A teen girl with blond hair got a dreamy expression on her face as if imagining the thrill of dating a cop, but the old woman next to me wasn't impressed.

"Some girls would say anything for a little nookie. Let's be honest. Duane Stoddard wasn't anything to write home about, yet he had a girlfriend."

"What was she like?" Susi demanded. "Skanky? I bet she was skanky, like those girls that hang out at the bowling alley. You'd think they weren't acquainted with a bar of soap."

"Not this one," the old woman said, triumphant. "She had long dark hair and dressed like a fairy."

That threw all of us. She searched our faces.

"You know. Like Tinkerbell. Flowing layers. And she moved lightly. She looked like she might float off any second."

That was an accurate description of Dymphna. I

glanced at June. Her jaw pulsed just like Bowers' did when he was holding it together. I had to do something.

"How do you know that was his girlfriend?" I asked.

"They were holding hands, and they had their heads together, the way people do when they have a secret. Or they're in love."

"Did you see their faces?"

The old lady's own face wrinkled in thought. "No."

"Then how do you know it was Duane?"

"It was obvious."

I forced out a chuckle. "Well, I'm not from here, but in Wolf Creek, if someone described a slightly pudgy, sandy-haired, balding man, it would apply to about ten people that I know, and I don't get out much."

Doubt crept into their eyes, so I kept going. "And those layered dresses are meant to hide figure flaws. The woman could have been skinny as a weed or on the plump side."

A middle-aged woman tugged self-consciously at the hem of her loose-fitting t-shirt, stretching it over her bottom.

"And dark hair, well, when the sun is shining, it brings out highlights, or shadows. So, she could have been raven black or a reddish brunette and it would have been hard to tell the difference."

"There wasn't any sun," the old woman insisted, refusing to give up ground. "It was nighttime."

I raised my eyebrows and nodded to show that made identification even harder. By now, those people weren't even sure she'd seen two human beings.

June sensed it was time to get out before other questions came up, such as if the couple had paused under a streetlamp. She grabbed the detergent from me and plopped it on the counter. "Ring me up. Marty's waiting in the car."

"And this." I slipped my candy bar in front of Susi and

handed June a dollar. She took it without looking and stuffed it into her purse instead of placing it in the wallet she held in her hand.

As we made our escape, a wiry man in a checked cotton shirt tucked into his jeans blocked our path. He wore the kind of flat cap my Irish grandpa wore, and he swept it from his head and held it in his hands, twisting it.

"Mrs. Baxter, I've just heard. I was wondering if there's anything I can do. I know it's not seemly, with Duane not buried yet, but I'm available."

"I'll let you know, Paul."

She snipped the words out, and if I were Paul, I wouldn't hold off applying for other jobs. He opened his mouth but decided against saying anything else and moved out of our way.

When we got back to the car, Bowers turned off his phone and dropped it into the cup holder.

"Who were you talking to?" June demanded as she pulled on her seatbelt.

He stared. "No one. I was looking at the scores."

"Well, maybe you should stay off the phone. Too many people are too accessible, and they've got too much to say. People need silence once in a while."

He sent a puzzled glance over his shoulder at me. I shrugged and took a bite of my candy bar.

June slapped one hand on her thigh. "What are you waiting for?"

When we got back home, Bowers' sister shot out of the car and headed for the house, leaving her laundry soap behind. I dragged it out and handed it to Bowers, and he took the last bite of chocolate away from me, too. As he finished it, he said, "What's bugging my sister?"

"Other than an old lady describing Duane's girlfriend, who was a perfect match for Dymphna, nothing."

He swallowed and choked.

"Are you going to talk to your sister again? She's obviously lying, but we knew that already. That heart necklace she wears sounds an awful lot like the one Duane's mother found in his pocket."

In a strangled voice, he said, "You think she killed him?"

"No! She wouldn't have the strength to wield a shovel, but I think she knows something."

He put his hands on his sides for one last cough and nodded. "I think you're right. But she's not going to talk to me."

I was facing the driveway, so I saw the vehicle first. An older model red hatchback crawled up the dirt drive and came to a stop behind Bowers' car. The door made a popping sound as it opened, and a small, slim woman with dark hair stepped out. Her thick lips were pulled back in a nervous smile that exposed little teeth, something I'd seen an English Setter do when nervous. She dipped her head to the side.

"Is this the Baxter residence?"

"It is."

Bowers didn't add anything, employing his *make them sweat until they talk* cop technique. She gave in first.

"I'm Terri. Terri Nila. Duane's girlfriend."

Things were about to get complicated.

FIFTEEN

Bowers didn't say a word. His expression didn't change either, but when he looked at me, I could see a message in his eyes as clearly as if he'd been a Doberman pinscher pleading to have a shot at the mailman.

I moved.

"So sorry," I said, backing away and bouncing on my toes. "I have to tinkle. Urgently. It's bad for you to hold it, you know."

Holding back from breaking into a sprint, I jogged to the house and through the kitchen, ignoring June when she asked me Marty's whereabouts. I found Dymphna in the living room seated next to Agatha on the couch.

"I need your help," I said, tugging on Dymphna's arm.

Her eyes grew wide and she looked to her sister for aid.

"Hold on." Agatha pried my hand off Dymphna's arm. "What's the rush?"

"It's an emergency." And just in case Agatha felt left out, I added, "I need you both to come to my room."

Dymphna stood. Maybe she was a sympathetic soul. Maybe she was curious. Or maybe she thought the sisters could better tackle and subdue me in the smaller space afforded by the guest bedroom. Agatha wasn't inclined to help.

"Explain first. Then I'll decide."

If that's how she met emergencies, Tom and Marc must have very frustrating lives.

I heard the back door open and searched the room, frantic. "This way." I pulled Dymphna toward the side door. Agatha stood, but only so she could hold on to her sister's other arm.

"That's not the way to your room."

"I changed my mind. I just need to talk to you privately, and my room was the first thing I thought of, but out here on the porch will be fine. It's better. Closer." I tugged harder.

From the kitchen, June's voice joined Bowers', and then Terri jumped into the conversation. Dymphna turned her head toward the sound.

"Who's that?"

"Who knows?" I said with a hysterical laugh. "Probably the postal delivery person."

June said Duane's name, and suddenly, I wasn't holding onto Dymphna's arm. It was as if she had evaporated and reappeared walking toward the kitchen, drawn by the name of her lover.

Needing something to hold onto, I clutched Agatha's arm. "Stop her," I hissed.

She studied my face, and something in my expression convinced her. "Dym, hold up."

But she was too late.

We joined the party in the kitchen and found Dymphna staring at Terri. Windy had joined her mistress and stood at her side with hackles raised. I could feel the rumble of a tiny growl in my chest, though the dog didn't make a sound.

I thought Bowers had the neutral cop face down to a science, but Dymphna had raised it to an art form. Her eyes were vacant, as if her soul had left her body.

June didn't notice. The elder sister looked pleased, and I'm sure she thought the entire episode in the mini mart had been a hallucination, and her sister had not been the woman described as Duane's date. Why wouldn't she? Terri wasn't dressed in a flowing dress, and she wasn't tall, but she had the requisite dark hair. Except it was short hair. But other than that...

"This is Terri, Duane's girlfriend."

Together, Bowers and I sucked in a breath and waited. Dymphna's expression didn't change. She merely said, "Oh," and left the room escorted by her pup.

We both exhaled, and Agatha gave us a questioning look.

"Marty," June said, "Terri wants to look through Duane's effects. Do you think that's alright?"

I caught the spark in his eyes as he said, "Certainly." He nodded at Terri. "I'll escort you."

She held her hands out to her sides. "If you could just point me in the right direction, I'd rather be alone."

"Then you'll have to wait for Marshal Kipper."

June's brow wrinkled. "But Marty, there's no need for that. Not when you're—"

"Happy to do it." He didn't apologize for cutting her off, and he ignored June's startled expression, took Terri's arm, and steered her out the back door. They didn't invite me, but I followed.

"I appreciate this," Terri said, gazing up at Bowers as we crossed the yard. "It has been such a shock."

"How did you hear about it?"

Now that he mentioned it, I realized the morning news on the radio had only mentioned a death.

"People talk," she mumbled.

"I'm sorry you had to hear about it that way."

The sun had begun its descent to the west and made a halo-effect around Duane's cabin, as if a holy man had been its last occupant.

When we got to his porch, we found police tape barring the door. Kipper must have put it up after his visit with June. He didn't trust us, I thought, as Bowers ripped it down and opened the door.

Teri took in the scenery with a slow gaze around the room, and then her knees gave out and she leaned against Bowers. He put an arm around her shoulders to steady her.

After my first wave of irritation at her damsel-in-distress routine, I wondered if she wasn't a victim after all. Duane was a two-timer. Maybe he'd been leading on both women, and Teri and Dymphna were *both* victims of his callousness. If so, his actions stunk. I could actually smell the stench. Or maybe the odor came from the old baked beans in the sink. The place hadn't miraculously cleaned itself since we were last here.

"Was this where it happened?" she whispered.

"The marshal is still investigating. Duane wasn't found here."

She gazed up at him. "Where—" She shook her head. "Never mind. I don't want to know."

As she stepped away from him and into the room, Bowers leaned against the door frame and watched. She wandered the room slowly, pausing to stare at some object or other, and I wondered if Bowers felt as bad for the woman as I did.

I studied his handsome profile, the straight nose, firm chin and lips, and I didn't see compassion written there. He must be used to other people's pain, and the idea unsettled me. Had his job made him callous? Had years of dealing with criminals and unsavory elements drained him of finer feelings? If I had a serious problem, I knew he'd do everything in his power to help me, but would it be instinct? Obligation? Would my helplessness irritate him?

Teri had moved on to some unfinished shelves that looked as if they had been part of the original shed. They held a few paperback books, a tin cup, a facsimile of a hot-air balloon, a rusty horseshoe, three shot glasses, and a deck of cards. She ran her finger over the paperbacks, took one down from the shelf and flipped through the pages. A piece of paper fell to the floor, and she picked it up, glanced it over, and replaced it.

I looked away, my heart hurting for Teri as I imagined her trying to replay the last time she saw Duane. Maybe reliving a conversation that had taken place in this very room. I couldn't imagine how sad I would be if something happened to Bowers.

When he suddenly stood straighter. I followed his gaze. Terri brushed her hand over Duane's dresser, and as she dropped that same hand into her pocket, I noticed she had palmed a piece of paper. A short while later, she nodded to us and moved to leave. Bowers blocked her way.

"I'm afraid you'll have to leave everything here."

She lifted her chin. "I did."

"What's in your pocket?"

She flushed and pulled out the piece of paper, showing it to him. "Just something Duane wrote for me. Something to remember him by."

I leaned in for a closer look. It was a poem. Not a

particularly good poem, but I don't think guys are naturally good at poetry, unless you count T. S. Eliot. Or Walt Whitman. Or Jack Kerouac. Okay. Maybe there were *some* male poets, but I still thought that average guys weren't naturally poetic. Duane's attempt proved my theory.

I look to the rising sun,
And I'm blinded by the rays,
But not as much as I'm blinded
By our two hearts, side by side,
Meeting in the center.

And then he drew an illustration of two hearts next to each other and a sloppy plus sign underneath them. Really, it didn't even make sense. Two hearts side-by-side wouldn't meet in the center. It defied logic, but then again, so did love. I chastised myself for being so critical.

"I'm sorry," Bowers said, folding the paper back up, "but this will have to stay until the marshal gives the okay. I'll let you know so you can come back for it, since I can't imagine he'll want to keep it."

She didn't want to agree, but she had no choice.

As we watched her drive off, I wondered how long it would be before Kipper finished with Duane's cabin and she could claim the silly but heartfelt poem from Duane, a memory I'm sure she would cherish. I frowned.

"How do we know the poem was for her?"

"I don't think it was for publication."

I nudged his side. "You know what I mean. What if he wrote it for Dymphna?"

He gave a small groan. "I don't know how I'm going to get her to tell the truth. I have nothing to hold over her."

I gasped. "You wouldn't blackmail your own sister, would you?"

"Frankie, it's so obvious you never had siblings."

He turned and headed back to the house.

"You have a few to spare," I called after him. "Why don't you lend me one?"

He stopped, turned, and studied me. In three long strides he was back, lifted me off my feet, and swing me around. "Frankie, you're brilliant."

"I am? I mean, I am. Yes. Glad you noticed."

He set me down. "Here's the plan."

By the time he finished, I was happy I'd been born an only child.

SIXTEEN

Dymphna's bedroom turned out to be the one next to mine. New Age instrumental music led me right to her door. I knocked and walked in. She sat on her bed with Windy in her lap, and she stroked the dog's fur, lost in thought.

I cleared my throat. "Dymphna?"

It took a minute for her to come out of her reverie, and then she looked up as if wondering who I was. Her flowing, layered dress spread over the bedspread, so I remained standing.

"How are you holding up?"

"*Mumble, mumble, mumble.*"

I held up my hand. "Maybe there's a reason you speak in whispers, like you're asthmatic and don't have a lot of air to put under your words, but if you don't speak louder, I'm going to have to sit in your lap."

Her startled expression was followed by a little smile, and when she spoke again, she had adjusted her volume from fey sprite to grown woman.

"I said I don't know why you, or anyone, would think I'm affected by this—this horrible situation more than June, or Cecelia, or Agatha. Naturally, I'm more sensitive than they are, but . . . ."

I scanned her room while she continued to tell me how uninteresting sordid things like murder were to a woman of her sensitive nature, and how the end of life on this plane was something to be celebrated, and blah-blah-blah.

On her dresser, a stick of cedar-and-spice incense burned, held in place by an ornate holder that resembled woodland faun. There was a brush, a small makeup bag, and a bag of rune stones that had been poured out and probably read.

Back in those happy days when I only pretended to communicate with animals, I'd investigated all things mystic to prepare for my role. Runes were flat stones with ancient symbols on them used by those who preferred to get advice from rocks rather than friends or wise elders.

It struck me that Dymphna must be a lonely woman. She had plenty of wise elders, but maybe not so many friends. And that explained why I was here.

Bowers had asked me to become pals with her hoping his sister would let a girlish confidence slip. He thought this because he was a guy. I knew better. It takes a long time to build up trust, and trust begins with truth. I made a decision and dumped Bowers' plan. Well, let's say I adjusted it.

"You and Duane were close. Windy told me."

Dymphna stopped petting her dog mid-stroke and looked down at the pup in her lap. Windy stretched her neck back to gaze adoringly at her master as if saying, *"Wasn't I clever?"*

"Told you what?" Her tone said there wasn't anything to tell.

I gave the woman credit for not wasting time asking me to explain how the dog had managed to tell me anything.

Instead, she got right to the point. I moved the folds of her dress aside and sat next to her on the bed.

"You don't have to pretend with me. Duane gave you that locket."

Her hand covered the gold heart that rested on her breast. "I haven't taken it off since I got it," she whispered, barely audible. She cleared her throat and spoke louder. "Sorry. Habit. You couldn't have looked inside. Can you read people's minds as well?"

"There was this one time—" I let Bowers keep his dignity. "No, I can't. His mother mentioned that she found it in his pocket around Valentine's Day."

On the words *Valentine's Day*, a light tingling filled my chest—a warning sign that an animal's thoughts were about to break through my mental door.

I know, I know. What's the point in having a door that is regularly bypassed by intruders insistent on having a chat? Because animals are a chatty bunch, and if I didn't block out their random thoughts, I'd be under assault 24/7. That's why.

When I began to pant, I suspected my latest visitor was Windy, especially when I caught her staring. I coughed, hoping to interrupt the message.

"Pardon me."

Windy wasn't about to be denied the chance to air her opinions. A scene unfolded in front of me. I was back in Duane's cabin. The small folding table from the front porch had been moved inside. June was right. Duane's cabin was neat enough to make any mother proud. And he was a romantic.

The table was set for two, including lit candles. Duane walked in carrying freshly grilled steaks just as Dymphna finished tossing a salad. The smell of the hot steaks and crispy, burnt fat caused my panting, and I clamped my mouth shut.

Bowers' sister sat down, but Duane walked to the neatly made bed and pulled a wrapped present out from under the pillow. She opened it, eyes shining with tears.

"Sorry it's late. I just couldn't get away last week."

Then Duane stood behind her and fastened clasp of the necklace with the gold, heart-shaped charm. Dymphna turned her head up to kiss him. The kiss heated up and the meal was forgotten.

"That's enough!" I waved my hands at the dog, who gave a little growl that said I had stopped her before she got to the good part. "You celebrated Valentine's Day a week late and Duane gave you the necklace then."

The dog whined, and Dymphna kissed her head.

"We got to talking, you know, about stuff—"

I held up a hand to stop her before she dug herself a nice hole. "Yeah. Sure."

She continued hurriedly. "And our steaks cooled off, so we cut them up for Windy." She held up the dog and kissed her nose. "So, it was a good time for snookum."

Her tone throughout this discussion had been too matter of fact. I narrowed my eyes. "You're taking this awfully well. I mean the bit about the dog talking to me. Aren't you surprised?"

Her expression turned all dreamy. "That we can communicate with animals? No. I always know what my little stinky butt is thinking. She just doesn't use words with me."

"Oh. Me neither. So far." I shook my head to clear the cobwebs. "Why don't you tell Bowers the truth? He's only trying to help you, and when the marshal finds out—"

"You can't tell him!"

I jumped, shocked at Dymphna's first sign of deep emotions.

"Uh, I think Bowers has an obligation to pass the information on. You know. Cop stuff."

She lowered her volume back to a whisper. "Then don't tell him."

"I can't keep secrets from him." My response lacked enthusiasm since I'd kept plenty of secrets from Bowers for my benefit.

Dymphna seemed to know what I was thinking because she nodded and smiled. "Just don't tell him."

"But I already told him—" I stopped before I described the passionate scene Windy had first shown me. "Windy mentioned you and Duane liked each other. Bowers already knows."

She shook her head, still smiling. "He knows that you told him my *dog* said we were friendly. He doesn't have proof."

Jabbing my finger at her necklace, I gave a triumphant snort. "He was there when Duane's mom described the necklace."

She toyed with the locket. "Phyllis describe *a* necklace. Who says it's this one?"

My hand shot out before I thought through what I was doing. I grabbed hold of the locket with both hands and tried to pry it open. Dymphna fought back, while Windy barked hysterically, especially when we fell off the bed and rolled across the floor.

"Let—me—see-inside!"

She bent my fingers backward, and I learned that Dymphna was stronger than she looked. "Ow!"

"Can I help?"

We froze at the sound of Bowers' voice, and I craned my

neck to see two boots almost touching my nose. Lighter on her feet than I, Dymphna bounced up and sat on the edge of the bed, her smile as serene as ever. Bowers held out a hand and helped me struggle to my feet. I shook my hand and stretched my fingers.

"What's going on?"

His gaze lasered in on the locket.

It was probably too late to salvage any girly relationship with Dymphna, but I tried. "We were having a tickle-fight," I mumbled, and I left the room with my head held high.

Bowers followed me to my room and closed the door behind us, breaking a rule of June's, I'm sure.

"That wasn't what I meant when I said get close to Dymphna."

"Your sister declined to bond."

"So, you attacked her?" He smirked.

"You're going to have to find another way to convince her to talk."

"I figured."

"It's not my fault. She—" I paused. Could I earn Dymphna's trust by not repeating our conversation and keeping my Valentine's Day vision to myself?

"She what?"

"Nothing."

He stared at me, a serious expression in his eyes. "Frankie, remember what I told you about lying to me?"

He'd caught me in one of many lies on the cruise last fall and asked me to never lie to him again. He kind of told me rather than asked me, but I'd agreed. Had I actually said I'd never lie to him? I must have because he was still talking to me. So, I could *not* tell him, as long as I didn't lie about it.

"Sorry. There *is* something, but I can't tell you. You're

the one who told me to get close to your sister, so I'm only following orders."

"And you think repeating what she said to me would break her trust?"

"Um, yes?"

He kissed my forehead. "That's good enough for me. I trust you. But you must remember, things could change. Kipper could get on to the fact that Duane and my sister were an item. If it comes to that, I may need to know what she said to protect her."

I nodded. "Understood."

He pulled me close and grinned. "Now, what was this about a tickle fight?"

"Don't you dare."

He didn't dare because there was a loud knock on the door. He sighed and pulled the door open. "Yes, June?"

She glanced at me, confirmed that we were both dressed and breathing normally, and told us to get ready for church.

SEVENTEEN

An hour later, the ten of us piled into three cars and drove to Holy Redeemer, a small Catholic church on the outskirts of downtown.

My mother had once referred to me as a Roamin' Catholic. It wasn't a compliment. Early in my adult years, I'd grown lazy and drifted away from religion. However, since I had nothing against the Church or Mass, I was happy for a chance to show the Bowers girls that I wasn't Heathen of the Year.

The church appeared like a mirage in the middle of open desert. Only a wooden cross perched on a small dome marked it as a place of worship, except for the sign at the parking lot entrance.

Built out of adobe bricks, the small building held about one-hundred worshippers, max. Inside, simplicity ruled, with wooden pews for the congregation and a plain alter behind a communion rail. The only sign of modernity came from a small synthesizer standing against the left wall.

The pews were only half full, and I learned later the parishioners followed an unspoken schedule. Those who worked the land and had animals attended Saturday evening Mass, which allowed them to rise early for milkings and feedings and such. The rest went to church on Sunday morning.

There were too many of us in the Bowers' party to fit in one pew, so our group separated. I wound up seated between my date and Cecelia, with Agatha and her family in front of me. Marc kneeled on the bench, hung his arms over the back of the pew, and theorized about Jesus' opinion of zombies. His mother poked him, and he retreated before I gave into the urge to laugh.

At the first notes of the entrance song, the congregation rose, and when the priest reached the altar, childhood training and the actions of the rest of the parishioners prompted me to sit, stand and kneel when appropriate. However, the verbiage had changed, so I closed my eyes and whispered my responses as if in deep contemplation to avoid slipping up and being overheard by Bowers' sisters.

When it came time for Communion, I panicked. I knew I couldn't receive the Eucharist. However, I didn't want to invite questions at the dinner table. I remembered hearing something about going forward for a blessing and thought I'd found a way out. It would have been less conspicuous if I had remained in the pew. Or fainted. Or left the building.

Not all priests were familiar with the blessing-at-Communion idea. When I was next in line, the celebrant held up the Eucharist and said, "The Body of Christ."

With a glance of apology at the Host, I leaned forward. "Just a blessing, please."

He lowered his hand. "What's that?"

His words echoed through the church.

"I've come up for a blessing. Since, you know, I can't receive right now."

"Why not?"

"I just..."

Glancing around, I caught the eyes of every parishioner as they waited to see the next move in this fascinating chess match.

"A blessing?" I squeaked. He continued to stare, so I nodded, curtseyed, and scurried, head-down, back to my spot.

"What happened?" Bowers whispered.

"Couldn't you hear?"

"Well, yeah. I heard." He put an arm around my shoulders and squeezed. "Don't worry about it."

Joe and Cecelia rode home with us, and from the back seat of Bowers' car, she said, "I think it's wonderful that you respect Our Lord enough to refrain from Communion when you aren't prepared. A lot of Catholics don't bother with a proper examination of conscience." She'd been behind me in line and had witnessed my humiliation up close.

Her husband offered a more practical explanation. "Father Zach needs a hearing aid."

As Bowers parked behind June's house, a gold Pontiac pulled in next to us. The driver's side door opened, and a balding black man about my height with a stocky build and a graying beard stepped out. He might have been shorter than me because his cowboy books made him taller. His plaid shirt was tucked into his jeans under a belt buckle of a cowboy on a bronco.

He walked around the car and opened the door for a woman I assumed was his spouse. She was his same age and had on a loose, navy-blue dress covered in a pattern of orange pansies. She wore her graying hair in a long braid, and turquoise- colored feather earrings dangled from her lobes. She broke into a smile as Bowers strolled over.

He shook the man's hand.

"Luther. Good to see you. You too, Ronnie."

Bowers took the glass baking dish from the woman so her husband could give her a hand up. Then my boyfriend wrapped his free arm around her and gave her a peck on the cheek, while she rocked him in a tight hug.

He motioned me over. "Frankie, this is Luther and Ronnell Jackson, our neighbors."

Ronnell looked up at me. "Let me see you." She made a show of inspecting me, and I straightened my shoulders and waited for judgement. She leaned forward. "What's a nice girl like you doing with this scamp?"

Bowers burst out laughing. "Scamp. That brings back memories. No one's called me that since I was twelve."

Luther closed the car door. "That's because you don't live with her."

The couple linked arms and walked with us into the house where they were greeted with hugs and laughter.

"Oh, dang it! They're here." June rushed forward. "I wanted to surprise you, but Father Zach's homily went on forever."

"It *was* a surprise," Bowers said, handing June the casserole dish.

She peeled back the cover. "Sweet potato hash. My favorite." She held up the dish in my direction. "Have you ever had sweet potatoes fresh from the garden, Frankie?"

"I haven't." I tried to put some enthusiasm behind my words. The reason I'd never had sweet potatoes fresh from the garden was because I hated sweet potatoes and avoided them like poison ivy.

"You are in for a treat."

June popped the rolls in the oven, set the timer, and then we went to the living room.

Ronnell and Luther admired Marc, commenting on how big he'd gotten and asking him about school. They made the appropriate noises when Agatha bragged about his grades.

Ronnell turned her warm smile on me to include me in the conversation, and I rustled up something intelligent to say.

"I noticed your farm as we drove by on Thursday afternoon. I didn't realize it was yours. I noticed a lot of trees. What is it you grow?"

"Almonds," the couple said at the same time.

"And sweet potatoes and peppers." Luther smiled. "The trees are almond trees."

"Almonds grow on trees?" I laughed, embarrassed. "If you'd asked me, I would have guessed bushes, like blueberries."

"They're an addition," Ronnell explained. "More of an experiment, since it takes several years before you see a return. But we were doing alright and thought we'd take a chance."

"They also have a petting zoo," June offered. "And a stand where they sell baked goods. You have to come back in the fall. Ronnie's cider donuts are to die for. Addictive." She rubbed her thick waistline to emphasize her point.

"It must be nice to have good neighbors," I said. "It could get lonely out here, so spread apart."

I was forced to get to know my neighbors after a crazed killer had tried to murder me in my home. It's the kind of experience that makes you think. How much time would pass before anyone noticed I wasn't around? Who would feed my pets? I introduced myself the next day.

Agatha grinned. "Lonely, my eye. They wanted to share labor."

As everyone laughed, June said, "And what better way to spend your summer? Kids without something to do turn to trouble."

Bowers explained. "Ronnie and Luther's kids came over here to help during harvesting, and we returned the favor."

"Kept you out of trouble," Carl said.

Ronnell turned conversation to me and Bowers. "How long have you two known each other?"

"Years," I said. "But we only started dating a few months ago."

"A few months?" Luther gazed fondly at his wife. "It took me two weeks to know I wanted to spend the rest of my life with you."

"Slow-poke," she joked, but I could tell she was pleased.

"Things have changed since we were young," June said. "I thought Agatha and Tom would never tie the knot."

The accused held up his hands. "Don't blame me. I kept asking."

His wife smacked his leg. "You did not. We were both busy getting our degrees."

I noticed Bowers was watching the banter, but not saying anything. Maybe talk about marriage made him uncomfortable. A sting of disappointment surprised me, but before I could give it too much thought, the timer went off, and we moved to the dining room.

EIGHTEEN

With the new guests, the seating arrangements changed, but only as far as the ends of the table. Carl sat at one end and Luther at the other, with their wives sitting to their right. Ronnell insisted on having Bowers next to her, so he sat across the table from me once again. Agatha and Cecelia managed to bookend me. It was becoming a bad habit.

In deference to the neighbors, Dymphna gave up the mumbling act. She was polite, but not a chatterbox. You'd never guess that she and I had been rolling around on her bedroom floor a short while ago. Quite the actress.

She didn't seem to mind talking about her relationship with Duane one-on-one, but that wouldn't do any good unless I could get her to have that one-on-one with Bowers. How long would that take? We were supposed to be on our way home tomorrow. I decided she would tell her brother everything before long, even if I had to steal that locket.

June set down a platter overflowing with a carved, roasted chicken, steamed carrots, and leftover green beans. She winked at me.

WHAT THE CLUCK? IT'S MURDER

"That fried chicken came from the freezer. You've never had fresh chicken, have you?"

"You are in for a treat," Agatha said, grinning at me from my left.

As June heaped servings of everything on my plate, I asked, "How fresh?"

"What time is it?" June called out to Carl.

"Six."

June nodded as if that sounded about right. "Three hours fresh."

"That's fresher than my sweet potatoes," Ronnell said with approval.

As Carl led the table in a prayer of thanksgiving, I tried desperately to think of a way out of eating this chicken. I couldn't say I was allergic. Not after the way I scarfed down a leg and two thighs yesterday.

"Amen."

Forks clanked and knives scraped as everyone dug in, but I stared at my plate and tried to block out images of excited chickens with bloody beaks.

"What's wrong?" Cecelia asked.

"I-I just . . ." Would it be bad manners to describe how I saw these chickens eating Duane last night? Not possible with Dymphna sitting at the table. Would eating the chicken, knowing it had swallowed a tasty bite of Duane, make me a cannibal?

June was the first to catch on. "You're worried about the way the birds carried on with Duane."

Carried on? That sounded romantic, not horrific. Luther and Ronnell exchanged glances. I could tell they didn't understand what we were talking about. Lucky them.

"Yes, ma'am," I admitted.

She barked out a laugh. "That bird would have pooped all that out long before slaughter."

Since her mouth was full, Agatha merely nodded vigorously, but as soon as she swallowed, she added, "They poop a lot. I mean a LOT."

Luther burst out laughing and nodded. "True. That's very true."

"Agatha! That's not appropriate talk for the dinner table," Cecelia said, her lips puckered in disapproval. "Especially with guests."

Luther grinned. "Toby has said much worse at our table."

"That's our eldest son," Ronnell added for my benefit.

It was Dymphna who convinced me to take my first bite. She methodically lifted her fork to her mouth and masticated. She wasn't enjoying her food, but I don't think her reason had anything to do with what June had served. Her mind was obvious on other things.

It surprised me she ate chicken because I figured her for a vegetarian. That seemed to go along with rune stones and fairy dresses and serenity. Still, I figured if she didn't have a problem with her dinner's connection to her late boyfriend, then who was I to throw a fit. Besides, the garlic and rosemary smelled wonderful.

"How are Toby and Sharon doing?" June asked.

"Four more weeks." Ronnell held up crossed fingers. "It's her third, so we don't expect any problems." She pinched Bowers' arm. "You're going to have to do some catching up."

Bowers kept his eyes on his plate.

To me, she added, "This will be our ninth grandchild."

I caught a wistful expression on June's face, and it occurred to me she and Carl had never mentioned biological children. Younger brothers and sisters were fine but no substitute for children of your own. At least that's what I assumed.

June changed the subject. "Frankie came to your defense today, Dym." June smiled at me. Dymphna did not.

"What do you mean?"

She'd gone back to the whisper-voice, so I didn't hear her, but her lips moved, and she raised an inquisitive brow.

Everyone stared at me, waiting for an explanation, and since Bowers had missed the conversation in the mini mart, he stared along with them.

I swallowed. "It wasn't a big deal."

June pointed her fork tines at me. "You're being modest." She looked to Ronnell and snorted. "Tallulah Lankershim had her big mouth running again."

"Poor soul," Ronnell said with sympathy. "She doesn't have any family to occupy her mind."

"She announced for everyone to hear that Dym and Duane were an item."

Luther frowned. "Duane Stoddard?"

"The same. Frankie put her in her place."

Dymphna's eyes bored a hole in me. She probably thought I had the perfect opening to reveal her secret. I *should* tell her secret, but something held me back. Pity? Nah. More likely self-preservation. I didn't want to get in the middle. The information should come from Dymphna herself. She saw it in my expression, and she gave me a private smile.

"Did you really?" Agatha punched my arm, knocking my fork out of my hand. "Good job. That old gasbag is always spreading gossip that isn't true." She made a face. "Ugh! Dym and Duane? Not a chance."

I know karma well, and she doesn't like me. The truth would come out, as would the fact that I'd known about Dymphna and Duane. Hadn't Bowers told me that June wouldn't tolerate lies? Rock, meet Hard Place.

I snatched up a forkful of sweet potato hash and almost bit the tines off the fork. "Mmm. These are delicious."

And they were. Smooth and buttery. Not killer sweet like my grandma's. Maybe I actually hated marshmallows, not sweet potatoes.

"Well," Cecilia said. "I'm happy you put a stop to that rumor."

"I was impressed with the logic of Frankie's argument," June continued. "Tallulah didn't have a chance, and once people thought about it, they realized how silly the idea was. If I hear anyone repeat it, I'll know just what to say."

June beamed at me, and I responded with a weak smile.

"I wish I'd been there to hear it," Bowers said, hiding a smirk behind his fork as he shoveled in some of those delicious sweet potatoes.

"Your loss, Marty. You shouldn't be so interested in your cell phone."

That sobered him up. "Sports. They can be addictive. You're right, of course. I'll work on it."

I narrowed my eyes at him. Bowers didn't give a hoot about professional sports teams, and he rarely checked in with the college teams.

So, what had he been doing on his phone?

NINETEEN

It didn't take karma long to catch up with me.

We were drinking our after-dinner coffee when trouble walked in. After nodding to everyone, Marshal Kipper asked to speak with Dymphna. Bowers, Carl, and Tom stood, perhaps ready to defend the women from the nice-looking marshal. Luther decided this was a family affair, and along with his wife remained seated, watching with interest.

Before Bowers' sister could do more than set her cup on her saucer, June said, "Anything you want to say to Dym, you can say in front of all of us."

"That's not how it's done. Now, I can take your sister down to the station to question her, or I can take her somewhere private in the house. Which will it be?"

It would take more than a marshal to intimidate June. She crossed her thick arms across her chest and lowered her chin. "Now you listen here, Sam Kipper. You can have your conversation in the kitchen like a civilized person. Doesn't my sister need a witness? Well? Doesn't she? Not that I'm suggesting you'd do anything underhanded, but we want to make sure Dym doesn't get confused or flustered."

She didn't look flustered to me. Her features rested in serene repose, as if we were discussing someone else. I knew not to trust that look. I got up and stood at Bowers' side.

Luther stood and Ronnell, dismay mixed with interest reflected in her eyes, followed. "This sounds private. We should leave you to it."

Kipper gestured with his hat at the silent fairy sitting at the table. "Is that what you'd like, Miss Bowers? To go to the station."

I caught the sudden firming of her jaw and the spark in her eyes and suspected Kipper was in for a tedious time. Bowers knew it too because he let out a long stream of air through his nose and his shoulders sagged.

"We might as well talk here," she said, softly, "because I have nothing to tell you."

Ronnie and Luther exchanged desperate glances. To leave or to stay?

The marshal pulled out a chair, sat, and rested his hat over his knee. "What was your relationship with Duane Stoddard?"

Agatha snorted coffee out her nose, and Cecelia cried, "That's an insult!"

A glance from Kipper silenced the outcry. "Well, Miss Bowers?"

"He was my sister's farmhand." Dymphna used her soft, whispery voice, but I was leaning forward with the rest of the witnesses and caught every word.

"I received an anonymous tip that the two of you were —" He paused and looked at Marc. "Friendly."

June squawked. "What did I tell you, Ronnie?" She glared at the marshal. "You've been listening to Tallulah

Lankershim. I thought you'd know better. At least Frankie had the sense to put a stop to that gossip right away." The lawman settled his interested gaze on me until I fidgeted before returning to the subject of his interrogation. "Well?"

Dymphna twitched her shoulders. "I'm nice to everyone."

"I'll vouch for that," June said. "Why, last Christmas in Phoenix, we were doing some shopping, and a panhandler high on crack tried to hassle her, and she just smiled at him. You know they're on crack, 'cause they smell like gasoline."

Agatha caught her son's saucer-eyed stare. "Cover your ears, Marc."

"But Ma!"

"Do it."

He raised his hands and cupped them over his ears, but everyone who's ever been a kid knows that old trick doesn't work.

Cecelia rapped on the table with her spoon like a judge calling the court to order. "Are you taking the word of a gossip monger over my sister?"

"No, ma'am."

Bowers tensed.

"Phyllis Stoddard gave us a description of a necklace and charm she found in her son's jacket around last Valentine's day. Someone thought the description sounded familiar. Now that I've seen it, I'd say the one you're wearing is a match. Do you mind if I examine it?"

All eyes were on the necklace.

"Let him see the darned thing," June said, but Dymphna declined.

Kipper sighed and nodded to Macoritto, and the deputy slipped out the door and returned a few minutes later with Phyllis Stoddard.

"Good evening, June." Phyllis took in the scene with a nervous glance, and she got a pained look in her eyes when she saw Ronnell and Luther, as if she were embarrassed to have additional witnesses.

It was obvious she didn't want to be here, and when Macoritto guided her forward, her feet stayed where they were until he gave a gentle tug.

Kipper stood and nodded at Dymphna.

"Is that the necklace you saw?"

Phyllis cocked her head and studied it. "Well, it *looks* like it. The only way to know for sure is to turn it over. There was an inscription on it. Two hearts next to each other with a plus sign underneath."

Bowers caught my eye, and we were thinking the same thing. That description sounded suspiciously familiar, like the drawing on Duane's love poem.

"Ma'am, will you show us, or will I have to assist you?"

I took a few steps back to stand next to Luther and Ronnie because if Kipper moved to *assist* Dymphna, there was going to be a brawl. I could see it in the expressions of Agatha, Cecelia, and even June. I reached out and guided Bowers backwards to stand next to me.

"You like being a cop."

Still looking at Kipper, he said, "I do."

"Remember that before you leap into the fray."

Luther snickered, and I felt Bowers relax.

Dymphna didn't force Kipper to act, but her choice of words was unfortunate.

"I want to confess."

Phyllis flinched as if someone had slapped her. "Did you kill my son?"

"Oh, Lord," Ronnie whispered.

"No. I loved him. And he loved me."

After a shocked silence, June said, "I thought that Teri woman was his girlfriend." June spoke in all innocence, and Bowers made a small noise in his throat. "You remember, Marty. You showed her Duane's cabin."

Kipper's posture went from casual to official.

Macoritto whistled. "A love triangle."

"No," Dymphna stubbornly insisted. "There was no one else. That Teri person is lying."

Kipper turned to Bowers. "Did you get her contact information while you were showing her around the cabin?"

Bowers let the criticism go and shook his head. "But I'm positive she'll be back." He motioned Kipper to the corner of the room, and the two of them held a whispering conference that ended with Kipper nodding.

The marshal stepped forward. "I want you folks to know I'm only helping on this case. Detective Deputy Robson from the Maricopa County Sheriff's Department is in charge. He thought you might be more receptive to someone you know, but if I don't make headway, he'll take over." And with that ominous warning, Kipper and Macoritto left.

Phyllis gave June an apologetic glance and followed the officers out the door.

"Dym, how could you!" Agatha said, voicing the thought written in all the sisters' expressions.

I slipped behind Bowers with the hope they'd forget about me.

"I can't say I approve of the relationship," June said, "but you're a grown woman."

"At least two of you recognize that."

I clutched Bowers' shirt in my fists.

"Who else knew?" Cecelia demanded.

"Frankie, of course."

June glared in my direction. "And how did she know?"

I held my breath. If Dymphna mentioned Windy, I'd have to drive myself home right now, with or without Kipper's permission.

"You used to talk to me." June's voice trembled. "But I guess that's in the past."

Bowers took away my hiding place when he turned to me, so I had to meet all the disapproving glares.

I shrugged. "Like you said. She's a grown woman."

Agatha huffed.

"I should say three of you," Dymphna continued, thoughtful. "Marty knew."

"Oh, Marty," June cried.

The corner of the accused's left eye pulsed, probably from the bad thoughts he was sending Dymphna's way.

Cecelia stood and went into the den, a symbolic washing of her hands.

Marc lowered his hands from his ears, and his next words proved he had been listening along with the rest of us. "Zombies remember their loved ones, Aunt Dym. They're the first ones they eat."

Agatha followed Cecelia out, dragging her son with her, though she paused long enough to toss a glare over her shoulder at me and Bowers. The men stood in an awkward circle, shuffling their feet, and staring at the linoleum floor. June ignored everyone and started baking something.

"I think we'll head out," Luther said.

Everyone crowded around them, apologizing for the display.

"We have children," Ronnell said. "It takes an awful lot to shock a parent."

She was being gracious. I doubt any of her kids had

been accused of murder. June and Carl walked them out to their car.

Dymphna stared, unseeing, at the wall. I slid into the chair next to her and put my hand on her arm. "Let's go upstairs." She nodded once and rose.

"Dym—" Bowers began, but she held up a hand. I gave him a look that said I'd take care of her and led her up the hallway staircase and back to the location of the alleged tickle fight. When I opened the door, Windy leaped off the bed and circled her mistress's legs. Dymphna scooped her up and held the dog close.

"I'm going to cry now," she said. "Would you mind taking Windy out? She probably needs to tinkle."

I gently pried the dog out of her arms. "Sure. No problem."

Either she had forgotten I communicated with animals, or she never believed I could.

TWENTY

When I returned to the kitchen, only Bowers remained. The rest of his family were having a spirited conversation in the den. I held up the dog and grinned.

"Look what I've got."

He didn't make the connection between the pet psychic and his sister's dog, brimming with information. Instead, he jerked his head toward the back door. "Come on. I need some fresh air."

Once we got outside and glanced at the dusky, wide-open space, I was reluctant to put the dog down. "What if she runs away? She'd be dinner. Maybe an appetizer."

"She'll be fine."

As soon as her paws hit the ground, Windy relieved herself on the side of the house. Then she hopped up the steps and growled at the back door.

"She's definitely not adventurous, but that's shouldn't be a surprise. Your sister doesn't seem like one to take risks, except with the police. Which is why—"

He let loose a harsh laugh and walked away.

Bowers wasn't prone to bitterness or sulking. He

typically put adversity in a headlock and reasoned it into submission. The cause of his distress couldn't be Dymphna's counterproductive attitude. She'd probably been that way her entire life. There had to be something more on his mind.

With a glance back at Windy, I followed him. It seemed more important to help Bowers through his funk than to talk to the dog.

We headed for the pasture beyond the chicken coop. Apparently, Windy didn't like to be alone because she followed. When we came to the wooden fence, Bowers leaned against it and watched the horses graze on Bermudagrass, Crested Wheatgrass and White Dutch Clover. My knowledge of desert grasses came from Bowers, who explained how Carl seeded the ground with a blend the horses enjoyed eating. I sat on the lower bar of the fence and leaned my face up to breathe in the cool air.

Since he hadn't spoken a word since his comment about Windy, I started a conversation with something objective.

"So, is Teri lying? Why would she? Unless she scans newspapers for recent deaths and then searches the houses of the deceased for trinkets to sell. And why are you so sure Teri is coming back? The poem wasn't that good."

He lifted his shoulders and let them drop. "Call it a hunch."

"Is that what you told Kipper?"

"Something like that."

I shifted my position so I could look at him. "Don't get all secretive on me. This isn't your case."

He stepped away from the fence and walked alongside it, away from me. "No. It's not."

Windy put her front paws on my leg and yipped,

beseeching me to pick her up. I hoisted her into my arms and followed Bowers.

"So?"

He stopped and turned to me. "So, what? It's not my case. I don't know everything Kipper knows. I'm not officially involved. I took my shot at getting Dym to talk to me, but that went nowhere. I just have to wait with the rest of you to find out how things unfold."

I snorted, and Windy, thinking I needed calming down, licked my chin. "Hello. I don't know if you remember me, but I'm the gal who regularly ignores your advice to stay out of things and causes the corner of your left eye to twitch."

"You can't get involved this time, Frankie. I mean it. You could be harmed, or cause harm." I assumed he stressed that last bit on behalf of his sister, Dymphna.

I scooted next to him and rested Windy's bottom on the fence. "How could I possibly get into trouble with you by my side?"

A bay mare approached and nuzzled Bowers' arm until he consented to scratch its neck. Windy growled, and to be safe, I pulled her close and stroked her back. She calmed down right away, so maybe she was jealous rather than frightened.

He still hadn't answered me. Since the horse was resting its head over Bowers' right shoulder as he rubbed the powerful neck muscles, I couldn't see his face, which meant he couldn't see mine. I left him to sulk and sat Windy back on the fence so I could look her in the eye. She returned the stare without blinking.

She seemed like a dog who would prefer the luxury of a soft pile to a dirt road, so I spread a padded carpet between her mind and mine and conjured up Dymphna and Duane having a heated argument.

The dog continued to stare, unaffected by what I'd shown her.

I added yelling, most of it coming from Dymphna.

Nothing. She kept those dark eyes fixed on me, but her unresponsiveness didn't have the same empty-headed disinterest I'd encountered in the chickens. It felt as if she expected me to explain myself.

I couldn't just ask her what had gone on between the couple. The average dog can understand up to two hundred words, but that didn't mean they could comprehend complex sentences.

Without shifting her position or showing any effort, the dog suddenly barraged me with images until my head swam with confused thoughts. Dymphna giggling at something Duane said. Kissing. Ugh! The dog agreed with me on that. The couple leaning their heads forward and whispering as lovers do.

Only one scene didn't fit with the others. Duane's lips moved, making garbled noises, while Dymphna listened, her forehead wrinkled, and pain reflected in her eyes. Or maybe it was fear.

My gaze went back to Windy, and this time, her little black orbs shone with wisdom. Or maybe I imagined it and the shine was because she was tearing up. She still hadn't blinked.

Windy had witnessed no yelling between Duane and Dymphna, which was something the chickens insisted on, but maybe Bowers' sister left the dog at home when she confronted her boyfriend. But why Dymphna's worried expression? Had Duane been breaking up with her? Had he finally told her about Teri? Did she kill him out of jealousy?

Dymphna had proved her skills as a liar which made this additional information...well, not so good.

Just like that, I had clarity. Bowers wasn't suffering from a fit of ego, nor was he upset about his sister's uncooperative attitude. He was freaking out because he thought she might have done it. Yikes.

I gathered the dog up again and moseyed around to Bowers' other side. Then I rested my bottom on the middle rail of the fence so I could sit the dog in my lap. To my surprise, he smiled, then laughed.

"You really think I could keep you out of trouble if we worked together? That's a tall order."

"If you think back, I've always had good intentions, and if we'd been working *together*, my information might have helped. Not that you don't always arrive at the same solution through your own methods, but if we shared information, wouldn't that make your job easier?"

He rubbed his chin. "Partners in crime, eh?"

"Not *in* crime. Unless you had something in mind you wanted to steal." I shifted Windy's weight. For such a little thing, she weighed a ton.

Bowers gave the mare a last pat and turned to me. "If we go forward with this, and God help me, I think we should, one of us has to be in charge, and that's me. If I tell you to do something, you need to listen to me."

"Sure."

"And if I tell you *not* to do something, the same rules apply."

"Okay, bossy-pants."

"Frankie, I'm serious. I know what I'm doing." He lifted his chin in mock importance. "I'm a professional."

I saluted. "Yes, sir. What's the plan?"

"I don't know. Let me think on it."

Patience isn't my strong suit. "How would you look at

the case right now if it were your case, and you didn't know anyone involved? Not even me."

He put his hands on his hips and shook his head. "It doesn't look good. Dymphna is the only person we know of who has a motive."

My eyebrows shot up. "I wouldn't say *only*. What about Paul? Wouldn't you question him? Didn't he blame Duane for his getting fired? And he obviously still wants his old job back, because he approached June about it when he saw her in the mini-mart."

He cocked his head and gave me an odd look. "I'm too close to this. My mind isn't clear. I didn't even think of Paul."

"You're right. You are too close. Because otherwise, you would have considered that Teri was the jealous woman, not your sister."

He groaned. "Man, I'm off my game."

I stood and gave him a friendly bump with my hip because by now it took both arms to hold Windy up. Since she was snoring, I thought it would be cruel to put her down. "You're just lost without your official notebook. You're probably having withdrawals."

The first time Bowers had interviewed me, he had his official notebook and pen at the ready. They must be departmental issue because Detective Gutierrez, his sometimes partner and always competition, had one.

I patted his back. "What you need is sleep. Right after we lock up the chickens."

He rubbed his eyes. "I forgot about the hens."

It was my turn to give *him* an odd look. I based mine on concern. Bowers the super cop forgetting things and ignoring suspects. He seemed . . . vulnerable. The world was out of balance, and I was arrogant enough to think I could quietly take charge and shepherd him through the investigation and directly to the murderer. In fact, I felt pretty chipper about it.

"It's getting late. Let's get the chickens over with and then you can relax. That's what you need. A glass of wine, put your feet up, and you'll be good as new."

"Here. Let me take her." He lifted the dog and hung her over one arm, where she flopped like a limp rag. He put the other arm around me and said, "Thanks, Frankie."

"No problem."

"And not a word to Gutierrez about this. Ever."

"My lips are sealed."

We had to walk around the run to get to the entrance, and once inside, we had little to do. Most of the chickens had settled on their roosts, and the few remaining skittered inside when I waved my hands. I latched the coop gate, and then Bowers snapped the padlock shut.

Agatha and Tom had taken Marc to bed and remained upstairs, and Carl, having to get up early to milk the two cows, had retired for the night. June darned a sock while Cecelia read a paperback book. I assumed Dymphna was still in her room because as soon as Bowers set Windy down, she shot up the back stairway.

I made Bowers take the remaining recliner and pushed the lever to raise his feet. Then I asked June if she had any wine. She looked up from her work.

"That's a good idea." Cecelia agreed, and she rose, but I insisted on serving them myself.

"It's in the pantry next to the stairs," June said. "Just use the regular glasses."

I found a large jug of cheap white wine and filled water glasses for me, Bowers, June, and Cecilia. I hugged them in my arms, so I only had to make one trip, and once I'd handed out the glasses, I settled myself on the couch.

June raised her glass. "What a day." It was as good a toast as any, and I sipped my warm wine, hoping it would relax me. It was a cloyingly sweet vintage, probably from this year.

"Can you believe Dym?" Cecilia asked, looking up from her book. "What is she thinking?" She snorted. "Love."

June sighed. "It shouldn't surprise me that she would pick someone like Duane Stoddard. Always has to be different."

It appeared Dym would be the target of their ire tonight, not me, so I felt safe asking some personal questions.

"What was Duane like? Everyone seems set against him, yet I haven't heard anything bad about him. Susi from the mini-mart liked him."

June dismissed that endorsement. "Susi likes anyone who will stop and chat with her. I must admit, I couldn't stand to be alone all the time."

"I just wondered. Was he rude? Lazy?"

"No, no. He was a hard worker."

"Duane wasn't ever *rude* to me," Cecelia admitted grudgingly.

"He drank too much," June offered.

I lowered my wine glass, feeling guilty that I was enjoying it even though it was muck. "Was he ever drunk on the job?"

She peered over the sock. With her glasses perched on the end of her short nose, she reminded me of Mrs. Santa. "No. I never actually saw him drunk, but he'd disappear on benders."

"How do you know that's what he did when he disappeared?" I pressed.

"Well, he told me. He apologized and said drink was the devil, and when he had one, it always led to two, and then it took hold of him. I admired him for knowing he had a problem, and usually, he kept it under control."

"How often did he lose control?"

"Only once or twice, not counting this last time."

I closed my eyes and brought up his Valentine dinner with Dymphna, courtesy of Windy. Duane brought in steaks. Dymphna tossed a salad. Windy waited patiently for leftovers. There weren't any wine glasses on the table. Odd for a man who liked his drink. Of course, I saw the setting through the eyes of a dog who couldn't care less about a nice Merlot.

"Are you defending him?" Cecelia asked in a dangerously light tone.

"Not really. I'm just trying to get a picture of him."

"Sounds to me like you're defending him. Had you ever met him?"

"Well, no."

"Frankie has a kind heart," June said.

"Really." That one word carried with it the same pronouncement—-that June didn't *really* know me. She gave me the smile of a guard dog coming in for the kill. "Is that why you kept Dym's secret from us?"

My back teeth ground together, but I kept my smile in place. "Isn't that the point? That it was Dymphna's secret to tell? Not mine?"

June stood and set her darning on her chair. "You must be so tired. I know I am."

I knew she was changing the subject for my benefit, but

I couldn't let it drop. "I heard he'd been in trouble with some friends. Was he ever in jail?"

"I have no idea," June admitted. "Phyllis will know."

Just the question I wanted to ask a grieving mother.

Cecelia closed her book. "Can't get any reading done in here with all the talking." She got up, said goodnight, and went upstairs. I picked up the wine glasses, shooing June away when she tried to take them from me.

"I'll only rinse these out and leave them by the sink," I promised, and that seemed to satisfy her. She headed for bed.

By the time I rinsed the glasses, made sure the back door was locked, and turned off the kitchen light, Bowers had fallen asleep in the recliner. I leaned over him and shook his shoulders.

"Bowers. Time for beddy-by."

He wrapped an arm around my shoulders and pulled me close, and putting a hand on my hip, he twisted me onto his lap so that my head rested against his chest. Then he kissed the top of my head and went back to sleep.

This position was extremely comfortable, but not one I'd want June to find us in tomorrow morning. I lifted my mouth to his ear. "Time to go to bed, Bowers."

His arms tightened around me.

"In your room next to June's."

That woke him up. His eyes opened and the legs of the recliner came down, almost flinging me to the floor. He blinked a few times, and I wrapped my arms around his middle and helped him to his feet.

"Come on, Mister Professional. Let's get you tucked in."

We parted at the top of the stairs, and I drifted off to wondering what it would be like to fall asleep in his arms every night.

TWENTY-ONE

Early the next morning—incredibly early by my internal clock—I got dressed in jeans and a t-shirt and slipped down the stairs. Bowers was stressed out, and so was the rest of his family. I had an urge to make life easier for them if I could, and that meant being proactive.

And yes. I had a selfish motive, too. This was supposed to be a weekend trip, but if Dymphna remained a suspect—and with the way she was withholding information, why wouldn't she? —Bowers and I weren't going anywhere. I can only wear my social face for so long before it cracks, and I was running out of clean underwear.

After closing the back door slowly so as not to make any noise, I turned around and got a face full of beauty. The sunrise painted the sky in purples and oranges, leaving the saguaro cacti and desert shrubs in shadow. I stared and wondered if I shouldn't get up early more often. Then I snorted. It would never happen.

Only the animals were awake. A nearby cactus wren warbled away in a song that reminded me of my car engine struggling to turn over during Wisconsin winters. His voice was joined by the rise and fall of a Gambel's quail.

A cow mooed from the large, red barn to the right of the house. This set off the horses lined up against the pasture fence, and they snorted in response. The goats joined in with a few bleats, and to round out the chorus, the chickens raised their voices. Cluck, cluck, cluck. That's where I was headed.

Last night, I'd seen Bowers hang the key to the run by the back door, and I pulled it out of my pocket, unlocked the gate, and stepped inside. Instead of opening the coop, I went to the trash barrel behind the coop, removed the lid, and began scooping feed into the pvc piping that funneled the yummies to the birds.

Once I filled it to the top, I went into the coop. I brought out the gallon buckets one at a time and filled them with water from the rain barrel. They were awkward to handle, because with the chicken nipples on the bottom of each bucket, I couldn't set them down.

By the time I finished, the legs of my jeans and the middle of my shirt were soaked. I never claimed to be coordinated. Finally, I tossed down a thin layer of mulch on the floor, left the door open so they could come out into the run, and admired my handiwork.

"Oh!"

I'd almost forgotten the eggs. I'd brought the basket with me, and I went through the coop and collected the early lays. Except for Lola, of course.

When I got back to the house, June bustled around the kitchen preparing breakfast. She smiled at me.

"Aren't you the early riser?"

Carl was already digging in, and June set another plate

next to him. I felt ridiculously proud, as if I had been moved to the grown-up table. When I finished eating, I told her to concentrate on the flapjacks and sausages for the late risers and I would set the table for the rest of the family.

I'd just put down the last fork when Bowers came into the kitchen. I was glad to see he looked awake and, if not happy, at least not depressed. He put one hand on my waist and leaned in for a kiss. June kept her attention on her cooking to give us some privacy. It was a sweet, soft kiss accompanied by a small smile that made my heart flip.

"Good morning."

My heart flipped again. There was something sexy in those benign words.

"I'm starved."

I grinned up at him. "Those of us who have been hard at work have already eaten breakfast."

Carl waved his fork. "Here, here."

Bowers stepped back and looked down at me with mock surprise.

"I've already fed and watered the chickens and brought in the eggs. And I put down a layer of mulch on the coop floor." Yes, I know I sounded like a needy schoolgirl waiting for a pat on the head, but I hadn't been this proactive in a long time. At least not voluntarily.

June walked over with a cast iron skillet and dished up breakfast to her baby brother. "We'll make a country girl out of her in no time."

Bowers pulled a chair out for me.

"I had no idea you were a country boy," I said as I scooted my chair up to the table.

His gaze rested fondly on his sister. "When my mother died, my dad was kind of lost with all us kids. Even though they'd only been married a few years, June and Carl invited us to move in with them."

June hushed him. "There was too much room for us."

Carl added, "And we wanted cheap labor while we were starting out."

"Who wanted cheap labor?" Cecelia came in from the den with the local newspaper folded under her arm. "You need to tell that paperboy of yours he needs better aim. Had to dig through the begonias to find today's edition."

June laughed. "My paperboy is sixty years old and does his route from the car, and if you question his aim, he'll make sure you really have to dig to find it."

"Good morning," Cecelia said to the rest of us, and seeing that Bowers had taken her usual spot next to me, she settled for the chair directly across from me. Or maybe she and Agatha saved intimidation for dinnertime.

Gesturing with her spatula, June said, "Marty was complaining about how hard it was to grow up here."

"Hard work is good for a person." Cecelia glanced at our plates. "Do you have toast, Junie?"

"In the pantry. And there's oatmeal in the slow cooker for Joe."

"Steel cut?"

June chuckled. "As if there's any other kind."

Cecelia got up to prepare their breakfast.

Agatha and Tom came next, preceded into the room by Marc, who was still in his ninja pajamas and leather slippers. I guess they didn't make zombie pjs. The kid stuck his face over Bowers' plate, gave a disappointed whine, and then slid into the chair next to his uncle.

"I wanted pigs in a blanket."

Bowers set down his silverware and rolled his sausage up in his maple syrup-covered pancake. "Pig-in-a-blanket."

The kid made a grab and Bowers pulled it out of reach and took a large bite. He turned to me, laughing and chewing. He had syrup on his lip, and I took my napkin and wiped it off. Female instinct. At least I didn't lick the napkin first.

"You goof."

He wiggled his eyebrows at me, and I laughed out loud. It was different seeing him so relaxed and happy. Bowers had a serious nature, and he rarely gave over to silliness. It was nice to see him smile so much. Our first few days here, he had worn his detective face and comported himself with the formal manner that went with the face.

I realized he might have been as nervous for me to meet his sisters as I'd been to meet them. I frowned. Was he worried I would embarrass him? Did he think they wouldn't like me? I took a deep breath and told Paranoid Frankie to go away.

The only awkwardness that morning came from Dymphna's absence. Maybe she was embarrassed about her relationship with Duane. Or maybe she was ticked over her sibling's reactions to her relationship with a mere farmhand, albeit a farmhand with a criminal record and a possible alcohol addiction.

Bowers laughed at a lame joke made by Marc, and he caught my eye and winked at me. I smiled back thinking how lucky I was. My man was handsome, strong when he had to be and gentle when it mattered. He could be protective, which I liked, probably because he didn't smother my opinions or act like a bossy-pants. Usually. He was funny, kind, and regularly surprised me.

After breakfast, June handed out chores. Everyone set about them without surprise or complaint, so I assumed this was the typical routine around the Baxter household.

She assigned me and Bowers the job of grooming the horses. She didn't apologize for asking me to pitch in as she did on my first day here. This acceptance of me as part of her clan made me want to live up to her expectations.

We accompanied Carl on his way back to the barn to check on the cows, which gave me the opportunity to increase my knowledge of farm life, starting with a question I'd been afraid to ask.

"Carl, can I ask you something?"

"Shoot."

My cheeks grew warm. I didn't want him to think I was criticizing. "Cows have to get pregnant to have milk, right?"

"Right you are."

"But, well, don't the calves have to eat, too?"

To my surprise, he laughed. "They sure do, and they eat a lot."

"Then why don't you leave them with their mothers? I mean, I haven't seen any calves."

"That's because of the three Cs." He held up three fingers. "Crushing, colostrum, and crap. Dairy cows have been bred to be docile, and they aren't always the best mothers. Sometimes they abandon the calves, and sometimes they wind up crushing them." He frowned. "Once you've seen a calf crushed by its own mother, it's not something you want to see repeated. So, we move the calf for its own safety."

"Yikes."

"Then we need to build up their immune system. We've only got a brief window to do that, and it requires colostrum. If we let the calf drink straight from the source, we have no idea if he's getting enough colostrum. We milk the mother after she's given birth and measure it. If there's enough colostrum in the milk, we feed it to the little guy. If there's not, we have to give 'em stored milk that we know has got enough."

"And crap?"

"Calves aren't born with a developed immune system. Not like human babies. And grown cows, well, cows go where they're at, if you know what I mean, which means lots of bacteria."

"The three Cs. That makes sense. Are the calves in the barn?"

"Good heavens, no. We're not set up to safely raise calves. There's a farmer not far from here who has a calf hutch. He's got two kids that love helping. Treat the critters like pets."

We entered the barn, and I got a whiff of urine-drenched hay and manure. The cows each had a stall, and there were several more stalls for the horses. Carl pulled out brushes, combs, a hooked instrument, and what looked like a small scrub brush.

Bowers took them from him. "Why don't you let me get Frankie set up with the horses, and I'll help you clean out the stalls."

"Wouldn't say no."

We walked to the stalls at the end of the barn and Bowers opened the first door. I gazed at the bay mare Bowers had been scratching last night. She seemed much bigger without the fence between us.

"Have you ever been around horses?"

"Sure. Penny and I used to ride Mabel." Mabel was about a hundred years old. We took her out, and she basically walked back to the comfort of the barn with us on her back.

He set the tools on a shelf, patted the horse on the neck,

and looked up at me. "Frankie, you're going to have to come into the stall to groom her."

"Right." I crept closer. "Good horse." I reached up to scratch her neck, and she nuzzled me.

"Have you ever groomed a horse?"

I hated being shown how to do anything, probably because the perfectionist in me thought I should do new things exactly right the first time around. Silly, I know, but tell that to the snotty voice in my head.

"I've watched Penny do it." I waited for the snort of derision, but it didn't come.

"That's good. Then you should pick it up quickly."

He took a brush and began stroking the horse. "This is Matilda. She loves being brushed. They all do, but—"

I saw—or rather heard—what he meant. Matilda made soft groaning noises of pleasure as he moved the brush down her back. When he stopped, she turned her head and nudged him. He rubbed her chin. "Greedy goat," he murmured. Then he handed me the brush and told me to give it a shot.

I slipped my hand under the handle and gripped the base as he had. Then I skimmed the bristles over her back.

"Put some muscle into it."

I leaned forward, giving my puny arms some backup.

"Shorter strokes. And flick your hand at the end."

He took the brush away and showed me. Dust flew up at the end of each pass.

"When you're done brushing her, you can move onto the mane and tail." He picked up a metal comb. Holding the hair at the base with his hands, he started at the end of the lock and combed, taking in more hair as he cleared the knots until he could stroke from root to end without a snag. He handed me the comb.

"Got the idea?"

The mane and tail. I walked back and was about to step behind the horse to get a better look at her tail when Bowers grabbed my arm and pulled me back. "Never do that. If you're going to pass behind her, keep your hand on her rump and talk to her so she knows you're there. Better still don't do it and walk around her front instead."

"I think I'll go back to brushing." I switched tools and started on her neck. "You seem to feel better this morning."

He picked up the comb I'd just set down and started back on her mane. "A little sleep can give one a fresh perspective."

"So? Do you have a plan of attack?"

He stopped to scratch Matilda between the eyes. "As you pointed out yesterday, we need to talk to Paul about how he got fired and where he was the evening Duane died. We also need to ask Phyllis about Duane's run-in with the law. How serious was it? Did he go to jail? Was it for something seriously criminal or simply stupid?"

He brushed away a horse fly. "My sister would be a great source of information, if I could only get her to talk to me."

I snickered. "Want me to try again?"

"No, thank you." He stopped combing to work on a knot.

"We also need to find out which bar he frequented and talk to people there. Had he said anything to them about being worried? Did he seem nervous? Scared? Who were his friends? Or who did he hang out with? What did he do in his spare time?"

I furrowed my brow. "Wasn't his spare time spent here? I mean, he lived here and ate here and worked here. How much spare time did he have?"

I bent over to reach Matilda's legs with the brush.

"June can answer that."

I finished the front leg on my side and looked up. Bowers was struggling with whether to spill. He'd spent so long keeping his own counsel that it must have been hard for him to open up to me, and I told him so. That did the trick.

"There was something about that poem Duane wrote that's bugging me, but I can't get my finger on what it is."

"A lot of soppy stuff about two hearts? You mean that could be a clue?"

He narrowed his eyes. "I wonder . . ." He worked the mane for a few minutes more. "How would you like to take a walk when we're finished?"

"Love to." I grimaced. "Exercise is my favorite thing."

The corners of his mouth curved up. "We'll be alone."

I stopped brushing the horse's hind leg and turned to him, fluttering my eyelashes. "Mr. Bowers, are you trying to tempt me into going?"

He stepped close and rested his hands on my waist. "Miss Chandler, I'm shocked at the suggestion." Then he lowered his head to kiss me, and he kept kissing me until Matilda, annoyed at the interruption in her spa treatment, bumped us.

"Meet you at the barn door in twenty minutes?" I said, a little breathless.

"There are three horses. It's going to take longer than that, but when we're finished here, we'll take off."

Time alone with Bowers put some zip into my brushing, and by the time he'd returned from helping Carl, I'd finished all three horses.

Their coats had a glossy sheen, at least in spots, and their manes and tales were more knot-free than my hair. After inspecting my work, Bowers gave me an approving nod. I accepted it in the spirit it was offered even though I'd hoped for a blue-ribbon. A gold star. Maybe a party. I decided country girls didn't expect rewards for chores done well and looked forward to my private reward —alone time with Bowers.

It had to wait until we cleaned their hoofs. All twelve of them.

TWENTY-TWO

Bowers and I weren't destined to have alone time. He grabbed two bottles of water from the house, and as soon as we took off hand-in-hand and headed toward the rising hills at the edge of June's property, a third wheel showed up on the form of Marc.

He broke through our clasped hands, his arms stretched out as if he had crossed the tape at the finish line of a close race, and then the kid circled back to us.

"Where are we going?" he gasped, breathless after his run to catch up to us.

Bowers ruffled the kid's hair. "Timbuktu."

Marc snorted. "My dad used to say that, but I looked it up on the Internet. It's all the way in Mali. We'd have to swim."

The Internet had ruined many a parental joke.

Bowers gaze held both admiration and disappointment. "Got me there. I'm just showing Frankie the property. She's never been here before."

Marc slid a glance in my direction, and I felt I was being evaluated and that there would be no second chance. I straightened my shoulders and lifted my chin, and as I did so, a gnat flew up my nose. I shook my head repeatedly and with violence while blowing out my nose like an angry bull into my cupped hand.

While Bowers patted my back, Marc went into hysterics, and his laughter only subsided when I expelled the invader into my hand and wiped it on the ground. I handed Bowers my water bottle.

"Open, please."

He did so, and I rinsed my hand off and wiped it on my jeans.

"That was cool." Marc grinned at me. I had passed the test.

Instead of putting his arm around me, Bowers reached out and pulled Marc to his side. "How ya doing, kiddo?"

Marc's expression turned serious. "Fine."

"Not having any nightmares, are you?"

"W-e-l-l..."

I gave my forehead a mental slap. How could I be so insensitive? Being around several murders had made me a tiny bit inured to death—at least when I'm not staring at dead bodies. I should have considered the effect news of a dead body would have on a child.

"I've been sleeping with the door open and the light on in the closet." He hung his head and mumbled. "Bet you think I'm a big baby."

Bowers squeezed his shoulder. "Nah. I've been keeping my closet light on, too."

Marc whipped his head up to stare at his uncle. "Seriously?"

"There's something very creepy about a sudden death. Not that we have anything to worry about."

"But I heard someone killed Duane." The kid gulped. "Ninjas. Or Zombies."

"If anyone started sneaking around here, the chickens would yell their heads off. Not to mention the dogs," he added with a nod toward the approaching Chauncey and Hero.

"But did they bark when Duane got killed?"

Bowers gave it serious thought. "You have to remember, there's a lot of land to cover. The dogs might have been busy all the way at the other end of the pasture. But, with two of them looking out for us . . . ."

"Don't you mean three?" I said, entering the spirit of things.

Marc frowned, and then he giggled. "You mean Windy? She can't do anything."

"She can bark. She's guarding *inside* the house."

He snorted. "She'd probably fart on them!"

I thought about it. "You don't mean—that's not how she got her name, is it?"

"Sure is. She farts all the time."

Good to know next time she wanted me to carry her.

We'd reached a rocky path that ran alongside a rocky hillside dotted with cacti that bordered one side of June's property. Bowers explained we were walking in was a creek bed that dried up long before June and Carl had bought the property.

The dogs darted back and forth, sniffing and marking as they went. Chauncey didn't have much opportunity to run around back in Wolf Creek because of the leash laws, and he was enjoying his freedom. He stuck his nose in a shrub, and while he had his face buried, a gecko lizard escaped and ran to the next shrub for cover. He finally snorted and gave up, happy to catch up with Hero and lick his new friend's face.

I watched, amazed at the transformation in my pup. Maybe I should get a second dog when I got home. Twice the food and twice the poop bags, but it would be worth it to see him this happy all the time.

Marc hopped from one smooth, gray rock to the next with ease, but Bowers took my elbow to help me navigate the uneven ground. Finally, he halted and searched the landscape. He pointed toward where the hill sharply receded as if someone had taken an ice cream scoop and removed a portion of the land.

"Up here."

I followed, not sure what he was looking at. Marc had more faith and ran ahead. As I navigated the climb at an angle, I noticed an opening halfway up the hill. When I was within thirty feet of the entrance, a second opening, hidden round the corner, revealed itself. Desert grasses hung from a dip in the ground between the two entrances, giving them the appearance of a heart—the kind of artistically challenged heart I might draw.

I sucked in a breath. "Two hearts," I whispered.

Marc ran inside despite Bowers' protest, and in a minute, the kid popped out the entrance of the second cave. We both entered less cautiously than we might have had Marc not just made it through alive.

Inside, the walls widened out to about twenty feet across, and thirty or so feet back, a narrow passage linked the two chambers together.

"Holy smokes."

Bowers nodded. "Two hearts, side-by-side."

"Duane's poem was about a place?"

"Or it's a coincidence."

Bowers didn't sound like he thought it was a coincidence.

Enough sunlight made it inside that we could see the basic outline. There were a few crumpled soda cans and candy wrappers in the corner that looked as if they had been here for a long while. Decades.

Marc ran by, followed by the dogs as they amused themselves running circles through the two caves. We sidestepped through the passage and found the second cave much darker and cooler than the first, as the sunlight entered this entrance at an angle.

Bowers pulled a small flashlight out of his back pocket and swung the beam around.

"A flashlight? What are you, a boy scout?"

"I grabbed it when I got the water." He sounded distracted, so I moved closer. He aimed the light at the ground, more specifically, at tire tracks. When he crouched down for a closer look, Marc skid to a halt and came over to see what Uncle Marty found so interesting. The dogs stuck their snouts on the ground and joined in, snorting up dust.

Marc snapped his fingers. "Cool. I bet I could get my bike up here and ride circles around this place." He stepped into the passage and held his arms out to his sides. He couldn't straighten them out, but he seemed confident there was room enough for a bicycle to get through because he dusted off his hands and grinned. "Cool."

"Could these be from a mountain bike?" Made sense to me. I'd often see teenagers—and even adults without sense—riding in the hills and valleys around Wolf Creek.

Bowers lowered his voice. "Not bike tracks. More like," he tilted his head, studying them, "a wheelbarrow." He pointed at the parallel tread marks.

My gaze flickered to the boy trying to climb the back

wall, egged on by his furry friends, but Bowers shook his head.

"He obviously didn't know about this place, and there aren't any other kids around here."

A shudder traveled over my shoulders. "What would adults be doing in a cave with a wheelbarrow? They would be moving something, obviously. Oh, jeepers. Do you think Duane was killed here and then moved to the chicken run?"

"That doesn't seem logical. No one visits these caves. Why not leave the body here, where it would remain undiscovered for weeks? Months even."

"If no one comes up here, maybe they've been around since you were a kid. Can you tell how fresh they are?"

He stood. "Not really."

When he shone the light around the dirt floor, it became obvious there had been a lot of shoes treading the ground recently, but the prints overlapped each other. I couldn't make out one clear print. He took a few steps to the entrance and looked back at the tracks.

"It rained a few weeks ago. June complained that her flagpole broke in the winds. That much wind and rain should have obliterated the tracks, or at least muddied the ground and made the indentations clearer."

To prove his point, he rubbed his fingers around in the dirt near the prints, and it pushed around like sand. He pulled his flannel shirt off and gently placed it over an area that had both track marks and footprints, and then he shooed away Chauncey and Hero, who had rushed over to investigate.

"Do you think this has anything to do with Duane's murder? Or was this just a meeting place where he and your sister could find some privacy?"

"Just the two of them and their wheelbarrow?" He shook his head.

He was right. Glancing around the cave, I didn't see anything romantic about it.

Marc approached us, and Bowers gave him a gentle push toward the entrance.

"Let's go."

Outside, the afternoon sun beat down on us, but it's a dry heat, right? Bowers stepped aside to make a call. Water, a flashlight, and a cell phone. My boyfriend *was* a boy scout.

He returned and the five of us headed back to the house, though I suspected that Hero and Chauncey were more interested in being fed than in the company.

By the time we arrived, Kipper and Macoritto were waiting. I wasn't surprised, since I couldn't imagine anyone else Bowers would want to contact after finding strange prints in a cave, though I did think he was overreacting.

He walked them over to the empty wheelbarrow resting outside the barn. While the men huddled in conference, I went upstairs to splash water on my face and apply moisturizer to the touch of sunburn on my nose.

I returned to the kitchen in time to find June preparing dinner. Chicken. Surprise.

TWENTY-THREE

If Bowers had wanted to keep the caves a secret, he should have gotten the memo to Marc. The kid waxed eloquent about our adventurous walk all through dinner, though he seemed to have forgotten about the tire marks except as they related to his anticipated biking adventure. Agatha immediately squashed that idea.

"Rattlesnake season is starting. It's too dangerous to go climbing around the hills."

"I won't be *climbing*. I'll be *biking*."

"Unless you plan on *flying*, the answer is no."

He squished up his face, and I could see the wheels turning as he contemplated how he might learn to fly.

"Are you talking about the Double Trouble?" June asked with an amused smile.

"Double trouble?" Agnes frowned.

Cecelia joined June in the joke. "Those two caves on the county land about a mile down the old creek bed. That place you young ones used to hang out."

"That's it," Bowers said.

"It was the only place we could get some privacy,"

Agatha said. "The only place *you* couldn't reach us." She grinned at me. "We used to sneak out and climb that hill into our own private clubhouse knowing that June would never bother to walk that far or climb up to get us."

Marc looked ready to cry. They'd just described heaven.

June stabbed a piece of chicken pot pie with her fork. "That's what I let you think because I wanted you out of my hair."

Dymphna got a dreamy expression. "Me and my friends used to smoke weed up there when we were in high school."

June paused before taking a bite. "I knew that too. You reeked of it."

"Does anyone go there now?" Bowers couldn't help himself. He sounded like a cop seeking information, and from the look Agatha and Dymphna exchanged, he had chased away any fond childhood memories. June didn't seem to mind.

"Not that I know of. Carl?"

Carl scratched his ear. "Can't remember seeing anyone. Not that I spend a lot of time at that end of the field."

Bowers leveled his gaze at Dymphna. "Did you and Duane ever go there?" When she hunched her shoulders and stared at her plate, he added, "It's important, Dym."

She blushed. "We were adults. We had no need to hide ourselves in a cave."

"I assume you two talked about things. Your past. You never wanted to show him your childhood hangout?"

"I didn't want him to feel awkward." She waved her fork toward June and then Carl. "Remind him that he worked for my sister. I agree with Agatha. Those caves are dangerous because no one goes there anymore. There could be snakes or mountain lions." She looked at Bowers. "You should stay away."

Conversation dried up, and we returned to eating our meal. When everyone moved to the den for coffee, Bowers and I stayed behind. "Did you believe her?" I didn't need to explain who *her* was.

"I can't see a reason she would lie."

"Did you tell Kipper about the tire tracks?" I made my voice casual, as if I had a million things on my mind and that one just happened to slip out.

He gave me a hard stare. "You know I did. Why?"

I tried to return the stare. "Because I can't see why a couple of tire tracks in a childhood hangout would make you call the local police."

He must have regretted the stare because now he wouldn't make eye contact. "It's just something out of the ordinary. There's been a murder, and you never know what matters."

I huffed. "Remember how we talked about lying? It goes both ways."

"What I said was absolutely true."

Now I had a dilemma. I considered that if I didn't share every detail I was thinking with Bowers, I wasn't lying. If I chastised him for keeping something back, I would have to apply the same rule to myself. I switched gears and nodded. "Okay."

His eyes narrowed because he suspected I had bested him again. Twice in one weekend. I was on a roll. But I couldn't afford to get cocky. Once we were away from his sisters, the mental fog would lift, Bowers would return to normal, and he'd make me pay.

"What now?"

"June told me which bar Duane said he used to hang out in, but I'm not sure I want to take you there."

I snorted. "Why? Are you afraid I'll drink myself into a stupor, come back here, and embarrass you in front of your sisters?"

"No. It's a bit rough."

I beamed at him. "But you're going to be there, and I know you wouldn't let anything happen to me." Bested, three times in one weekend. Darn, I'm good. I grabbed our jackets and let him tell June we were stepping out to see the nightlife in Cave Bear.

We passed the mini mart on the way to downtown, and through the glass windows, I could see Mary leaning against the counter with her chin on her fist. She straightened up and waved as we drove by.

Poor woman must be bored out of her mind, I thought. Then I realized that a bored woman killing time in a mini mart probably amused herself by noticing every car that drove past. She was a fount of information waiting to be tapped, and I wondered why Bowers hadn't suggested we talk to her. However, I was eager to check out The Black Stallion, Duane's bar, so I saved the thought, intending to ask Bowers on the way back.

When we drove to June's house from Wolf Creek last Thursday, we approached from the other side of her homestead, so I hadn't seen downtown Cave Creek. It was adorable in a small-town way. The store fronts had wood siding to make the main street look like a scene from a Western. Many of them were family-owned restaurants with quaint names like The Trough, Granny's Table, and

The Squirrel's Nest. The sign in the last place proclaimed it was a Vegan's delight.

Artsy places like Balls of Yarn, The Bead Corral, and The Gelded Gallery stood alongside a gun shop, a bank, and a realtor's office. The sidewalk, especially around the restaurant entrances, teemed with people out to socialize.

We passed out of downtown and into open space. After another five miles, I spotted numerous cars parked in the dirt off the side of the road. Bowers pulled over next to a gigantic red pickup truck covered in mud splatters. He locked the doors and we headed past about a dozen more pickups in various colors and sizes until we reached the doors of The Black Stallion.

Dwight Yoakam's *Guitars, Cadillacs* blasted from the front door as a drunk man pushed his way outside to the amusement of several Stetson-wearing men smoking cigarettes. The woman with them wore a cowboy hat as well, but she merely gazed up at one man the way Chauncey looks at my plate when I'm eating pot roast.

Inside, the wood dance floor was covered with couples doing the two-step, twirling and scooting as if they were born moving that way. Tables and booths lined the edges of the dance floor, and these were packed, as was the bar to our left. The place smelled of stale beer and old cigarette smoke.

Bowers took my hand and we scooted past tightly packed chairs and groups standing in conversation until we made it to the line waiting to order from one of two bartenders.

"This place isn't scary," I said. And then I took a closer look at the clientele.

Most of the women were in skin-tight pants and leather, laced-up vests or sleeveless shirts despite the evening chill, and many of them sported tattoos on their shoulders and necks. There was a hardness in their expressions—tight lips and heavy eyeliner—even as they seemed to be enjoying themselves.

A man stumbled as he got up from a barstool and splashed the front of my shirt with beer. He grinned at me showing a few missing teeth before he belched.

Bowers placed an order for two beers, and while I waited, I cracked open a peanut I'd snatched from a bowl on the counter. At first, I thought I'd swallowed wrong and the nut was stuck in my throat, so I coughed a few times, but the ache wouldn't leave, and my eyes teared up.

Bowers handed me my glass. "What's wrong?" He swore under his breath. "I knew I shouldn't have brought you here."

"It's not that." I took a sip of the mild brew. "I just suddenly feel so sad."

"Oh." No man knows how to respond to that, so I didn't take it personally when he brushed it aside. "The bartender said he didn't remember Duane or know any of his friends. I assume he's lying."

"What are you going to do?"

"Wander. Listen. The man just died, so he might be a topic of conversation."

And so, we wandered, which was kind of difficult because it was so crowded. I tripped over a chair leg and apologized to the woman sitting there. She had slick, unnaturally black hair pulled back tightly into a bun, enough eyeliner and mascara to fill the cracks in my driveway, and white skulls dangling from her ears, which, along with the breasts popping out of her shirtfront, was not my idea of how a woman in her fifties should dress. She turned her head to give me a penetrating glare but otherwise ignored me.

Most of the conversation I picked up had to do with three topics: irritating children, misbehaving boyfriends and husbands, and problems associated with horses. No one was talking about Duane.

A little farther on, three men in leather jackets and pants stepped into Bowers' path. The man who appeared to be the leader stood a few inches shorter than me and was built like a box. His blunt features were not improved by the half-circle scar on his cheek, as if someone had tried to grind a broken bottle into his face. That's what kept me from giggling at the pink bandanna on his head.

His sidekicks were obviously the muscle. The bald one was Bowers' height with an open leather vest. His biceps bulged every time he moved his arms, which he did often, as if he were posing for a weightlifting magazine. The third man was a bearded mountain with long, shaggy hair. Gigantic. Just . . .huge. If Grizzly Adams had worn a leather jacket, this man would be his twin.

"Haven't seen you here before," the guy with the scar said.

"That's because I haven't been here before," Bowers said, his voice deceptively pleasant.

Scar stepped forward and his backup followed suit.

"What's the sudden interest?"

Bowers put an arm around my shoulder. His voice stayed casual, but I could tell from his tight grip and the way he clamped me to his side that he expected trouble.

"Not that it's any of your business, but I'm showing my girlfriend around Cave Bear."

The guy sneered, and I realized that Bowers was at a disadvantage. I thought he looked great, but he could hardly come off as an invincible threat and defender of all that is good and holy while dressed in a blue, untucked flannel shirt over a white t-shirt and khakis. In that outfit, he might even be mistaken for a pushover.

If Scar started something, I couldn't expect Bowers to take on three guys and get me out of here alive, especially when one of them was a living land mass. I put my animal behavior knowledge to work. If these three stray dogs smelled weakness, they would pounce and probably tear us to shreds. So, like any dog feeling threatened, I faked bravado.

Instead of lunging and snarling on the end of my leash, I tugged on Bowers' arm and put on my bored face. "I can't imagine why Duane liked this place. Let's go."

The effect wasn't what I'd hoped for. The threesome stepped closer, and the chatter at the surrounding tables quieted to low murmurs.

"Did you say Duane? As is Duane Stoddard?"

Bowers stepped forward, and they were almost nose-to-nose, except Scar's nose only came up to Bowers mouth. If the worst came to pass, Bowers could bite him. "He worked for my sister."

"Good for you. That doesn't explain why you're nosing around here."

I shoved myself in between them with difficulty and smiled. "Duane's mother asked us to hunt down—er, find his friends to make sure they were invited to his memorial service." I glanced around the room.

"That's really nice," the moving mountain said, and his sincerity gave me the confidence to continue.

"We heard he hung out here, so we assumed his friends did, too. And you do. At least, I assume you were his friends."

The mountain nodded. "I liked Duane."

The muscle-bound, vest-wearing sidekick looked like he agreed with the mountain but needed permission from Scar to do so.

"Is one of you Tommy Kincaid?"

Mr. Muscles eyebrows shot up. "Do I know you?"

"His mother mentioned that you were his close friend." I leaned in to share a confidence. "Phyllis is broken up by his death. Of course, she wants answers, and she wondered if he had been depressed or nervous during the last few weeks of his life."

"Not that I noticed," the mountain said, and Tommy shook his head in confirmation.

Scar looked at me. "When is it?"

Darn. I hadn't thought this through, but Bowers came to the rescue.

"Phyllis hasn't set a date yet. The police have to release the body to her first. We'll let you know. I assume we can find you here?"

"That's right."

Scar stepped aside to let us pass, and his parting words were, "And now I know where to find you, too."

As we turned the corner back toward the bar, Bowers, who had been gripping my arm, leaned in and whispered. "I'm getting us another round. Drink fast and we'll get out of here."

I nodded and waited at the corner of the bar. And then I saw the source of the ache in my chest. Against the wall sat a bird cage, and someone had the bright idea to use the cage as a home for a large squirrel. From the shells surrounding the cage, I assumed patrons amused themselves by tossing the poor thing peanuts.

Our eyes met, and I winced at the appeal in the little

guy's eyes. I couldn't leave him there. It wouldn't be right. I only hoped I could convince the squirrel I was acting in his best interests.

Blocking out Garth Brooks' *Friends in Low Places*, I slipped open the mental doorway until it stood wide open. I imagined a beam of light traveling from my mind to the squirrel's. In my imagination, I acted out unzipping my jacket, unlocking the cage door, and inviting the squirrel to come inside. Then I walked out the front door and set him free.

His tail shot straight up. I think he got the message. Unfortunately, the guy next to me noticed the squirrel's sudden movement and started throwing peanuts into the cage. I counted to ten to keep from yelling and then inched closer.

"That girl at the end of the bar—see the blond? She was checking you out a minute ago."

He jerked his head in that direction and eyed the buxom beauty sipping a margarita by herself. He shook his head. "Out of my league."

That was probably true. He wasn't bad looking, but he didn't look tough like the rest of the crowd. No facial hair. No tattoos. "You'll never know if you don't try. Go on. Introduce yourself."

After toying with a peanut for a few minutes, he tossed it back in the bowl—ew—and pushed away from the bar. "Why not?"

As soon as he moved, I slipped around the corner of the bar and pretended to admire the mascot. I wiggled a finger at him and flipped up the door's lock as I did so. Then I unzipped my jacket and stretched it out to my sides as if my fondest desire were to shrug it off—providing cover as I did so. The squirrel shot inside, and I bit my lip to cover a squeak as tiny claws dug into my shirt. Then I acted as if I was suddenly cold and wrapped my jacket around me, hugging the squirrel to my chest. Anyone who saw me might think I was a flake, but I don't think they could have seen the squirrel's escape.

Bowers walked up with two beers. I took them from him and slid them in front of a couple farther down the bar. "On the house." They looked up in surprise but didn't question their good fortune. Then I grabbed my date's arm and dragged him toward the door.

"Should I be worried," he said in a low voice.

"Are you armed?"

"Aw, hell."

The cold air hit my face as we pushed our way outside. The drunk guy who had stumbled out before was leaned up against the wall with his eyes closed, but the group in the cowboy hats had left. Before we made it five yards, the harsh-looking woman I'd tripped overstepped in front of us.

"I saw what you did."

"What *did* you do, Frankie?" Bowers hissed in my ear.

"Nothing. This lady is mistaken."

"The name's Dee-Dee." She rubbed her nose with her palm. "I've been worried about that squirrel ever since Bart first showed him off. Dang fool. It has been a cloud over my good time ever since."

I sighed with relief.

"You stole their mascot?" Bowers said through gritted teeth.

Dee-Dee jerked her chin toward The Black Stallion. "I heard you talking to those guys in there. Mort and Tommy and Bub. Those aren't the guys you should be talking to if you're looking for information about Duane. You want

Slick. They don't move a muscle unless Slick tells them to jump, and then they only ask how high."

"Do you know where we can find Slick?"

Dee-Dee considered Bowers as if she were memorizing his face, since she knew this would be the last time she'd see him alive. "If you really want to, The Painted Pony is a body shop. He owns it."

I was just about to thank her when the bartender burst out the doors. "Someone took Henry!" His gaze rested on my guilty face and he started over. Dee-dee stepped around us and pointed and the drunk guy.

"He was foolin' around with something. Might have been Henry."

We didn't wait to see what happened. It seemed to take forever to get to our car, and I held my breath until I strapped myself in. Bowers started the car and the back end fishtailed as he turned onto the road.

I unzipped my jacket and out popped Henry. He gave me a look of betrayal, so I held him up so he could see The Black Stallion recede over my shoulder. After that, he rested his front paws on the dash and his back paws on my chest and stared out the front window, his flicking tail tickling my nose.

"Where do you think you're taking him?"

"Home. I mean, to June's place."

"That's a rock squirrel. They eat eggs, and he might go after the chicks if June decides to expand the flock." He glanced at my horrified expression. "I suppose we could release him by the hillside. They like rocky areas."

"I'll take him there myself."

"I don't want you wandering alone at night."

"Then we'll take him."

He drove on in silence. I could feel the tension in the air, and I knew what was coming. He didn't disappoint me.

"If you're going to come with me places—places like The Black Stallion—then I need to know you won't compromise me."

Compromise. What a nasty word. "I headed us out the door the minute Henry was safe," I protested.

"What if I'd started a conversation with someone? One that was leading somewhere. Not only would I have lost out on gaining valuable information, but I would have been in a tight spot if Henry's disappearance had been discovered before I was ready to leave." He grinned to take the sting out of his words. "Two guys I can handle. Three, I'm not so sure. Four would have been over my limit."

"Oh my gosh. I didn't think about that." I reached out and touched his arm. "Bowers, I'm so sorry. They could have hurt you."

That ruffled his manly pride. "Let's not exaggerate. I'm sure I would have figured a way out of it. But it would have been more difficult because I would have been distracted worrying about your safety."

Unlike me, I thought, who hadn't given a care about his. When he parked the car out back of June's house, Henry plastered his body against the window. As soon as I opened the door, the squirrel took off into the darkness. There wasn't a thing I could do about it, so I shrugged. Bowers sighed.

We checked on the birds who were tucked in and locked up for the night.

"June must have taken care of them herself." Bowers seemed disappointed that his sister hadn't trusted him to keep his promise to check on the birds once we returned.

After we hung our jackets on the pegs inside the back

door, Bowers pulled me into his arms and kissed me. "That's for coming up with the idea of the memorial. Pretty good for an amateur."

"Is that you, Marty?"

Bowers released me as June wandered into the kitchen wearing a flannel nightgown and mule slippers. "I forgot to give you a key, so I waited up."

"You didn't need to do that, and I would have taken care of the chickens, too."

"Someone else took care of them for me," she said a little too lightly.

Bowers locked the back door, and the three of us climbed the stairs together, which meant I didn't get a kiss goodnight.

TWENTY-FOUR

Anyone who says that life is boring should trade places with me for one day. Not long after a filling breakfast of French toast and bacon, I stepped outside and came face-to-face with June's former employee, Paul Jones. He stood there in his wrinkled t-shirt and dirty jeans and grinned at me. It was a friendly grin, though I found it sinister since he was a guy who had a very good reason for wanting Duane dead.

"You must be June's new sister-in-law."

I felt the blush move over my cheeks. "I'm Bowers'—Marty's girlfriend. Um, can I help you?"

"Nope. Doing fine. Is there something I can help you with? Did you want to take out one of the mares? I can get her ready for you."

"Um, no." I was saying *um* a lot. "I was on my way to feed the chickens."

"Already done."

"Okay. Um, thanks."

I turned on my heels and headed back into the house. Bowers was still in the kitchen finishing up a second helping of breakfast. It's not fair the way men can pack it in without gaining weight more easily than women, who enjoy their food just as much. When I explained my encounter with our suspect, June interrupted.

"Paul always was good about starting early. I daresay he's fed all the animals by now."

Bowers set down his fork. "You rehired Paul?"

His sister barked out a laugh that lacked humor. "Didn't know I needed permission."

"Not at all. I'm just surprised, after his carelessness."

"I got to thinking about that. It only happened once, and maybe he was right. Maybe Duane did forget to lock up the hens, and it wasn't Paul's fault."

"I thought Paul had already locked them up for the night, and he accused Duane of letting them out again." Never mess with Bowers' memory.

This ticked June off, since she had already rehired Paul. "I'm not going to discuss it. Everyone deserves a second chance. Otherwise, people wouldn't make mistakes and learn from them. I don't remember you being perfect, Martin Bowers."

He held up his hands in surrender. "I was just asking."

"Well, now you know."

Bowers pushed away his plate and stood. "I need to stretch my legs."

His sister shook her dish towel at him. "You leave Paul alone. He's got a job to do."

"Frankie's coming with. She'll make sure I toe the line."

June's glance didn't hold much confidence in me, so I nodded my head and held up crossed fingers. "Scouts' honor."

We found Paul in the barn putting down fresh hay.

"Looks like you got your old job back." Bowers patted

the neck of the dapple-gray horse who was getting a hay upgrade.

Paul stopped working and leaned on his pitchfork. "June and Carl need the help. It's a lot of work to keep this place going, and now that Duane's not here...."

Bowers smiled. "The day he replaced you. You told June you put the Guinea Hens away the night before and you suspected Duane let them out to make you look bad."

The farmhand poked at the hay with the pitchfork, and I wondered if he was imagining Duane's face. "To be honest, I don't know why Duane did what he did. All I know is I got sacked and he got my job, which makes me assume that's what he was after."

"You worked together for a few months over the summer. Did he seem as if he was angling to replace you?"

"Not at bit. Duane and steady work weren't exactly friends. He started helping out here more as a favor. Phyllis, his mother, talked to June and heard we were extra busy, and she suggested Duane."

"What was he doing at the time? Did he have another job?"

Paul leaned his head back and squinted, looking into the past. "Near as I can remember, he was working for that fella who owns the automobile shop. The one that does a lot of paint jobs. Painted Pony. That's the place. But he got let go there right after the cops tried to bust the place up. Said there were stolen vehicles, but Slick—that's the guy that owns it—he lived up to his name. They took him to the station, but he had receipts and invoices and papers enough to convince the marshal that if there were any funny business, he was an innocent party. Everyone knows that's nonsense, but what can you do when a guy's got papers? Anyway, Slick probably had to mind his manners for a while which meant less work. So, he let Duane go. All he did for Slick was drive the cars, and anybody can do that."

It was time for me to earn my position as Bowers' partner. "Didn't it make you mad when Duane pulled that trick on you?"

He raised his brows. "I was peeved, but more surprised. I didn't expect to get stabbed in the back by Duane. He didn't seem that type."

"What's that mean?"

I seriously wanted to know. The Bowers girls had pegged Duane as trouble. Drinking. Stealing silverware. A bad influence on Marc. Yet not one thing they said qualified as proof. Now Paul, who had been betrayed by Duane and had every reason not to like him, didn't think he was a bad guy.

Paul shrugged. "Didn't seem motivated enough to want my job. In fact, he complained non-stop when he was around me. And we seemed to get along all right."

"I'm sure Kipper asked you where you were three nights ago," Bowers said. "Did you have a good alibi for him?"

This made Paul snicker. "I sure did. Hard to refute five men, especially when one of them's the mayor of Cave Bear. Our poker game went into the early hours of the morning. Mayor Honeywell got something other than sweetness from his wife when he got home. That's what I heard, anyway."

"Where are we headed next?" I asked as we returned to the house.

"I think we should pay a call on the bereaved mother."

"Do you think it's too soon? I mean, if this were your case, you'd have a reason."

"All we need for a sympathy call is food."

"So, we're headed to the store?"

I don't know which annoyed me more. The sarcastic

Duh, or the wry look that went with it. "The day my sister June doesn't have something baking in the oven is the day I retire."

Sure enough, June had an angel food cake cooling on the countertop. Lemon by the citrus smell filling the room and the fact that the lemon tree at the side of the house was in danger of breaking from the weight of its fruit if steps weren't taken.

She agreed to our plan, but she made us wait until she drizzled it with icing before she would allow Bowers to wrap it up. As he was doing so, Agatha came into the room and all hopes of a quick escape went out the back door—where we should have been.

"Hey! That's dessert!"

"Yes, it is. Just not *your* dessert."

What followed had something to do with Bowers' smug smirk.

"June," Agatha whined. "You're not going to let him take it, are you? I've been looking forward to your lemon angel food cake all day."

It was only ten a.m., but I took her point. "We can pick something up from the store."

June gasped as if I had suggested poisoning the grieving mother. "Don't you dare. Phyllis needs it more, Aggie. Besides, I've still got time to bake another."

That mollified Agatha, but only a little. She folded her arms over her chest and sneered at her little brother. "Is Marty playing detective again?" When he ignored her, she inched closer, like she was approaching an unchained tiger. "Do you think Marshal Kipper would like to know what you're up to?"

He turned and took a quick step forward, and she skittered back. "June!"

Tom walked in from the den, and Agatha said, "Don't you touch me, Martin Bowers, or my husband will whip your butt."

Tom, his lanky body relaxed and an easy smile on his face, said, "Who am I whipping? Oh. Hi Marty. Frankie." He pulled out a chair and sat at the kitchen table. "It's between you and your brother, Aggie, whatever *it* is."

June's gaze caught mine, and she shook her head. "Last time Marty punched his sister, he was nine."

"And she hit me first," Bowers said, grinning.

Agatha slipped behind her husband's chair. "A lot of help you are, Tom. What about defending your wife?"

"You like to talk about equality. Well, here's your chance."

"He's taking the cake!"

Tom frowned. "Oh, well, if it's over the cake . . . ." He half stood.

"I've already started on another," June said, giggling.

"Oh. Well, good." He sat back down. "That was a close one, Marty. I might have had to act."

"I'll thank my guardian angel tonight." Bowers took my hand. "Speaking of angels, we've got a cake to deliver."

When Phyllis greeted us with raised eyebrows and then peered around my shoulder to look around the yard, I didn't take it personally. She didn't really know Bowers, and she knew me even less. It wasn't a surprise she would look for June.

Bowers held out the cake. "My sister sent this over."

From the expression of uncertainty on the woman's face, I assumed dropping off two food items within twenty-four hours was considered overkill and threw the entire mourning protocol off kilter. She rallied, though, and invited us inside.

I hoped we could find out about Duane's escapades and leave before the cake cooled. A house in mourning is depressing.

"We'll only stay for a minute," Bowers said, relieving her of the duty to offer us something to drink. He set the cake on the coffee table so she wouldn't even have to leave the room.

She sat down, invited us to join her, and once we had taken our seats and declined an offer to taste the cake, she gave a small gasp and reached out a hand toward Bowers. "You've found out something about Duane's death. That's why you're here."

"Not yet, ma'am, but I wanted to ask you a few questions. If you're up to it."

Frowning, she said, "But I can't think of anything I haven't already told Marshal Kipper. Surely he shared the information with you, since you're working together."

Bowers only flinched a tiny bit. "I believe I explained Cave Bear is out of my jurisdiction, but I'm doing what I can to help. I specifically wanted to get some details about the time your son worked at The Painted Pony."

"Duane didn't work there that long. He made a career move." She nodded, assuring herself that her son had been on his way to better things.

A harsh laugh came from the hallway leading to the bedrooms. A plump woman with the shade of sandy hair as Duane's came in and leaned against the wall just inside the living room.

"Nancy!" Phyllis scolded. "Your brother is dead."

Nancy moved to take a seat on the couch next to her mother and put her arm around the older woman's shoulder.

"If you want the man to help, you need to tell him the truth." She seemed to sense who had the power because she ignored me and looked directly at Bowers. "My brother was allergic to work."

"My sister isn't a pushover, and she hired him."

"Maybe I should clarify. He worked hard when he had a job, but he tried not to fall into that situation often."

"He was a free spirit," Phyllis murmured.

"Free from responsibility."

I could see how it would irk me if I had a sibling who skated by while I was the responsible one.

Nancy held up a hand in truce. "You know I loved him. I'm just telling it like it was without the frills."

Bowers nodded. "And I appreciate that. Were you close to your brother? Did he confide in you?"

"Not really. We talked once a week if he was around when I called for mom. The last time we talked was about a month ago. He seemed frustrated, but he'd just lost his job, so it makes sense."

"Did he ever talk about Slick? Or Mort, Tommy or Bub?"

She threw back her head and laughed. "Those three morons?"

Phyllis pursed her lips and shook her head. "Not nice boys. Tommy disappointed me when he led my son astray. I thought they were friends. I was happy when Duane went to work for June and stopped hanging around with them."

I frowned. "I thought you didn't know his friends other than Tommy?" I added, "Ma'am," since I had just accused her of lying.

She gave me a kindly smile, as if I was a simpleton. "Those weren't friends. They were coworkers."

"I'd heard about some trouble, but I don't know the details." Bowers looked hopefully from one woman to the other.

"Neither do I," Phyllis began.

Nancy raised her hand. "I do. Those crumbs talked him into working for The Painted Pony. *You'll only have to deliver cars.* What they didn't tell him is those cars were hot. Well, maybe not all of them, but some of them were stolen and given new paint jobs, and when he delivered a Mercedes to some guy in Scottsdale, the police were waiting. It took some convincing before they believed Duane was just the dummy driving the cars. His so-called friends were nowhere around to help him out."

"You think the other three knew what was going on?"

"No doubt in my mind. Those three are born criminals. Of course, the police got nowhere. They took Slick in for questioning, but they had to let him go. That's because he lived up to his name. The man is a slimeball."

"You've met him?" I asked. She didn't seem intimidated by him, so maybe what we'd heard so far was an exaggeration. I could hope.

"Only from Duane."

I pressed the point because it would make me feel heaps better to find we weren't dealing with a monster. "Was he scared of him?"

Nancy considered my question. "Not that I noticed. He seemed more annoyed at being used." She leaned forward and clasped her hands. "The thing you need to understand about Duane . . .he didn't scare easily. Not because he was brave. He just didn't think about consequences. The only thing that mattered was what was in front of him. He had a job delivering cars. He got paid for it. That's all that mattered. When something ruined that for him, it just annoyed him. Then he forgot about it and moved on."

Bowers took a deep breath and hesitated. "Would

Duane get so focused on something that he wouldn't care about the impact his actions had on other people?"

Phyllis sat up. "My son didn't have a mean bone in his body."

"Maybe he wouldn't see himself as being mean but just doing what he had to do."

Nancy nodded. "Paul Jones."

Bowers eyebrows went up. "He talked to you about his . . .circumstances?"

Phyllis flushed. "That man showed up here and accused my son of stealing his job. If he didn't do his job right, why shouldn't he lose it?"

"Paul claims that Duane made him look bad on purpose by letting the Guinea hens out after Paul had locked them up." He looked to Nancy. "Would he have been capable of doing something like that if he had wanted Paul's job? Or maybe he thought of it as a joke."

She spread her hands. "Impossible to tell. It depends on the situation. That would be a mean joke, and I can't see Duane killing chickens for a joke, or even to get what he wanted. He loved animals, and leaving hens out overnight around here is certain death. Still, I see what you're asking. In that situation, I'd have to say no."

"So, Paul is lying."

For the first time, Duane's assertive sister looked uncertain. "I didn't get that impression. And Paul's known as an honest guy. None of it makes sense."

TWENTY-FIVE

Duane Stoddard's character didn't become clearer as Bowers and I discussed Nancy's opinions on our way home. We ignored Phyllis's observations. She had a blind spot for her son.

"So, Duane wouldn't hurt a flea, but Paul wouldn't lie about Duane stealing his job."

"Perfectly clear." Bowers grimaced. "Unfortunately, Dym holds the key, and she isn't talking."

"I wonder who she's protecting?"

He shot me a quick glance. "Are you saying my sister knows who killed her boyfriend? Why would she keep that a secret?"

"If it were someone she cared about, she might."

"So, one of my *other* sisters killed Duane?"

I twisted my fingers in my lap. "No-o-o. But she might protect herself."

If he planned on protesting, the possibility I was right stopped him. Instead, he redirected the conversation.

"Slick didn't have a reason to want revenge."

"You're right. I'd like him to be our guy because he's

already a bad guy, but it's not as if Duane ratted on him. It sounds like Duane didn't even understand he worked for a crime ring."

"Crime ring?"

"And even if Duane had turned his boss in to the authorities, it's not as if Slick got arrested." I wondered if Bowers realized that this could eliminate yet another suspect, leaving Dymphna the star of Kipper's show.

He might have because he responded with the one thing that could take my mind off murder.

"Do you want some chocolate?"

I stared. "Are you trying to win my heart forever?"

He glanced over as he pulled into the mini-mart parking lot.

"Is that all it would take?"

I fluttered my eyelashes. "Does that make me sound cheap?"

He turned off the car and gave me a quick kiss. "Never."

The sound of the bell above the door brought Susi out of her living quarters and to the counter. The strains of a television program escaped through the open door behind her.

"We won't keep you long," Bowers said, pulling out his wallet.

"No hurry. There isn't anything worth watching. I was just killing time."

I moved to the candy display and selected two Cruncho bars to keep Bowers from filching any of mine. When I set them on the counter, my boyfriend was praising Susi's keen observation skills.

"I bet no one enters or leaves Cave Bear without you knowing."

Exactly what I had been thinking last night.

"That's probably true," she said, trying to keep the pleasure out of her voice. "I bet you're going to ask me about the night Duane died. That would be Friday, right?"

"Observant *and* smart. Susi, you're a rare jewel."

"Flattery will get you everywhere." She leaned her elbows on the counter. "Let me see. I know that no one other than cop cars passed by after eleven. Before that I saw a station wagon drive by, the one that belongs to the family with five kids. It was still early then. Around seven. But closer to eight, a black pickup truck stopped here to gas up. I didn't get a good look because Tallulah Lankershim was here. She dropped a bottle of Amaretto and I was cleaning up the mess. They didn't come inside. They were probably passing through to Phoenix because I didn't see them come by again. Oh. I saw your sister drive by just before that. Looked like she was headed home."

Bowers and I exchanged a glance.

"June couldn't have driven by. She was with us."

"Not June, silly. Dymphna. She was headed toward her apartment. Like she was headed home from June's house. Didn't you see her there?"

In the words of Bowers, aw, hell.

"What time was this?"

She squinted her eyes. "Seven-thirty? No, after eight for sure."

Back in the car, Bowers turned to stress eating and shoved his Cruncho bar down his throat in two bites. I finished mine almost as quickly but because I'm a piggy when I have a candy craving.

I took the wrapper from his fingers and crumpled it up, licked the remaining chocolate from my teeth, and said, "Why is Dymphna staying at June's house if she has an apartment in town?"

My companion seemed grateful for the chance to talk about something as mundane as living arrangements. "It's outside of town. About a thirty-minute drive. June wanted this to be a reunion weekend of sorts and invited everyone to stay. Like us."

"Nice of her."

Silence.

"Very nice."

More silence.

"Are we going to—"

"No."

So, we weren't going to talk about this surprising development even though we were supposed to be partners. I knew I shouldn't point this out, but I couldn't help myself.

"We're supposed to be partners."

"About that—"

Uh-oh.

He grimaced. "It's not you. It's me. I'm used to working on my own. Having time to think things through."

"You've worked with Gutierrez before," I said, voicing my hurt pride like a teenage girl. Call it professional jealousy.

"She knows me well enough to give me space, and I do the same for her."

Ouch.

"If you pull over, I could walk the rest of the way home. You know. To give you space."

"Don't be like that."

I folded my arms. "Like what?"

He nodded at my defensive posture. "That. This isn't personal. I'm not attacking you. I'm just used to working a certain routine, and when things get stressful, it helps to fall back on routine."

My choices were to be the understanding girlfriend who backed off and let him work his magic alone, or be the harpy who refused to understand, which I did. Understand, I mean. Only, if we were going to be a team, we should be united throughout the entire process, not just when Bowers found it convenient. Suffer together. That's my motto. I used my nicest tone when I explained that to him.

He disagreed.

"Being a team means taking into account each member's idiosyncrasies, and methods of working, and strengths—"

"What's my strength?"

I was looking directly at him, so I saw how his eyes opened wide in surprise. Or should I say panic, because he took his time responding.

"Well . . .I haven't had you at my side during an investigation, so I don't really know. Yet."

I made an uncomplimentary noise.

"Hold on. You're tenacious and fearless when an animal's welfare is at stake. Remember how you attacked that trainer when you thought he was trying to poison your pets?"

Not one of my finer moments, and Bowers had to pull my attacker off me before he finished strangling me. Yes, I had thrown myself on Tyler Watts without a thought for my safety—or any thought at all, if I'm honest, which was not the brightest way to approach someone intending to kill your best friends-. But I had been brave, hadn't I?

"Come here," he said, reaching out an arm and pulling me to over in a side hug, which kind of hurt with the console digging into my hip. Still, I appreciated the intention and rested my head on his shoulder.

He kissed the top of my head.

"I don't want to argue with you."

"We weren't arguing," I said primly, dismissing the irritation that I'd been feeling. "We were discussing."

He slipped me a sideways glance. "It was headed that way."

After pulling into June's parking area and shutting off the car, he turned his upper body toward me and embraced me in a full hug.

"Now, are we going to talk about your sister?" I said, my chin on his shoulder.

His arms tightened. "Is that really what you want to do right now?"

When he nuzzled my neck and worked his way to my mouth, I responded with enthusiasm. Five minutes later, we were both breathing heavily. I didn't think we were breathing *loudly*, but apparently, we were heard, because the back door opened, and we broke apart.

Bowers leaned back against the headrest. "She must have heard the engine when I came up the drive."

She referred to June, who was now leaning out the open back door. "Marty, is that you?"

He rolled down his window and leaned his head out. "No!"

Ignoring the frustration in his voice, she giggled. "You nut. I just set lunch on the table."

"We're coming," he assured her.

We headed inside without ever talking about Dymphna, and I realized I'd been played. I took comfort in knowing the score was still three-to-one in my favor.

Once we finished lunch, everyone scattered, even Bowers, who said he had calls to make. I asked June to direct me to the laundry machine. I was wearing my last spare pair of underwear, and my jeans were on day five.

Once I got a load started, I sat on the back steps and took stock of the current situation.

I had called Seamus McGuire and asked him to hold on to my cat, Emily, for a while longer. He was happy to do so since Emily loves men and shows them both a courtesy and admiration she would never bestow upon me. Still, he probably wouldn't want to keep her forever.

Since I worked for myself, I didn't have to clear my extended vacation with a boss. I also didn't have vacation pay, and if I didn't start taking clients soon, I'd have to dip into my meager savings.

I didn't think Kipper would mind if we returned to Wolf Creek, but before Bowers would leave, his sister Dymphna had to be so free from suspicion of murder that at the mention of her name birds would break into sweet song. How close were we to finding out what happened to Duane?

He worked for a criminal named Slick with coworkers who resembled the Three Stooges in leather. When the cops had caught him driving a stolen vehicle, no one had come to his aid. That sounded like a reason for Duane to commit murder, not be murdered.

His mother thought he was a saint, without cause. His sister seemed more realistic. She probably resented him, which seemed natural to me. Refer back to the mother-thinks-he's-a-saint comment.

It was odd, though, that Nancy thought her brother's work ethic didn't include playing dirty tricks to get a job, yet she thought Paul was telling the truth when he said Duane had done so just to work on June's farm. I liked June and

Carl, but shoveling poop and feeding animals wasn't much of a prize.

Agatha and Cecelia both disliked him, also without cause. June believed he was a part-time drunk, but only because he told her so.

Paul had a reason to want Duane out of the way, but he also had a solid alibi, unless the mayor was in on the murder. Unlikely.

That left Dymphna. The woman who loved him. The woman who Duane might have dumped in favor of Teri. The woman who looked unhappy at something Duane said in my vision. The woman who was seen driving past the mini mart on her way home from June's around the time Duane was killed.

Not looking good.

Feeling restless, I went back into the house. When I passed the den, I saw Agatha sitting on the couch with Dymphna, so I wandered in determined to manipulate information out of one or both. And forge a lasting relationship with two of Bowers' former guardians if possible.

They stopped talking and looked up at the outsider breaking into their private talk. My resolve to interrogate them dissipated and was replaced by an embarrassed flush that spread over my face as I sat down in June's chair.

"So, is this the weekend you were hoping for?" Probably too sarcastic for an opening line, I thought, but Agatha joined in.

"More than a weekend."

With Kipper focused on a Bowers girl, all plans to return home had been cancelled.

"The weekend from hell," I muttered.

Dymphna just sat and looked down at her folded hands.

"At least you can go home for a change of clothes, since you're only half an hour away." I plucked at my purple sweater, which was making its second appearance.

She looked up. "How do you know where I live?"

Sucking in my bottom lip, I furiously considered how to get out of the mud puddle I'd stumbled into by trying to be pleasant. Reassuring, somehow, to know my dislike for mingling with people wasn't just the unfriendly preference of a woman who thought humans were often the pits but a wise tactic for keeping out of trouble. It's hard to stick your foot in your mouth if the latter isn't open.

What would Bowers do? Would he want Dymphna to know we were on to her? Or would he hold that card close until required? If only he'd discussed the subject last night like I wanted. Without his guidance, I flipped a mental coin and proceeded.

"When Bow—Marty and I were at the mini-mart last night, Susi mentioned she'd seen you drive by last Friday night. And of course I thought you came from out-of-town for the weekend, so Bowers—Marty—told me where you lived."

She frowned.

"Generally. Just a vague idea."

She stared at me with her mouth open. I squirmed in my chair. You would think we had searched her underwear drawer.

"It's not as if we went to your house or anything like that."

She rallied, sat straight, and smiled. "I was checking in with June to find out when dinner was planned for the next night."

I couldn't stop nodding my head and grinning, something Agatha noticed.

She narrowed her eyes. "That makes perfect sense."

And I really wanted to agree with her and then invite them both to bake cookies or whatever gal pals did when they hung out, but I couldn't turn off my brain or shut my mouth. "Not really, because you were seen driving home around 8:00. We were all here, but you didn't come in."

Agatha turned on me. "Well, maybe she saw we were busy and decided not to interrupt us."

"But I didn't hear a car drive up. Did you?"

She snorted and mumbled. "Some people should mind their own business."

"Who's business?" Bowers strolled into the room and Agatha glowered at him. "What did I do now?"

Dymphna stood. "I need some fresh air."

When Bowers sent a questioning glance my way, I glowered too. If he had been willing to discuss our approach to Dymphna, I wouldn't be sitting here feeling like a crumb.

Marc called for his mother from upstairs, and she swept out of the room without another word. Bowers took her spot on the couch and sighed. "What have you been up to?"

"Making friends."

"I can see that. Want to tell me about it?"

"It's not my fault. I was trying to make nice with your sisters, and then the subject of where Dymphna lived came up—"

He narrowed his eyes. "Came up how?"

I explained how talk had gotten around to Dymphna's apartment— innocently—and by the time I got to the bit about Mary seeing her on Friday night, Bowers was rubbing his eyes.

"It's not my fault! I wanted to discuss our game plan yesterday, partner."

"Yes, you did." He sat rubbing his knuckles together and

thinking, and then he stood and held out a hand. "Well, partner, want to take a walk?"

He pulled me to my feet and put a comforting arm around my shoulder as we headed outside.

"It was sweet of you to try with my sisters. They aren't always the easiest to get along with."

"Was Dymphna always . . . like she is now?"

"You mean flaky?"

I protested, but he squeezed my shoulder. "She started in on that airy-fairy stuff in high school. I think it's because she wanted to be different. Make her own mark. The rest of my sisters were . . .assertive."

"How else is she different, other than her style of dress and the whispering? Does she drink tea made from roots she's gathered under a full moon?"

He laughed. "She likes her comforts. I can't see her running around in the dark and digging things up."

"I don't even know what she does for a living."

"She got a teaching degree but decided she didn't like children. At least not other people's children. Marc's the exception. Since then, she's flitted around trying things out. Right now, she works in a flower shop making arrangements."

"I can see that. She has an eye for what goes together. Take her outfits. They wouldn't be my choice, but they go together, jewelry and all." I sighed. "Not one of my gifts."

This was the moment for Bowers to tell me he thought I looked fine the way I was, but he didn't. I don't think he'd heard a thing I'd said for the last few minutes, because he was focused on what lay ahead. We were approaching the Double Trouble.

Windy sprinted down the hill and greeted us with joyous barks, jumping on my leg until I picked her up. I pointed her butt away from me just in case Marc was right about how she got her name.

Dymphna appeared at the opening of the first cave, frowned, and then disappeared inside.

"Why don't you keep Windy company while I talk to my sister."

"Nope. Partners, remember?" I handed him the dog. "You carry her. She's heavy."

I led the way up the hill to the caves and entered the one I'd seen Dymphna standing in. Once inside, I had to let my eyes adjust, and even then, it took a minute to locate Bowers' sister.

She sat against the wall with her arms wrapped around her knees. In that position, I got a peek at the sulky teen she must have been. She glared at me and then looked away.

"Dym," Bowers said from behind me. He set down the dog and approached her with his hands in his jean pockets, pausing a few feet from her. "So, you and Duane *did* come here."

"I told you we didn't," she muttered.

He crouched down and rested his elbows on his knees. "Just hanging out here because it's such a nice spot?"

"It's the only place I can get some peace. Or it was."

Bowers sighed, stood, and walked to the wall. He slid down it until he was seated next to her. Windy scooted around the back passage into the neighboring cave, and I followed so they could have some privacy. I had a subtle exit in mind, but Wendy doubled back, and I tripped over her in the passage. They ignored my cry and the following thump, so I called out, "I'm alright," just in case they cared.

The thing about caves is sound travels, so their conversation wasn't as private as they thought. I sat down and rested against the wall with the dog in my lap and pretended not to listen.

"*I'm trying to help you.*" That was Bowers.

"*You could help me by leaving me alone.*"

Big sigh. I recognized that frustrated noise as one Bowers regularly made around me.

"*Okay, Dym. You're not a kid, so I'm going to be blunt. You were seen driving away from here the night Duane died. There's probably a good explanation, but people who don't know you as well as I do might think it looks funny.*"

"*Ha-ha.*"

"*I'm serious.*"

"*Mumble, mumble, mumble.*"

I was relieved when Bowers said, "*What?*"

Dymphna raised her voice. "*I said I came here to see him, but I couldn't find him.*"

"*Did you have a date?*"

"*Sort of.*"

"*Where were you going to meet?*"

"*At my place, but he didn't come.*"

"*Was it locked?*"

"*No.*"

"*Was it a mess inside?*"

No answer.

"*Dym, when I saw his place, it been searched. Did it look like that on Thursday night?*"

"*Searched? No. What would anyone be looking for?*"

When she said this last bit, her voice was high and followed by a tinkling laugh. A lie.

"*Anyway, he wasn't there, so I waited for a half hour, but he never showed. So, I went home. End of story.*"

Susi saw Dym around eight o'clock. Duane had been dead for two hours. I gasped. If Bowers' sister didn't kill her boyfriend, did she find his body? No, no, no. The idea was too horrible. Plus, she would have raised the alarm.

I shifted my weight to adjust Windy, and my head brushed against a divot in the wall. I craned my neck to look and brushed at the rough spot to smooth it down, and the wall crumbled. At the center of the patch was a small hole that seemed too round to be natural. Since I'm not crazy enough to stick my finger into strange places and let creepy things gnaw on me, I felt around until I found a rock and then used that to dig. Imagine my surprise when a flattened bullet fell out.

I pocketed it as I struggled to stand with Windy in my arms and then headed back for the first cave. Bowers was asking his sister about Duane's friends.

"What do you know about those three knuckleheads that hang out at The Black Stallion? Weren't they friends of Duane's? Phyllis said at least Tommy was." Since Dymphna only shrugged, he added, "And what about that Slick guy? Did you ever meet him?"

They say animals pick up on the emotions of people. Apparently, emotions stink, or at least the chemical reaction that accompanies them gives off a smell that animals can detect. A point of interest; animals also mimic their masters. If you're a hothead, your pup will probably develop into an out-of-control troublemaker. Similarly, if your mistress typically shrugs off her police detective brother's questions about nefarious characters, her dog will play it cool . . .on the outside. But just like her mistress, Windy couldn't control the turbulent emotions inside. Instead, she sent them my way.

After a zing in the chest that left me clenching every muscle, my knees began to shake, and my hands trembled.

The dog wisely jumped out of my arms before I dropped her.

"There you are." Bowers got up and walked over. "Ready to go?" He leaned in. "It's pointless to keep talking to her when she's decided the conversation is over." He put his arm around me, and then he looked at me in surprise.

I glared at him. I didn't mean too, but rage overwhelmed me.

He steered me out in a hurry. He wanted to stop just outside the cave entrance and let me get hold of myself, but I pushed on until we were back on the dirt road. Finally, he blocked my path, took hold of my shoulders, and bent his head to meet my gaze.

"What?"

I rubbed my face to stop the tingling. "Anger. Massive, overwhelming anger."

He looked back at the cave. "My sister? She didn't want to talk, that's for sure, but I wouldn't say she was furious."

"Windy. As soon as you said Slick."

He still wasn't getting it. "The furball was angry?"

"Trust me." I gave one last shiver.

"What would a dog know about a chop-shop villain?"

I raised my brows. "Nothing, as far as I know." I hooked my arm through his and started walking. "You're asking the wrong question."

"Which is?"

"What does *Dymphna* know about Slick? Windy was only reacting to what your sister was feeling."

He stopped. "And she was feeling anger?"

"I'd say rage is more accurate. If he killed Duane, and Dymphna *knew* he killed Duane..."

"Kipper says Slick has an alibi. But if Dymphna doesn't know that, she might do something she'll regret."

I thought he was overreacting. What could she do? Seek out Slick at the Painted Pony and whisper him into submission? Still, I couldn't argue away a brother's concern for his sister.

He jogged to the bottom of the hill under the cave. "Dym. Dym! I forgot. June sent me to get you."

She emerged a minute later, hands on her hips. "I'm remembering why I moved out of the house. Privacy."

Bowers grinned and shrugged. "I'm just the messenger."

While Windy ran ahead and yapped at lizards, the three of us marched back to the house in silence. I wondered if I could get a do-over weekend with Bowers' three remaining sisters, because it might be time to write off Agatha and Dymphna.

The latter ran ahead of us into the house, I assumed to ask Joan what she wanted, which was nothing. Bowers turned to me.

"I don't suppose there's any point in me asking you to stay here while I talk to Slick."

"You'd be right."

Bowers steered me toward his car explaining the entire time how these types of guys were not as considerate and polite as he was, and he opened the passenger door for me to make his point.

I slid inside and buckled myself in. "Good. If he's a brute, then I won't be required to be polite and keep quiet like a good girl."

Closing the door with more force than necessary, he got in and started the car.

TWENTY-SIX

Bowers parked on the street in front of The Painted Pony, but he didn't get out right away. I assumed he was strategically casing the place. Looking for fast exits and sizing up the opposition.

The body shop was on the outskirts of town, past cute shops and neat landscaping and up a side street lined with auto repair shops, tire stores, and smog check stations. The front office faced the street, while the rest of the building, accessible by a drive, stretched out behind.

There were two steel garage doors, one open and one closed. A tall man in red overalls leaned up against the closed door, smoking a cigarette. When we parked, he looked our way, flicked the cherry off his ciggie and sauntered back inside.

"I would prefer it if . . ." He began again. "It would be a great favor to me if you stayed in the car while I talked to Slick. He might be a murderer."

I opened my door. "It's harder to bury two bodies. Maybe my presence will make him think twice about killing you."

He got out and slammed his door shut. "It's not as difficult as you think."

Bowers seemed distracted. Distracted and serious. Not that I was afraid, but I took up the rear position as we entered the office. Inside, the place seemed smaller. It reminded me of when I'd broken up with my ex and moved an entire apartment's worth of stuff into a spare bedroom.

The counter was barely visible under all the brochures and paint sample books. A coffee pot full of dregs sat on an old, wooden stand, and two chairs that had seen many bottoms were angled so close together that the occupants would have touched knees. The narrator of a nature special droned on from a television that hung precariously from ceiling opposite.

A bell jangled as we entered, and the guy who had been smoking outside walked in, wiping his hands on a greasy rag.

"That looks like a cop car," he said, nodding toward Bowers' dark-blue Crown Victoria.

Fully expecting Bowers to pull out his badge and take advantage of his authority, I said, "You got us there."

The employee narrowed his eyes in response, but it was Bowers' reaction that interested me. The expression in his blue eyes turned cold and hard—enough to make me shiver—and he shifted his shoulders slightly forward in a way that made him look intimidating. When his upper lip curled in a slight sneer, I swear I saw a scar form.

He casually flipped open the book of paint samples. "Got it at an auction. Why? Are you making me an offer?"

His voice, normally a smooth baritone, had a flat edge to it that made it sound lower. The voice of someone you didn't want to offend.

A little guy with a beard wearing a matching jumpsuit came in. "There's a cop car parked out front."

Smoking guy shushed him.

Bowers held up the book and pointed. "How do you think it would look in cherry red?"

I remembered reading how hippos would push their babies onto the backs of alligators just to dare those enormous jaws to make a move. It was a way of establishing that the babies were off limits. Bowers question had that same taunt in it.

Bearded Guy guffawed, but Smoking Guy elbowed him and put an end to the laughter. "Whatever you want, we can do. Cherry's nice. Makes a statement."

I opened my mouth, but Bowers turned that intimidating gaze on me, and the words stuck in my throat. I swallowed and took a step back, and it was another ten seconds before he turned his attention back to the employees.

"Is one of you named Slick? Someone told me I should talk to Slick."

Smoking Guy, though not comfortable asserting himself, was obviously more worried about offending Slick than Bowers. "Who told you that?"

"Duane Stoddard."

"Duane's dead," Bearded Guy squeaked out.

Bowers favored him with an ill-humored look, and the guy moved his gaze to his feet. "He made the recommendation before he died, obviously."

"Duane recommended you come here and talk to Slick?" Smoking Guy asked the questions slowly to make sure he got it right.

All three of us jumped at the crack the book made when Bowers slapped it shut. "Why else would I be here? There are three other body shops in town, two of them on this street."

"Was there, um, something special you were looking for?"

Bowers' thin smile lacked any signs of joy. "I won't know until I talk to him."

Smoking Guy made up his mind and got professional. "He's not here right now. Where can he reach you?"

Bowers rattled off a number I didn't recognize and stressed that he wouldn't be in Cave Bear for long. I'm sure their gazes followed us all the way to the car. Once inside, I turned and stared.

"Who are you?"

Keeping his expression serious, he started the car. "I'm the man who's going to kiss you as soon as we're away from here."

He pulled out from the curb, did an illegal U-turn, and drove off at what I would call a casual pace. He drove on until we got to the mini-mart, and then he parked around the side next to the air and water stations. As promised, he delivered a solid kiss filled with a passion that surprised me. But then he broke away and tucked my hair behind my ears.

"I wasn't sure which track to take, but then you forced me to make a choice when you mentioned the car. And then when you stepped away from me when I tried to shush you? Perfect." He pulled me to him and kissed me again. This time I pulled away and sent a quick, embarrassed glance around the parking lot. Bowers didn't notice.

"It was like we'd rehearsed."

"So, that was a performance?"

He leaned back and frowned. "I wouldn't say performance. It's useful to have a few personalities you can pull out without too much thought. That one's based on

June's behavior after another parent threatened to hit one of us kids."

I let out a breath. "Your face changed. Even your body. And you didn't sound like you."

He smiled, pleased. "That's useful feedback."

"Seriously. You were scary. And don't laugh, but I swear I saw a scar form on your upper lip."

He sneered, and I saw it again. Then he grinned. "I got that from an unfriendly dog when I was ten." He pulled down the overhead visor to look in the mirror and ran his finger over his lip. "You can't really see it anymore."

"I didn't recognize the number you gave him."

"It's a burner I keep. Comes in handy if I want to be anonymous."

"Does that happen often?"

"That reminds me. I should turn it on." He reached in front of me and popped open the glove compartment. After digging through his registration and several maps, he found a small, black flip-phone and turned it on. Nothing happened.

"Damn thing's dead."

He pulled a portable charger out of the console, removed the cigarette lighter and plugged it in. "I don't expect he'll call right away." He grimaced. "I hope he won't."

I jumped when someone rapped on my window. Mary waggled her fingers at us while Bowers rolled it down.

"June called and said if I saw you to tell you to get home ASAP. She said it was an emergency."

It's a good thing Susi stepped back when Bowers started the car because he kicked up gravel as he shot out of the parking lot and onto the road. The speedometer jumped to seventy, and in minutes, we turned into June's drive. I thought he might ram through the wooden gate before it opened, although, once through, he slowed down to a reasonable speed as he approached the house.

June waited on the back steps, and she wrung her hands as she scurried to the car. Bowers jumped out to meet her halfway, and I heard him ask, "Is Dym okay?"

His sister's eyebrows shot up, and she looked at me as if I might know what he was talking about. "Why wouldn't she be? It's Carl who's hurt. Someone hit him on the head while he was repairing the west fence. Had another hole cut in it. Someone snuck up behind him and walloped him one. When he didn't come back for lunch—" She gave a small gasp at the memory. "I sent Paul looking for him."

"When did this happen?"

"We just got him back to the house about a thirty minutes ago. The doctor had a look at him and congratulated him on his hard head."

The tears finally broke through, and Bowers enveloped her in a hug. Thinking I should do something, I rubbed and patted her back like I'd seen mothers do with infants.

"Oh, Marty. Who would do such an ugly thing? And to Carl!"

As he led her back to the house, he said, "Why don't we find out?"

Carl sat in his recliner with the legs up. He didn't look any different to me. Only tired. As we came into the room, the older man raised a hand in greeting.

"Has June been making a fuss? I've gotten harder knocks from the cows."

He bowed his head so Bowers could inspect the spot where the blow had landed.

"Doc says I might have a mild concussion, but I wasn't even out cold."

"Did you see them?"

"No. But I heard them as they were leaving."

"Leaving?"

"I guess they wanted to use the hole I'd just patched up. There were a couple of them. Two. Maybe three. One of them objected on my behalf after I got slugged. I appreciated that, but it would have been better if he had made his views known beforehand. Anyway, I was only there a few minutes when Paul found me." He grimaced. "Had some trouble standing up."

Bowers looked around. "Where is he now?"

"I sent him to feed the cows."

"Marty," June said in warning, "you let Marshal Kipper handle it."

Bowers ignored her, and I scurried to keep up with him as he headed for the back door in long strides. He took a detour back to his car. I jogged to the passenger side because I didn't want him to leave without me, but all he did was open a slim compartment attached to the passenger side of the counsel. I gasped when he pulled out a gun.

"Do you really need that?" I called after him, scurrying to catch up.

"I won't know unless I do, and then I'd rather have it." The gun was in a holster he clipped to his waistband, and it's the first thing Paul's eyes went to when he straightened up from leaning over a bin of feed.

"What happened?" Bowers' voice sounded calm, but the muscle in his jaw pulsed.

Paul cleared his throat. "June sent me to find Carl, and I did. She sent me to the front acres. He was on his hands and knees and looked to be in pain. I helped him to his feet, and he asked where they went. I asked who they were, and he told me what happened."

"Did you see anyone?"

"No." He scrunched up his face, giving him the appearance of an old potato. "I might have heard a truck. That's what it sounded like, anyway. I didn't know how many there were or if they'd be back, so I asked if he could walk, he said yes if I helped steady him, and we came back to the house. That's all."

"Which direction did the truck head?"

"South."

"This isn't about stolen chickens, is it," I called out to Bowers as he walked away.

The front acres met up with Cave Bear Road, so it surprised me when Bowers turned in the opposite direction and headed for the caves, the ones June called Double Trouble.

"Is this smart?" I panted as I tried to keep up with his long strides. "If there are several of them, and they all have guns, and you only have one gun . . .I don't like them odds, partner."

He wasn't in the mood to joke. "Go back to the house, Frankie."

"No. I'm not leaving you to—to deal with whoever it is by yourself."

He spun and grabbed my shoulders. "Frankie. Honey. Please. Don't argue."

My voice cracked as I tried not to cry. "You listen to me, you—you hothead. There is no reason on earth why you shouldn't wait for Kipper."

"You heard Paul. They drove away, and there isn't any access to the caves from the road. So, they're gone."

"Then why are you headed this way?"

He snorted in frustration and rubbed his forehead. "You don't give up, do you?"

"That's my one feminine trait."

He turned his head and looked down the creek bed, the opposite direction of the house.

"At the edge of this land is a gravel road that gives Luther access to his fields. It's possible that's where the truck was headed."

"Don't you think they would avoid the Double Trouble after attacking Carl? I mean, once we discovered him, there would be people all over this place looking for clues."

"You make a point."

"Great. Then you can wait for the marshal. And if you don't, I'm coming with you."

I really, really hoped he would go back to the house because the primary emotion I felt at that moment was fear. Something moved in the hills over Bowers shoulder. I stiffened, and he dropped his hand to his holster and turned to look. As Chauncey and Hero came loping toward us with tongues hanging out, my laughter had an edge of hysteria.

"That's that," he said, turning toward the house. "If there were strangers around, the dogs would have smelled them." He looked at Chauncey's drooling face. "At least Hero would have."

The aftereffects of all that adrenaline left my knees shaking, but I played it cool and focused on getting one foot in front of the other.

"Did it occur to you that Paul might have attacked Carl and there wasn't a truck full of hoodlums?"

"Of course."

"Oh. Okay. As long as you keep it in mind."

Kipper and Macoritto met us halfway, and this time, when Bowers sent me back to the house, I went.

TWENTY-SEVEN

Technically, I didn't return to the house. Between the attack on poor, sweet Carl, the worry I'd seen reflected in the usually cheerful June's eyes, and the new determination that Bowers and his gun had to find the killer, I felt it was imperative that I get an animal—*any* animal—to tell me what in the name of Diggity Dog was going on. So, when I came upon the three mares lounging in the pasture closest to the house, I approached the fence and waited.

They turned their heads toward me, and their ears twitched with curiosity. They'd seen me with Bowers, so they didn't feel threatened, and when Matilda moved toward me, the others followed.

While they approached, I took several deep breaths and cleared my mind of irritation and fear. I imagined the gigantic wooden door I used to keep the constant babble of animals out of my head, and I opened that sucker wide. By the time the horses made it to the fence, I was ready for anything.

I was immediately overcome by a feeling of sadness that

I associated with the fact that my hands were empty of carrots or apples. Even a sugar cube would have been nice.

I didn't have time for bribery, so I snapped my fingers and said, "Listen up." Matilda nudged my hand until I scratched her cheek, and then the other two pushed their faces forward and they forced me to use both hands and alternate between cheeks, necks and fuzzy noses, which made it difficult to concentrate. Finally, I took a step back.

"Pay attention, please."

They looked at me with interest, and then I was barraged by thoughts of me surprising them with carrots hidden in my back pocket or pulled from thin air. Note to self. Always bring carrots when paying a call on horses.

I ignored them, closed my eyes, and imagined delivering a jpeg file from my head to theirs. The image in the picture was Duane. I waited for a response.

I learned Duane *always* carried carrots, the dapple gray had a secret spot in front of her left ear that, when scratched, gave her extreme waves of pleasure, and the third horse, a chubby dun with black socks, thought Duane had been stingy with the oats.

Now that we'd established the subject of our conversation, I realized I didn't know if they had been pasturing or in their stalls the night Duane was killed. I turned back to get their view of the barnyard, and then, using that perspective, I played out a movie of Duane being attacked with a shovel in the chicken run. I made it a little fuzzy to take into account the fencing around the run.

Their ears swiveled forward, and I got the sense they thought I was telling them a story. I tried again, this time going by my memory of what the inside of the barn looked like and my point of view as I was grooming them. I gave them an audio of a fight between Duane and a woman, since that had caused a reaction in the chickens. Nothing. Apparently, they weren't witnesses to Duane's death.

Tired from my foray into their heads, I leaned back against the fence and let them nibble on my shoulders and hair. I wondered what Bowers and the law were up to right now? There were three of them, so if they ran into the three men who had attacked Carl, at least they were evenly matched. Maybe they were checking the caves for additional prints to see if—

I stopped breathing. The horses had been listening to my thoughts, and as soon as I mentioned the caves, they started pawing the ground and snorting.

Their tension transferred to me, and I paced and dug at the ground with the toe of my shoe. I froze as the darkened Double Trouble caves came into focus with incredible clarity. Lights flashed inside the cave. They must have been flashlight beams. Or exceptionally large fireflies.

Male voices droned on in a conversation comprised of inarticulate words, which was not surprising as the scene was from the perspective of horses. But one thing was certain. The voices were angry.

I jumped when a shadowy figure loomed into my peripheral vision. It stooped and picked up a stone, shouted, "Scat", and threw the stone.

This seemed to excite the horses because they snorted and tossed their heads. When they started rearing back and pawing at the air, I got realized again how powerful these animals were, and I got scared.

I still had control of the conversation—I hoped—so I swept away the flashlight beams and the ornery shadow with a fondness for rocks. Showing my audience the empty, clean caves finally calmed them down.

To thank them for sharing, I gave them extra nose rubs

and scratches, and by the time I left, we were back on carrots again. I promised to bring some on my next visit, which they reluctantly accepted as my best offer.

I wanted time to digest our session, so I sought the privacy of my bedroom. When Bowers returned to the house ninety minutes later, I'd had plenty of time to get worked up over bad men and my boyfriend's willingness to put himself in danger. Fear had taken over. Actually, I was fuming, too. And sulking. It was quite a combination, and by the time Bowers knocked on my door, let himself in, and closed the door behind him, I was ready for a fight. He headed me off.

"I need you to listen to me carefully," he said, his firm tone matching his expression of barely controlled anger. "When I tell you to leave, I mean it. I'm not being a chauvinist. I'm not sharing my opinion. I'm not opening up a debate. I'm telling you what I need you to do for both your safety and mine."

The skin on my face flushed warm. "Just say yes like a good little girl."

"No. Like a woman who isn't trained for the situation."

"I don't need training to know you shouldn't run into danger without backup."

"Ideally, yes. But there isn't always going to be backup."

I stood. "Then let them go. Does it really matter? Duane's not coming back to life. Carl's okay." Even as I said it, I didn't agree with myself, and Bowers, no surprise, didn't either.

"This time. You can't seriously expect me to risk my sister June getting attacked next. Or you. Or what about Marc?"

That was a low blow, but he had a point. I crossed my arms. "I don't like it."

He gave me a tired smile and brushed his fingers through his hair. "If you did, I'd worry."

Seeing how affected he already was by worry awakened my compassion, but I didn't want him to think I was a pushover. "Well," I said gruffly, "at least you've got a gun. They seem to prefer rocks."

"What's that?"

Explaining took too much effort, so I gave him the short version.

"How many were there?"

"I only saw one. But I could hear the others talking in the cave."

"What did they say?"

"I couldn't understand the words because the horses couldn't."

I stuffed my hands in my jean pockets and felt something small and hard in one of them. I pulled out the bullet I'd found in the cave.

"I forgot." I held it out and he took it. "I found that in the cave's wall while you were talking to Dymphna."

He held it up and rolled it between his fingers. I walked to the window. When I glanced over my shoulder to see how Bowers was taking this information, I was staring at an empty room.

I found Bowers in his room finishing a phone call. He tucked his cell phone in his back pocket and said, "Sorry about that. It was buzzing, and I had to take it."

My gaze traveled around the forbidden room. I brushed off my disappointment, but Bowers caught my expression.

"What?" He searched the room, looking for something worth frowning at.

"Nothing. I just expected it to look as it did when you

grew up here. You know. A shrine. Track trophies on the wall and band posters . . . or girlie posters."

Bowers smiled. "My choices of wall art were Marilyn Monroe and movies like *Phantasm* and *Night of the Living Dead.*"

I arched one brow. "So, you prefer blonds?"

He took my hand. "You want to see where I spent my childhood?"

On the first floor, Bowers opened the door to a small closet off the den. "In here."

"Seriously? Your sister locked you in the closet?"

He pushed aside the hanging sweaters and jackets and got down on all fours. "Come on." Then he disappeared into a small passage. I crawled in after him, bumping nose-first into a wall three feet in.

"Over here."

I turned a sharp corner and found a small area under the stairs that held several cardboard boxes. Bowers was sitting with his knees up, resting against the wall. It was a tight fit, but I positioned myself next to him.

"I used to bring my comics in here and read them by flashlight. It was the only quiet place in the house. Agatha tried to follow me once, but when I turned off the flashlight, she freaked out. Swore she felt something crawling on her and never tried it again."

I jerked my hand off the floor, but he took it in his and chuckled.

"There weren't any spiders. It was me tickling the back of her hand to scare her."

"Were you lonely?"

"Surrounded by sisters?"

"Well, yeah. Didn't you have guy friends?"

"Toby, of course, but his parents kept him busy, and

now he's got a family of his own. Gary Hall and Brett Roman. We were on the baseball team together, but they lived in town, so I didn't see them often. Gary's married with three kids and is an attorney. Brett just kind of drifted away in high school. Died of a drug overdose four years later."

"I'm sorry."

"You're very lucky to have Penny." He referred to my recently married best friend.

I agreed. "If it wasn't for her, I'd still be in Loon Lake, Wisconsin, trying to live down my ex-boyfriend's—what he did to me."

Bowers knew the story, though he hadn't heard it from me. Like an idiot, I had moved in with a guy who hinted at marriage *some day* when the moment was right. The right moment came when he met up with a bimbo reporter. They bonded over an article using things I had told Jeff in private. They twisted my words to tell the world I was a fake, which I was at the time, but still. It left a terrible taste.

Bowers' thumb had been stroking the back of my hand. He stopped. "Do you still think about him?"

Since we hadn't brought a flashlight, he couldn't see me gape. "Not at all. Only when the subject comes up, like it just did, and then my only reaction is one of those head-slapping chastisements. You know. *Stupid-stupid-stupid.*"

He leaned in until our heads touched. "Good. I don't mean it's good that you think you were stupid. You should let that go. Everyone makes mistakes. I mean, it's good that you don't think about him at all."

I got a funny feeling in my stomach and hoped I wouldn't regret my next question. "Do you have a mistake you regret?"

"One. I trusted someone who wasn't worth it."

"And do you think about her?"

"Not for years." He sounded surprised.

June's voice called out from another room. "Marty!" She was on the move, and the next time she called, her voice came from the den. She pushed the door all the way open and leaned in. "Oh, for heaven's sake. Are you in there?"

"No one here but us mice."

She gurgled out a laugh. "Marshal Kipper is here to see you. Do you have room for him?"

Bowers nudged me and I crawled out.

Kipper must have been in a hurry because he had followed June into the den. He didn't bat an eyelash when we came out the closet door on all fours. Bowers helped me to my feet.

"The marshal and I have business to discuss. We'll step outside. Frankie, could you help June with dinner? Please?"

Since he asked nicely, I agreed even as June protested that she didn't need any help. That was good news, since I didn't have much to offer.

TWENTY-EIGHT

As I entered June's kingdom, I tried to recall every recipe I'd ever scanned, which was a very short list, as well as every piece of wisdom imparted by my mother while we bonded in the kitchen. Usually, Mom ended our time together with the same words. *"I'll take care of this. Why don't you set the table?"*

The kitchen might belong to June alone, but all of Bowers' sisters had made it clear that the ability to provide nourishing, delicious meals for their baby brother was high on the girlfriend suitability chart.

Within minutes, June had vegetables lined up in front of me on a rectangle cutting board with instructions to wash and chop them into half-inch pieces. She handed me a vegetable scrubber shaped like a potato, and I got through that with no injuries. Then I sized up my waiting victims.

While June was busy defrosting frozen homemade stock in the microwave, I bent my pointer finger and held it up to a potato. The space between the second and third knuckle measures approximately one inch, so I made two little marks with the tip of my knife for a guide. Once I got the first piece the right size, I used it as my template.

"Marty sure likes you," June said as she put the lid on the pot and turned the burner up.

"I like him."

I finished the potatoes and moved on to the onions. Focusing on my task, I fell into a rhythm and picked up speed. A few more days in the kitchen and I'd be a pro. Or at least not in danger of maiming myself.

"What are your intentions toward him?"

The knife slipped. I sucked in my breath and pulled my finger back. Fortunately, I'd only nicked the fingernail.

"You mean do I plan on having my way with him and then tossing him out like a used napkin?"

She laughed. "Something like that. I practically raised him, you know. I'm fond of Marty."

"Um, me too."

"He's a tough nut to crack. Always on the quiet side." She made a t'cha noise. "When he was little, he thought it was his fault our mother died."

"Oh my gosh!" I brushed the pieces of onion aside and started on the carrots. "Why would he think that?"

"Because that's what Agatha told him."

"That b—" Agatha was her sister, so I amended my statement. "That bad girl."

"She *was* just a girl. Barely a teen. That age when a girl wants her mother, and she was feeling the loss. I tried my best, but I wasn't Mom."

I stopped chopping and turned to her. "I'm sure you gave them a lot of love, and that's what kids need."

June stirred the stock and tasted it. "That they do." She replaced the lid and gave me her full attention. "I just want you to understand that beneath that tough cop exterior,

Marty is sensitive. He's a good man. He's also not casual, if you know what I mean. I wouldn't want to see him hurt because you didn't understand that." Her voice got that throaty sound of someone who might cry.

Last month, I'd realized I loved Detective Martin Bowers. However, it didn't seem appropriate to share that news with his sister, especially since I hadn't told him. My experience with Jeff had left me skittish about making myself vulnerable, and so much depended on this weekend. If his sisters didn't take to me, I figured it would doom the relationship, and I wasn't about to expose myself only to have Bowers end the relationship. That would be pathetic. I felt my own tears well up.

"Yes, ma'am. I understand perfectly."

"Good." She sniffed. "I got the feeling you would."

The subject of our conversation stepped inside just then, alone. He looked from me to June and read something ominous in our expressions. "What?"

I gazed at his face, weary once again from worries. I noted the permanent creases around the corners of his blue eyes, the ones that crinkled when he smiled. The firm mouth that I thought was fixed into a permanent frown when I'd first met him. I learned how quickly those lips could soften into a smile. I swallowed hard. I would hate to lose him.

"It's the onions," I said, pointing with the knife at my handy work.

June moved over to check the results.

"Good job. Now dump it all into the pot."

Bowers lifted the lid to inhale the delicious scent and held it while I swept the veggies into the stock. "Chicken noodle soup?"

June laughed. "Vegetable. I thought you two could use a break."

I gave her an impulsive hug, and she squeezed me back, tight. One sister down. Six more to go.

With the attack on Carl, I hoped the marshal would focus on an explanation for Duane's death beyond lover's spat. Something more nefarious. Not because I reveled in conspiracy theories, but because that moved the investigation away from Bowers' immediate family. Then we could leave.

As much as I looked forward to getting back to what passed for normalcy, leaving soon also meant I had limited time to endear myself to these women who mattered most to my boyfriend. They *would* love me by the time we left if I had any say in the matter.

While he went upstairs to shower, I sought the sister I thought would be easiest to tackle—or should I say win over? —next. Cecelia was in the den, reading her book.

Why her? She hadn't been particularly friendly, and I didn't know of any common interest we shared. However, I always found older women more reasonable, and I hadn't yet offended her by scandalizing her young son with my near nakedness or rolling around on the floor and trying to snatch her jewelry.

I took a seat on the couch and smiled, which might have been a nice opening if she had looked up from her book.

"What are you reading?"

She sighed and closed the book, using her finger as a placeholder. "Are you interested in archeology and Indian artifacts?"

I thought about faking it. "Um, not really. I mean, if you had something interesting to share, I'd love to hear it, but as for researching it myself, no."

She gave me a tolerant smile. "At least you're honest."

I only knew one thing about Cecelia, and I used it to entice her into a conversation. "I'm curious what got you started on the organ. June said you played. I mean, you wouldn't just run across an organ sitting around and test it out."

She chuckled. "Especially not a pipe organ."

I frowned. "You mean those gigantic organs in churches?"

"And theaters. They used them in theaters a long time ago. Preservation is difficult but allowing them to fall into disrepair is a crime."

And that's when I discovered Cecelia had been a teacher before she retired. But do teachers ever retire? I think not. It's in their blood.

The retired teacher informed me that organs originated in Greece when an engineer came up with an instrument called the hydraulis. Then the Byzantines got involved and the instrument finally wound up in the West. And thank goodness for the Middle Ages because someone came up with a portable version so people could enjoy them at home. Kind of like the first personal computers.

As she moved through history, she hummed examples of the music. They all sounded the same to me, though I recognized Bach's *Toccata in D minor*.

She dragged me through the Renaissance, Baroque, and Classical periods, and by the time we made it to the Romantics, my mind had wandered onto the ingredients in her perfume. Was the citrus smell from oranges? Lemons? Limes? Limes got me thinking about margaritas.

She pulled my attention back by mentioning something I could relate to—the 19th century. But then she got technical. Cecelia waxed eloquent about the pipes, stops, keyboards and couplers. My neck ached from nodding, and my vision clouded. When she started on composers, I held up my hand.

"I won't remember all this."

She laughed, a low, chuffing sound. "I promise not to test you." Her features softened into a dreamy look. "Knowledge is more than handy tips. There's the pleasure of learning and the pride of recall."

Like I said. A teacher. I never found any pleasure or pride in knowing that twelve was the square root of one-hundred-forty-four, but it's stuck in my head.

Fortunately, June called us in for dinner, and I could escape.

CHAPTER 29

Once we were seated in our usual places, I glanced around the table. As I smiled at Tom and said hello to Joe, it occurred to me that I'd been so concerned about the women in Bowers' life I'd ignored potential allies. The men.

Cecelia's husband Joe rarely spoke, so after June had dished out the soup and everyone had buttered their fresh bread, I asked him how he and Cecelia met.

He had a sweet, shy smile, and I prepared myself for a sappy love story.

"I had her arrested."

His wife gazed at him fondly, as if he had just paid her a compliment.

"At least I had the phone in my hand and was dialing the police. She was trespassing on my property. I thought she was one of those animal cruelty fools protesting outside my business. Had to have a vet come in once and lecture the idiots on the health advantages of properly fitted shoes."

Was consulting a vet instead of a podiatrist a form of alternative medicine? Bowers picked up on my confusion.

"Joe's a farrier."

That didn't help.

"A blacksmith who specializes in shoeing horses."

"Turns out Cissy just wanted a look at my bellows. Not that we use them these days, but I give historic demonstrations on the weekends so folks can see the conditions blacksmiths used to put up with."

I nodded. "Because of the organs."

She beamed at me and I felt foolishly pleased, which increased my confidence. I looked at Tom and asked him to share how he met Agatha.

"Oh, I'll let my wife tell you that story."

She had claimed her seat next to me, so I only had to turn my head to see her frown. "It was no big deal. At a Prince concert."

Tom's grin told me there was more to the story, but I let it alone because I suddenly sensed danger. I'd led the conversation to where they would naturally ask about me and Bowers. These were the same women who had taken against Duane based on hearsay. They'd never seen him drunk on the job, but they believed he had a drinking problem. They didn't know the details of his brush with the police, but they had pronounced him untrustworthy. They'd eat me for dinner.

"How about you?" Agatha said, smiling sweetly.

She had jokingly referred to me as a criminal Bowers had rehabilitated. How would she take the actual story? I didn't think she'd be as receptive to animal communication as Dymphna had been. Bowers saved me.

"Frankie consults on some of my cases." He didn't even flinch as he repeated the lie I'd told Marshal Kipper. Instead, he dunked a hunk of homemade bread in his soup and took a bite. It touched me he would lie to his family to protect my reputation. Or maybe he was protecting *his* reputation. Either way, I was touched.

"I thought you said you worked with animals," Cecelia said. Trust a former teacher to remember details.

"Does Marty call you when the case involves an animal?" June smiled, and I wanted to hug her.

"Yes." I nodded. "The police can't waste their time with animals left at the crime scene when there are criminals to catch."

"So, are the animals witnesses?" Dymphna made this surprisingly perceptive—and catty—comment. She hadn't forgiven me for snooping on her. Her lips twitched as she took in the reaction to her comment.

Agatha snorted soup up her nose, and June shook her head.

"Dumb witnesses, you mean," Cecelia said. "Just like that Agatha Christie book."

"Animals talk, if you can speak their language." Dymphna continued to stare at me as she said this, so, in defense, I threw her suggestion back in her face.

"Do you talk to Windy?" I asked sweetly.

Her shoulders twitched. "Of course. But I can't understand her as well as if I had *your* ability."

Heads swiveled my way.

I let out a dramatic sigh. "You wouldn't believe how many animal behavior books I've had to study to get to where I am now. And I take continuing education classes. Constantly." I turned to Joe. "What would you do if a horse pinned its ears back?"

"Get the heck out of the way."

"Congratulations. You've just had a conversation with a horse."

Carl winked. "I get ya. Just takes practice and being around animals."

I winked back. "Exactly."

"I never thought of it that way," he continued. "I'm talking to animals all day long. What do you think of that, June?"

She returned his affectionate smile. "You're a regular animal whisperer."

"I talk to my turtle, Bob." Marc glanced around the table, shyly, as if he never would have admitted to this if the adults hadn't made their confessions first.

Agatha leaned her head toward her son. "What does he say, sweetie?"

Marc lowered his voice. "Give me some grubs." He snorted with laughter.

If Dymphna kept pushing, she would cement her reputation as a flake. I caught Bowers eye and grinned. Success.

It never pays to get cocky.

TWENTY-NINE

Bowers took me aside after dinner on the excuse that I missed my time with the chickens. June, loving her chickens, bought it.

"They do grow on you."

We both had on long sleeves—me in my blue, cowl-necked sweater, and Bowers in a fawn-colored pullover—so we skipped the jackets. I noted the bulge under his sweater where the hip holster rested but made no comment.

"I should have cautioned you about Dym."

I hooked my arm through his. "That's alright. I thought I handled her pretty well."

He grimaced. "N-o-o-o. You put off the inevitable. You challenged her, and Dym never forgets a challenge. She'll dedicate the rest of your time here trying to prove that you talk—really talk—to animals."

I snorted. "That's hard to prove. You still don't believe it. Not one-hundred percent." When he protested, I squeezed his arm. "It's okay. Most days I think it's a mistake. At least until one of the little buggers invades my mind."

He seemed cheered by the difficulty of proving something like animal communication, and maybe that's why he offered to give me an insight into his working methods.

"It's useful to go back to the first witness. Sometimes they remember something once they've calmed down and don't feel pressured into coming up with spectacular insights for the police."

"That's nice, but we're the first witnesses. Are we going to take turns interviewing each other?"

"Not quite."

He swung open the door to the chicken run.

"You don't mean . . .."

"I do. We have additional information. Maybe they'll have new responses."

My eyes narrowed. "You're taking the idea of talking to chickens awfully well. What's changed?"

He focused his gaze on a spot of wood on the side of the coop and picked at it. "Nothing. I'm being methodical. That's all."

Methodical my eye. Though he tried to cover it, a tension hung about him. He couldn't deny it any more than he could deny that he was carrying a weapon around his sister's homestead. However, if he wanted me to think he was fine, so be it.

Wandering the edges of the run so as not to step on anyone, I spread the mental net wide, since I wasn't sure which chicken I should target. I began with specifics, such as images of each of our suspects starting with Dymphna. The birds practically cooed when they saw her face.

"Does your sister, Dymphna, like the birds?"

Bowers leaned his head back and rubbed the bridge of his nose. "She likes all animals. Why?"

"They like her back."

They had no opinion of Tina or Paul. Since I'd never met Slick, I couldn't show them his face, but I gave them a peek of his three minions. No response. I scratched my chin. How would I feel if someone were attacking me, assuming I had enough time to have a reaction before they hit me with a shovel? I chose fear.

In response, my chest got tight. A few clucks followed this but only lasted for a moment.

Anxiety was close to fear. Since the killer struck Duane on the back of the head, he might not have seen it coming, but that scenario didn't give me anything to work with. I decided they had cut him down trying to escape. Okay. So, maybe he was out of breath. Panicked. Had high adrenalin. How would I go about generating those feelings?

Sticking to the edges of the run so as not to run over the birds, I sprinted until I reached the coop, then turned and ran along the fence until I reached the opposite side of the coop near Bowers.

"Should I join you?"

"Quiet," I panted, and then I turned back and did it over again. By the time I made it to Bowers the sixth time, my heart was pounding, I was sweating a little and my limbs shook slightly. I don't do a lot of sprinting. Then I sent out what I was feeling in a wave. The wave kicked back.

My knees buckled and Bowers caught my arm.

"What the—?" I looked up at him.

"Well?"

"It's coming from inside."

"Inside your head?"

I made a face and led the way into the coop. The frantic response had left a reverberating wave, and I followed it until I stood in front of the wannabe mother, Lola. I gave her another dose of the feeling and attached it to Duane's face, and boy did she have something to say about that.

Suddenly, feathers and hay filled the air along with angry avian screams. I'd entered the scene mid-commotion, so I couldn't see the cause. A hand brushed my face, and I snapped my beak and heard a male voice swear.

Someone was after my children, and I had to stop them. My claws went into overdrive, kicking and swiping at the invader.

"Frankie!"

The vision stopped as abruptly as it had started. As my eyes focused on the calm, quiet coop, I noticed my hands were slapping and swiping at Bowers' chest. He gripped my arms tight and shook.

"Frankie."

I blinked a few times and let my breathing return to normal. When I looked up, I saw an angry scratch on Bowers' cheek. I reached out, but he jerked his head back.

"Did I do that?" I whispered.

Satisfied I wasn't about to claw at him again, Bowers let go of me and pulled a tissue from his pocket. He dabbed at the spot and looked at the blood.

"Bowers, I am so sorry." I gasped. "I didn't bite your finger, did I?"

"I asked for it," he said, tucking the tissue away. He studied me in a disappointed daze, like a man who's seen his date's underwear drawer and found she wore the same brand as his mother.

"You went a little crazy. You screamed, sort of. More like a screech. Then you started hitting me."

"I was in Lola's head."

He reached out for me and changed his mind. "So, you saw what she saw?"

I shook my head. "It's too stupid."

"We're standing in a coop talking to chickens. Nothing's too stupid."

"Lola seems to think Duane was after her eggs. She says he attacked her."

"Maybe she attacked him first."

"No. He picked her up and threw her around. Tried to murder her darlings."

"Did she look manhandled to you the day we found his body?"

"No. And there wasn't hay tossed around or feathers on the floor." I looked down at the mulch and the stray feathers and hay from the nesting boxes. "Or maybe there was, and I didn't notice."

"She didn't respond by braining him with a shovel, so the episode doesn't seem to have anything to do with the murder. We are, after all, investigating a murder. Can't you just ask them if they saw anything that night?"

"Sure. The minute they start using calendars and the English language."

He squeezed the bridge of his nose. "This was a waste of time."

"You have a better idea?"

He let his hand drop. "If I did, I wouldn't be standing here."

"So, I'm the last resort?"

He sighed. "I hurt your feelings. I'm sorry."

"Don't worry about it. I'll survive."

As we left the run, I asked if he had heard from Slick.

He hesitated. "No."

"You didn't give them your name." I gasped. "Why didn't they ask for your name?"

"Because they already knew who I was. Is that what you're thinking? It's possible. If so, he's not going to call."

"Is that why you're carrying your little friend around? Because they know where to find you?" I grabbed his arm. "That goon from The Black Stallion said he'd know where to find you."

"No. That's not it. I'm carrying because I've got to finish the job Carl started, and I don't want anyone sneaking up on me. Not that I think they'll come back."

I stopped walking. "You're not going alone, are you?"

"Nope. So, stop worrying."

The sun was already behind the hills, putting a shadowy golden glow on the landscape.

"Hadn't you better get moving? Otherwise, you'll be out in the dark."

"June has work lights I can use." He moved to kiss me but adjusted his trajectory so his lips landed on my forehead. "Stop worrying."

And that's when I really started to worry, and not just about the mystery.

I didn't get to sleep until well after midnight. That's because Bowers didn't get back from fixing the fence until then. Not wanting to worry June, I went to my bedroom, waited until the house was silent, and then sneaked to the window at the end of the hallway where I had a view of the front field.

I thought I could make out lights in the distance, which I assumed were the work lamps Bowers had mentioned. It might have been a trick of the eyes, but the bright dots seemed to move.

After an hour, I went back to my bedroom. The floor creaked when I paced, so I sat on the edge of my bed and swore I wouldn't lay back on the inviting mattress, not even for a minute. That soft, hand-stitched quilt and those fluffy down pillows would have to wait until Bowers was in his own bedroom down the hallway, safe and sound.

Maybe a quick minute wouldn't hurt.

I jumped up, opened the window, and hung my head out into the cold, night air. A coyote yipped once, but otherwise; the wildlife was still. Probably asleep on soft piles of leaves, snuggled up to other warm bodies.

One weakened glance at the bed convinced me I could prop up the pillows and sit up. There wasn't anything wrong with wanting to be more comfortable during my vigil. In fact, being comfortable would probably sharpen my senses since I would stop thinking about my tired feet.

I wasn't sure what pulled me back from the edge of slumber. It was either the motion from my chin hitting my chest or the voices I heard coming from the parking area below. I slid off the bed and crept up to the window to hear better.

My room was dark, so I risked leaning forward for a peek. Bowers leaned against the side of a black pickup. His body blocked the driver, and the passenger was a mere shadow. He tapped the top of the truck twice, and it backed up at a curved angle, straightened out, and headed down The Old Road.

The back door clicked shut, and my first impulse was to run down the stairs and meet him there. Fortunately, I remembered my mother's words—something about men needing space and how they didn't want to feel their woman was their babysitter.

The stairs creaked as he climbed them, and his footsteps paused at the top of the steps. I held my breath, hoping he would drop by and tell me about tonight, but his steps headed the other direction. Finally, I heard his door close. It took fifteen minutes before I relaxed enough to fall asleep.

THIRTY

By morning, my curiosity had chased away all thoughts of giving Bowers his space. As soon as breakfast was over, I dragged him outside for a walk down the driveway.

"Tell me."

After a moment of silence, Bowers said, "Do you want to see the fence? Maybe I could teach you how to fix it. It would make you indispensable and Carl's favorite gal."

"Would it make me valuable to your friends?"

He shot me a sharp glance. "Were you watching us?"

It sounded like an accusation. "Not through binoculars, but only because I don't have a pair." Not the right approach. I sighed. "I was sound asleep and heard a truck pull up behind the house. Naturally, I was concerned. Worried." His expression didn't change. "And a little scared."

That did the trick. He put an arm around my shoulder and squeezed. "You didn't want me out there alone, and I decided you had a point. So, I called a few friends to help."

"I didn't think you had friends around here, except the attorney."

"There are close friends and then, well, friends. I told you about my best childhood friends, but that doesn't mean I grew up in a hermetically sealed bubble. I know lots of people."

My only friend had been and still was Penny. I never considered my situation pathetic. I thought I was lucky, but I realized not everyone saw it that way.

"Did your friends have an opinion on the fence?"

"Guys always have opinions. That's what we do."

"I wasn't talking about ways to mend the fence. I meant about who did it and why."

"Oh, you know. Vague rumblings and accusations. Nothing worth listening to."

"I noticed one of them drove a black truck. Coincidence, huh?" I said it quickly, hoping to throw him off.

He stopped walking and turned to me. "Frankie, most people out here have trucks. Black is a favorite color." He grinned. "It's manly."

I shook my head. "People don't want black vehicles. Even the smallest amount of dirt shows up on black."

"I thought we were talking about men."

He had a point. We cut through the pasture until we reached a patch at the far side of the property. The men had replaced the barbed-wire fence at the bottom with regular wire. They wouldn't get an A for neatness, as the wire was looped and tied for security in several thick knots and didn't match the surrounding fence.

"Nice job," I said.

"It will hold."

"Have you decided what they're after?"

"Rural areas aren't immune to thieves."

"But what would they be after?"

WHAT THE CLUCK? IT'S MURDER

"Your typical thieves are after animals. Tools. Equipment. Anything that's not nailed down."

"Tell me, why wouldn't the thieves just climb over the gate? Seems like less trouble."

"The security lights," he said. "And whatever they were stealing might be too heavy to lift."

I laughed. "How heavy could a chicken be?" I knew we were past chickens, and I hoped he would correct me with the truth.

He smiled back at me, distracted. "You're right. But we'll never know until we ask them, and that means catching them."

"What are you going to do? Stand guard all night?"

He averted his eyes. "Some of us will take turns."

I swallowed down the fear. "Sounds like a lot of trouble over some chickens."

He frowned the frown of every homeowner, rancher, or farmer whose private property rights had been violated. "It's the principal."

"Sure, sure. I see that." I slid him a glance, already knowing the answer. "Which shift do you want me to take?"

He put his hands on my shoulders and kissed my forehead. "None. You're a guest. You just relax and get to know my sisters."

Liar, liar, pants on fire. Bowers was full of poop. I knew it, and he knew I knew it. We had agreed to be partners on this investigation but he was still keeping me in the dark.

That's why I felt justified in making my next move.

Since Bowers was going to hold things back from me to protect my fragile self, I figured he didn't need to know everything I was thinking either. In his distracted state, it wasn't difficult to wrangle the car out of him under the guise of getting a present for Seamus McGuire, the animal trainer who was watching my cat.

He insisted I bring my cell phone with me in case I got lost, something I intended to do anyway, but my purpose in bringing it was so I could track down my quarry on the internet.

When Teri Nila had arrived at the Baxter house and dropped her bomb about being Duane's girlfriend, I'd noticed a sticker on the back window of her red hatchback. It was two knitting needles crossing each other over a ball of yarn. Or maybe they were crochet hooks. They were implements of crafting, and that's what I searched for when I pulled off the road just outside of downtown Cave Bear.

It took me seven tries before I turned up the Knot for Fun knitters' group and recognized their logo. They had a shop on Euclid Street, and the map showed this to be a block off the main road.

I parked in the small lot behind the shop. The entrance had glass windows lined with handcrafted scarves, sweaters, and purses. Inside, the place appeared to be a co-op as well as a meeting place. Goods hung from display racks and bore little tags that showed big prices and the name of the artist who created the item. As I wandered through the wares, I noted a table at the back of the room where several women worked on projects. None of them was Teri.

A woman with short, sun-streaked hair wearing a tank top made from variegated yarn in tones of blue and coral approached me with a smile.

"Can I help you find something?"

"Everything is so beautiful," I said, earning a bigger smile. "But, actually, I'm looking for Teri Nila."

"She's not here," she said, edging me toward a rack of sweaters. "Here are some of her designs."

Teri may be a liar, but she was a gifted liar. I touched a jacket with a brown and teal pattern and couldn't resist pressing the soft fabric to my cheek.

"Wonderful."

"Do you want to try it on? We have a changing room in back."

After a glance at the six-hundred-dollar price tag, I reluctantly let go and straightened the sweater on the hanger. "Maybe next time." I smiled. "Teri promised to find me some wool."

The woman gestured to a wall covered with bins of yarn. "We have a lot to choose from."

"I needed a specific color. I don't have the sample with me," I added to keep her from offering to search, and to make my story more plausible, I mentioned the one kind of wool I'd heard of from a friend. "Alpaca."

Her gaze turned to one of respect. "Huacaya or Suri?"

"God bless you," I said, laughing. She was serious. It was time to backpedal. "I'm just a beginner. Teri knows what I need."

She frowned. "Are you sure you want to start out with such an expensive wool?"

"That's me. Dive right into the deep end. Do you know where I can find her?"

The bell over the door jangled, and in walked Teri Nila with a backpack slung over one shoulder.

"There she is." My helper gestured and returned to the table.

Teri's eyes opened wide at the sight of me. "What do you want?"

I hooked my arm through hers. "Just a talk. You know, about Duane."

"I'm teaching a class in ten minutes." She jerked her arm away.

"That's okay. We can reminisce in front of witnesses. I don't mind. They might like to hear your story. Women love romantic tragedies. Star-crossed lovers like *Romeo and Juliet*. Sad endings, like that movie *Love Story*. I forget. Does she die, or does he? And then there's—"

"We can step outside, but only for a minute." She raised her voice and called out to the other ladies. "I'll be right back."

It was lucky she'd interrupted me, because I had run out of fictional examples of love stories. I'm not a fan.

She took me round back and to the farthest edge of the parking lot where casual passers-by wouldn't see or overhear us. By then, she had put on her sad girlfriend persona and smiled at me. "Are the police going to let me back into Duane's cabin?"

I shrugged. "Search me. I'm more interested in why you pretended to be Duane's girlfriend."

"Pretended?" She sniffed. "How could you be so cruel."

"The police have the poem. Since that's what you tried to lift from Duane's cabin before Bowers caught you, I assume that's what you were after. So why not come clean? Who were you acting for?"

The blood drained from her already pale face. "Acting for? What do you mean? I wanted a memento of my dead boyfriend."

I studied her. She may spend her spare time creating beautiful women's fashions, but she seemed rough around the edges. A tattoo of a pair of lovebirds snuggling on a branch peeked out from under the sleeve of her black t-shirt. She had a tiny diamond pierced into one nostril, something she'd left at home when she came to the Baxter's house. Her hair hung limply, and her small mouth fell into a natural frown. Definitely not the sweet thing she had pretended to be.

"Look. You seem like a fairly normal person, and dropping by the cabin of a recently murdered man isn't quite nice. So, I think you did it because someone made you."

"No one makes me do anything I don't want to," she growled. For such a tiny person, she gave off an aura of toughness. I wasn't one to dismiss sinewy muscles. Everyone knows that the best wrestlers are beanpoles.

"Then you did it as a favor." When she clamped her lips together, I nodded. "But who? Who would be interested in Duane? Who would attack Carl?"

"Somebody got attacked?" She raised her brows, and I saw panic in her eyes. "Were they hurt?"

"Yes. An elderly man who is one of the nicest people I know." I narrowed my eyes. She seemed concerned. Worried. Maybe worried that the attach involved someone she knew?

Carl thought there might have been two men. Possibly three. The trio from The Black Stallion knew where Bowers lived. Had they come to show him who was boss, and Carl got in the way?

But the squirrel-loving woman from the bar had said none of the three made a move without their boss's approval. Were they sent to the Baxter's to do Slick's dirty work? My knees shook at the thought.

"What do you know about Slick?"

"Slick?" She batted her eyes and played dumb. "Slick who?"

"He owns The Painted Pony."

"Oh. That Slick." She shrugged, but her nostrils flared. In fear? Or was she worried because I had made a connection.

"It must be him," I muttered. "Or at least Scar and his two knuckleheaded sidekicks doing Slick's bidding."

"Mort is not a knucklehead." Teri bared her teeth at me. "He's a nice guy, so don't you dare call him that."

Ah. I had my connection. Did Teri come to find Duane's love poem to help Mort the moving mountain? What would he want with the information? And what did that have to do with tire tracks in the Double Trouble caves?

I needed to think.

"You should get back to your class."

She looked at her watch and appeared frustrated that we had run out of time, which was odd considering how little she had to say to me.

Unfortunately, when she dug her cell phone out of her purse and dialed, I assumed she was calling Mort.

THIRTY-ONE

Instead of leaving downtown Cave Bear after my talk with Teri, I went into a few shops to search for the gift I'd mentioned to Bowers. I finally settled on a hand-painted coffee cup with an image of a bear on the front and *Cave Bear, Roaring since 1920* on the back.

As I walked back to my car, I passed by an alley between two strips of shops. Suddenly, my feet weren't touching the ground, because on either side of me, the two mechanics from The Painted Pony carried me by the armpits.

"Hey!" I yelled, struggling to hold onto my purchase. "Put me down!"

They did so in a recess behind one shop, and we had company. A handsome, muscular man of medium size with skin the color of deep chestnut, close-cropped black curls, and a menacing mustache leaned against the wall across from me, his arms folded across his chest.

"Miss Chandler," he said with a nod. "I hear you've been asking about me. Well, here I am." His tone sounded as if he were ready to challenge me to a rumble. Was it possible he saw me as a threat? I didn't want to be a threat to anyone.

I cleared my throat to keep my voice from cracking. "That depends. Who are you?" I asked even though I suspected.

He smirked at the two mechanics, sharing a joke. "My name is Slick, and you've been using it in vain."

I shook my head. "Nope. Not me. Teri got confused. Easy to do when you're emotional."

He cocked his head at me. "Teri?"

"Someone I was talking to. Not a friend as much as an acquaintance. Your name came up, but only in an ancillary way, and since that's the only time you were mentioned in any conversation I've had—and why would I talk about someone I've never met?—it seems logical that Teri was the one who repeated our conversation to—to someone. They must have misunderstood, and it got back to you. Don't you hate gossip? The message is always twisted in the end. Like in that game Telephone. Did you ever play it?"

His eyes had glazed over, but once I finished talking, he straightened up and took a menacing step forward. "Make sure it doesn't happen again. I'm sensitive that way."

"Me too!" I gushed. "That's why I normally avoid people. They drive me nuts. I much prefer animals—"

Slick didn't care about my preferences. "Next time, I'll be forced to stop the chatter." He jerked his head and his two minions walked on either side of him back toward The Painted Pony.

It took a few minutes before I could trust my legs to carry me back to my car. There wasn't any sign of Teri's red hatchback in the Knot for Fun parking lot. I tossed my bag inside and tore out of there.

I should have been happy. I'd confirmed that Teri wasn't

Duane's girlfriend and that there was a solid thread that linked her to the nefarious Slick. Instead, I wondered if I had invited more trouble to June's house.

By the time I pulled into The Old Road, my breathing had returned to normal. Bowers had given me a code to punch into the keypad to open the gate, but I didn't need it because he was leaning against the fence, waiting for me. He pushed himself straight and got into the car on the passenger side.

"What took you so long?" He asked the question without any warmth.

I nodded to the bag he had pushed aside to sit down. "Seamus's gift."

He pulled out the mug and held it up. "It took you almost two hours to pick out a coffee mug?"

"Men are hard to shop for." I forced out a laugh aware that Bowers wasn't in a laughing mood.

"What else did you do?"

"Not much. Peeked into a knit shop. You wouldn't believe how much a hand-knitted jacket costs."

I pulled up next to Cecelia's camper and turned off the ignition. "So, what have you been up to?"

His jaw pulsed. "Anything else you want to tell me?"

"Nice to see you?" Again, I smiled, and he didn't. "If you wanted to shop with me, you could have said so. I wouldn't have minded the company." I sighed. "Shopping bores me stiff."

Snatching my purchase from him, I got out of the car. He obviously suspected something untoward had happened. Was he having me followed? Did he have spies?

He closed the door carefully after he got out, which told me just how angry he was.

"Susi called."

"Susi from the mini-mart? I didn't go there."

"Two men were manhandling you."

I imagined that scenario and rejected it. "How would Susi leave the store? She's the only employee I've ever seen there. And she lives there."

"She's not a prisoner."

"Did she close the mini-mart? Who watched it while she was gone? Or is everything on the honor system when she steps out?"

He didn't rise to the distraction. "I'm sure she has it worked out. The point is you getting accosted."

Should I tell him about my meeting with Slick? No. Because then I would have to tell him how Slick had found out about me, and I didn't think he'd be pleased about my interview with Teri.

"Did she use that word? Accosted?" I giggled. "That must have been when I tripped, and these two nice men grabbed hold of me to keep me from falling."

"They dragged you into an alley."

"They took me to a chair outside of a shop so I could catch my breath. Wasn't that nice of them?"

His jaw twitched again.

"Look, Bowers. If Susi really thought something was wrong, wouldn't she have come to my aid or called the police or something? As it is, here I am without a scratch."

When I held my arm out, he took my wrist and pulled me closer so he could glare into my eyes and catch me if I blinked. "As long as you're alright," he said in a tight voice.

I smiled without blinking. "I'm fine. And it's so sweet of you to be concerned."

He flinched. I'd used the ultimate kiss-off word. Sweet. The word that was usually followed by a qualifier. *I think you're sweet, but I don't like you that way. What a sweet gift, but I would have preferred a pony.*

Frankly, after the afternoon I'd had, I was too tired to fix my error. I held up the bag. "I need to pack this, so I don't leave it behind." I grimaced, acknowledging the lameness of my gift. "Seamus would be devastated."

I wasn't sure what the score was by now, but one thing was certain. Bowers and I were now heavily invested in lying to each other. Should I be worried?

THIRTY-TWO

Bowers and I didn't have much opportunity to discuss our lies further that afternoon. June had asked for my help in the kitchen, and I could hardly turn her down, though out of her available selection of helpmates, I should have been her last choice.

When I came back downstair after tossing Seamus' lame gift on the bed, June had several bowls of dry ingredients as well as butter, oleo, a wooden rolling pin, and a cutting board lined up on the counter. And a notebook and pen.

"I'm better if you just tell me what you want me to do," I said, deciding to be direct.

"Frankie, honey," she said, and then hesitated. "I don't want to insult you, and you can tell me to mind my business if you like, but it has occurred to me you don't have a lot of experience in the kitchen."

"I only have myself to cook for," I began. "And my animals. Chauncey will eat anything."

"Exactly. Everything takes practice, and I've had a lot of that between the kids and farmhands." She hesitated. "Do you want a few tips?"

I couldn't count on Bowers to cook every time I asked him over, and it would be nice to surprise him. Shock might be a better word.

"Sure." I sent a wary glance over the ingredients. "But I don't know how good a student I'll be."

"Like I said. Everything takes time." She smiled. "Are you ready?"

It occurred to me that Bowers might have begged his sister to teach me how to cook. Not that he ever complained. Then again, we always went out to dinner if he was too tired to cook.

I gasped. Poor Bowers. Because of my poor culinary skills, I'd left him with a choice between spending his meager policeman's salary on take-out or slaving away over a hot stove after a long shift at the Wolf Creek Police Department. What a selfish beast I'd been. Unintentionally, of course.

Firming my jaw, I nodded. "Ready and determined."

June started simple, at least simple for her.

"Don't worry yourself over different types of flour. All-purpose is fine, and when you bake more, if you do, you can branch out and try bread flour and pastry flour and worry about self-rising, whole wheat, rye, gluten-free and the rest."

They weren't interchangeable? I bit my lip, doomed before I'd started.

"All-purpose flour," she said slowly. "That's the only one you have to remember." She pointed to a bowl of white powder. "You know what we use baking soda for?"

"Um, cleaning?"

She gurgled with laughter, explained the difference between baking soda and baking powder, and then she got down to business.

"Tonight's menu is steamed carrots with dill, yeast rolls, tossed salad, and steaks on the grill with apple pie for dessert." She smiled. "I thought your first lesson should be simple."

I glanced at the clock. "It's already three. Is there time?"

"The men have some silly idea of patrolling the grounds, so we're postponing supper until right before they go out. They may be bored, but at least they won't be hungry."

"Bowers mentioned something. What do you think they'll find?"

She laughed. "A lot of cow patties. Now, let's start with the rolls."

I had to concentrate on the task at hand, which turned out to be kind of fun. Like playing in the mud but with purpose.

She let me toss the ingredients for the rolls together and get my hands full of mushy, warm dough as I kneaded it, dipping them in extra flour when necessary. Afterwards, I understood why women made fresh bread. It was a workout and tension reliever rolled into one. June had to stop me before I kneaded the dough into leather.

Then we rolled the dough into one-inch circles and placed two of them together into each section of a muffin tin.

"The kids used to call these butt rolls. You'll see why when they're done."

"Did you teach Bowers how to cook?"

"Marty was one of my best students."

"So, he *likes* to cook?"

She turned to me. "Frankie, I don't know what you and Marty have planned for the future, but every man, woman and child should know how to take care of themselves in the kitchen." Her lips pressed together to push down a smile. "If Marc is right and we're due for a zombie apocalypse, you might find yourself the last person alive, trapped with only flour and baking soda to survive on. What would you do then?"

"Well, if I had cream of tartar, I could mix two parts to one part soda and make baking powder," I said, repeating one gem she'd shared.

She nodded. "Very good. I like working with fast learners."

Grinning with an unseemly amount of pride, I moved to the next task. I already had peeling and chopping down, so the carrots were a cinch, but when it came time to make the pie, I took the spectator role after I dropped my pie crust on the floor while transferring it to the pan.

My favorite part of making the salad was the spinner. I carried it outside and swung it over my head, spraying water on the door, the steps, and the grateful plants. It was like doing the shot put in track but without the danger of knocking anyone unconscious.

All too soon, we were ready to put the steaks on the grill. I had a grill in my tiny backyard. It seemed like a necessary step in home ownership. However, I'd never so much as lit the grill, so this part of the process slightly terrified me, but then June pulled over two baking pans lined with foil. After salting and peppering the room temperature meat, she lined up the steaks on the pan.

"You're not grilling them?"

"I call them grilled steaks, but between you and me, I hate lighting the thing. No, I bake 'em and then sear them in a cast iron skillet on top of the stove. No one's complained yet."

If this experienced home cook feared the flame, there might be hope for me yet.

I'm pleased to say that nobody choked on dinner. In fact, the compliments rolled in. June winked at me.

"Frankie made dinner tonight."

I was tempted to take the gaping expressions and sudden silence as an insult. Perhaps they feared doling out compliments to the newcomer might infringe on June's rightful place as Queen of the Kitchen. I smiled. "June supervised. I only did as I was told."

Everyone relaxed now that all was right with the world. The only reaction I was interested was Bowers'. He raised his brows and thanked me for the delicious dinner, but it was a half-hearted compliment. He seemed distracted.

I hid my smile. Soon he would make excuses and slip out of the house, ignorant of my intention to follow him and his buddies. In fact, when he approached me and said we needed to talk, I played the role of understanding girlfriend to an award-winning level.

"We're just going to walk the perimeter and make sure there aren't any more gaps, and if there are, we'll stop and fix them. It will be boring."

"It sure will be, and that's why I'm going to catch up on my reading. I brought a few animal behavior books with me that I haven't had a chance to look over." I pinched his waist. "You've been distracting me, you little devil."

Even as the words came out of my mouth, I knew I had overdone it. *You little devil?* Who says that? Not Frankie Chandler in her right mind. His narrowed eyes confirmed I'd stepped out of character.

I dropped my voice to a bored tone. "Actually, I'm tired. It has been a full day. Shopping wears me out." I slipped him the look I might have given him if I were trying to hide something, which is the look he would expect from me. I knew darn well he was aware of my confrontation with Slick but was afraid to admit he had his spies watching me.

He relaxed and kissed my forehead. "That's a good idea."

Someone knocked on the door, and I caught site of Luther. They must be turning a simple property patrol into a men's night. Carl called out to Bowers, and with one last look in my direction, he headed out the door. Tom and Joe went, too, which surprised me. It also made me certain they didn't expect to run into trouble. Tom wasn't exactly fighting material, and Joe looked like he'd topple if I pushed him with my pinkie.

I made my excuses and went to my room, allegedly to retire early. I expected at least half-hearted resistance, but no one tried to argue me out of it, which was disappointing but not surprising.

Instead of changing into jammies, I slipped on my black slacks and my purple sweater, which was the closest thing I had to black. My forest green quilted vest gave me more freedom of movement than a jacket would. A pair of tennis shoes were waiting by the door as I sat on the bed and counted the minutes.

June was the first to retire, followed by Cecelia. When Agatha put Marc to bed, she returned to her own room rather than go back downstairs for a glass of wine or nighttime television. Dymphna was already in her room, and I gave it an extra half hour to make sure she didn't have to take Windy for a tinkle. And then I made my move.

The hardest part was unsetting the lock on the back door without making too much noise, but I finally stood on the back porch and breathed in the cool night air.

I gazed upon the familiarity of June's backyard, the

chicken coop, Duane's cabin, and even the barn, all blanketed under the glow of the security lights. Beyond them? Only darkness.

Most of the trouble had come from the front pasture, so I assumed that's where the men would focus their rounds. I slipped between the house and the barn and stepped into unfamiliar territory.

THIRTY-THREE

Fields do not have the advantages of a well-trimmed backyard. The kind of place you might lie on your back and stare at the stars.

"Dang it!"

My ankle twisted as I stepped into a hole and then stumbled over a clump of tall grass. Other dangers included stones and the many cow patties. However, I wanted to keep to the center of the pasture because I assumed the men would walk the periphery. I wanted to spy on them, not join them.

A shadow moved to my right. I froze. It was about twenty yards away, and it was joined by six other shadows. That made seven.

I'm not a mathematician, but Bowers plus Carl plus Joe plus Tom plus Luther, even adding Paul, made six, not seven. Maybe Marshal Kipper had joined them on their walk. That made me feel better. With the law around, surely the bad guys would stay away.

They walked in silence along the edge of the pasture in the opposite direction of Cave Bear Road. Perhaps they were coming in for the night. I stood still until they passed me, and then I followed.

When they kept going past the house, I assumed they were headed for Double Trouble, but that made little sense. The only field they could watch over from that vantage point was the one they used for the horses. Unless they were dealing with horse thieves. But no. You couldn't fit a horse through the gap the thieves had made in the fence. Maybe they were walking Luther home. Unless...

That brat! Bowers had suggested they would be patrolling to make sure the fence didn't need repairs, which would naturally make me think they would be in the front field. He must have suspected that the thieves were accessing June's farm from the Jackson farm.

If they were planning to steal equipment or livestock, it made more sense to go this back route along the creek bed. Maybe they only came through the front fence to do reconnaissance.

When I finally came to the hillside under the caves, I regretted my decision to leave my cell phone in my bedroom. Walking on an uneven creek bed without seeing the path had proved difficult enough; uphill seemed impossible. However, the flickering of flashlight beams in the closest cave felt like a taunt and spurred me to action.

A few feet up, the toe of my shoe stuck in a crevice. After freeing myself, I jumped back, panicked, certain that I'd just awakened a slumbering rattlesnake. I let out my breath when nothing attempted to kill me and returned to hiking up the hill.

By the time I reached the cave entrance, the knees of my jeans were dusty from falling, there was dirt under my fingernails from grabbing ground to get my balance, and I hated every man in that cave for having his own flashlight.

Before entering, I straightened my vest, ran my fingers through my hair, and threw back my shoulders, ready to stroll in and surprise them in the act of being macho. I readied my quip. Something that would tell them how easy it had been to follow them in the dark. Something that would make them feel foolish.

As I stepped inside, all flashlights turned my way, blinding me. I held my hand up to block the glare, since they made no move to point them elsewhere, which would have been polite.

"What's the matter? You've never seen a girl before?"

The loud *har-de-har* that answered me didn't match any of the voices I knew, and I didn't think it was necessary to use the language another man used in front of me and said so.

"Pardon me, princess."

That voice I knew, and I took a step back.

"Oh, no you don't." Slick stepped forward and grabbed my arm. "We can't have you wandering around in the dark, sweetheart. You might hurt yourself."

He wore the same expressionless mask that Bowers often used, but on him, there was a menacing aspect to it. Probably because I knew he was a criminal. And because he threatened me in the alley.

I pretended that strolling inside had been my idea all along and stepped forward, shrugging him off. "Could you get those lights off my face?"

Slick nodded, and they complied. As my eyes adjusted, I noticed Smoking Guy and Mustache Guy from The Painted Pony, out of uniform, and Scar and his two buddies, Tommy and Mort, from The Black Stallion. I think the guy who laughed had been Mort the Mountain.

"Put her with the other one," Slick said.

"No."

A man I didn't recognized stepped out of the shadows, and my insides quailed at someone standing up to Slick.

"They'll be out of the way here," Slick said. It worried me he felt it necessary to explain himself to the new guy rather than ordering him to obey, because that meant the new guy was more powerful—and probably more frightening—than Slick.

I studied his face—what I could see of it. He stood the same height as Slick, and he was just as solid, but he had the skin of someone who'd lost a battle with teenage acne, and his black eyes reminded me of something dead. They were the eyes of a shark.

"They can be our insurance policy if we run into trouble."

Insurance against what? Frightened as I was, my brain processed a tidbit of information. Slick had referred to *the other one*, as in I wasn't the only unwanted person in here. Had they captured Bowers? Carl? Tom? Tom didn't seem very tough, so I put my money on him. Of course, I didn't think Joe could outrun even me. Maybe he was their hostage.

Slick shrugged, and he stepped into the dark at the back of the cave. I heard someone grunt, and when he moved back into the light, he held Dymphna by the arm.

"What are *you* doing here?" I demanded. I couldn't hear her answer. No surprise there.

"Let's get this over with," the new evil guy said, and we processed out of the Double Trouble caves and into the unknown.

The new guy's name was Bryce, which didn't sound very tough.

While we were standing outside the cave entrance, two dark shadows loped up. Chauncey and Hero snuffled my hand and then did the same to Dymphna.

I heard a menacing click and shouted, "No!"

Hero growled, and I stepped in front of them.

"They won't be any trouble. I promise."

I grabbed their collars and said, "Quiet!" Hero obeyed the command, and Chauncey, always a follower, imitated his buddy. I stroked their heads.

"They just want to be around people."

"You shoot, Bryce, and it will echo," Slick said, sounding irritated.

The head honcho glared as if he didn't appreciate the advice. "First wrong move and I'll take care of it." His words were a threat he'd be happy to carry out.

Dymphna took Hero's collar so I could hang onto Chauncey. When our heads were together, I hissed, "These guys are armed. What the what! And why are you here?"

"Quiet," Slick said, not sounding as menacing as Bryce, but meaning it.

As we descended the hill, Dymphna went before me, and I noticed that she had left the fairy dress at home and opted for black leggings and a black turtleneck topped off by black boots. She had out-dressed me for night stalking, which made me think she had come out with the same intention—to follow Bowers and company. But why? Her man was dead. Did she simply want to irritate her baby brother? Or had she innocently taken an evening stroll to the caves to reminisce about Duane? If so, I hoped she wasn't destined to meet him again tonight.

As we marched along the creek bed toward the

farmhouse, my back ached from the strain of bending to reach Chauncey's collar. Dymphna had to feel the same, as she was even taller than me.

When we were about twenty yards from the chicken run, the leader of the gang separated the two Painted Pony guys from the three Black Stallion guys.

"I want every inch of this place covered. You three take Duane's cabin. Check the floorboards. Pull the furniture away from the walls. Check under the bed if you have to, but by the time you're done, I want something that tells us where he put them."

Those were his instructions to The Black Stallion trio. To The Painted Pony duo, he said, "You get the barn. Check the loft first." He swung those dead eyes toward me and Dymphna. "Is there an animal in that barn that's especially mean?"

It took an effort, but I met his gaze. "They all scare me."

Dymphna gave a haughty tsk. "They are all sweet, beautiful creatures. Unlike *some* people."

"Check the stalls, too."

"They're full of crap," the mustached Painted Pony employee whined.

"You want me to find you something easier to do?"

The two men took off, but Bryce held Slick back. "You're with me."

"What's left?"

"The coop."

Slick made a noise. "The coop? It's not that big, and it's full of chickens. There's not enough room in there to hide my lunch, let alone—"

"The coop," Bryce repeated.

"It's locked." It slipped out, and the two men looked at me. "I mean, the run is locked."

Bryce stared. "I don't think that will be a problem."

I gulped. Probably not. I just hoped he didn't intend to shoot the lock because that would bring people running, including Bowers.

"I'll get the key." I just couldn't keep my big mouth shut.

"You mean you'll go in the house and call the police."

"No. Everyone's asleep. The key is right inside the door."

Slick nodded his approval. "It will keep things quiet. She can leave the door open so we can see what she's doing."

I didn't realize anyone could look so mean when they smiled. Bryce held up his gun. "I'll be watching."

I hoped that's all he'd do.

While I approached the back door, the rest of our party remained by the gate to the run. I'd convinced Bryce that it would be better for everyone if I took the dogs with me and locked them in the house.

"You're very thoughtful."

"I'm thinking of the dogs," I snapped.

"It's not a bad idea," Slick said. While Bryce's gift was terrorizing innocent women and not-so-innocent thugs, Slick seemed to have all the brains.

"You better come back," Dymphna hissed.

I assured her I would, and when I got the go-ahead, I hurried to the house as best I could while lugging two large dogs, praying the entire time that Bowers and Carl and the rest of them were far away. I held onto Chauncey and told Hero to stay while I opened the back door because it was more probable that Hero would listen to me. He looked across the yard at Dymphna, and I could feel his confusion.

I pushed their rear ends inside, grabbed the key, and

closed the door behind me. Then I rushed down the hill to the run, holding the keys out in front of me like an offering.

Bryce waved his gun at me and nodded at the gate. I was about to unlock the door when the sound of male voices came to my ears. I froze, recognizing Bowers low rumble. He was headed in this direction. Dymphna gasped.

Bryce raised his gun, ready to take aim. I admit what I did next should not be an example to anyone in the same situation. Clenching the keys between my fingers, I launched myself at the bad guy's face and screamed, "Bowers, look out!"

It took Bryce half a second to grab me and twist my arm behind my back.

"Frankie?" Bowers stepped from the side of the house and into the light. He was alone.

Not to be outdone by a mere girlfriend, Dymphna shouted. "Marty, run!" I didn't know she had it in her to yell so loud. I glanced nervously at the house to see if any upstairs lights turned on and breathed a sigh when they did not.

"Not so fast," Bryce said, which was a silly thing to say, since Bowers hadn't moved. The bad guy grinned. It was a shame that such a nice set of teeth were wasted on an ugly, menacing smile. "Looks like we have a family reunion."

"Technically," I explained in a haughty voice, "I'm not family. I'm only the girlfriend."

"You're more than any old girlfriend," Dymphna said. "Marty hasn't introduced us to anyone since—in a long time. That means something."

I placed my free hand on my chest. "That's so sweet of you to say." Sweet can be taken literally when women say it to other women.

Bryce growled. "Shut up."

"That was rude," Dymphna said in my support, and I swear Slick's lips twitched, fighting back a smile.

"I assume you have a weapon, Detective Bowers. Take it out slowly and set it on the ground. No quick moves, or I'll have to decide who to shoot first."

Bowers complied.

The scumbag Bryce knew Bowers' identity. I wondered if going to The Painted Pony had been a mistake. All the employees had to do was write down Bowers' license plate and they could find out all the background on him they wanted, including his employment with the Wolf Creek Police Department.

The trio from The Black Stallion appeared just then. Scar took in the scene and pulled out a gun, and Tommy followed suit. Mort the Mountain didn't need a weapon.

"What's going on?" Scar looked from Bowers to Bryce.

"Did you have any luck?"

"Nah. We turned the place inside out. There's nothing there, not even under the floorboards."

The head honcho stepped away from the gate. "Why don't you do the honors?" he said to Bowers, waiving his gun at the run. "And keep your hands where I can see them."

With his arms out to his sides, Bowers slowly walked to within three feet of Bryce, who jerked his head at Slick. The man I had thought of as the most dangerous guy around until meeting his boss took the keys from me, handed them to Bowers, and stepped back.

"Are you ladies okay?" Bowers' voice had an edge to it. He might have resented the way Dymphna and I had practically offered ourselves as hostages. I was going to hear about this later, if we survived, which is why I offered a hearty response.

"Fine, just fine. Making new friends. You know I have a gift for it."

With the gate open, Bryce motioned us inside, and Scar and his friends as well as The Painted Pony employees joined us. The latter looked to Slick for an explanation, but he only shrugged.

The exchange caught Bryce's attention. "I assume you didn't find anything either." He made a noise of disgust. "Did you even look in the stalls?"

"Sure we did," the mustached guy said, which was confirmed by Smoking Guy.

Bryce scanned the chicken run. "Where was Duane when you caught up to him?"

Scar answered. "Coming out of his cabin. I made nice with him, and he said he had to lock up the chickens, so I followed him in here. When he insisted he didn't know where the stash was, I let him have it and put the body where no one would find it, at least not right away."

Scar now ranked higher than Slick and Bryce on my list of scary men because he had actually killed someone.

"That was smart," Bryce said in a tone that made Scar wince. "Now we can't convince him to share the information."

"Maybe we should go over his cabin again," said the Smoking Guy.

The normally silent Tommy took offense. "What? You think we're blind? We already looked."

"It just makes sense, since that's where you found him," Smoking Guy said, trying to sound reasonable. I noticed the Painted Pony team, presumably following their leader, still hadn't drawn weapons. "I once found a stash of drugs hidden in a septic tank." He turned to Bowers. "You got a septic tank out here, don't you?"

"We do."

Smoking Guy looked at Slick. "Septic tank makes more sense than a chicken coop. There isn't much room in there."

"What about under it?" Slick asked, moving forward. "Where's the tools?"

"The cops took the shovel," Scar said with a snicker as he started walking. "The rest are back here. I'll show you."

While we waited for them to return, I tried to catch Bowers' eye, but he stared at Bryce without blinking. Dymphna kept her gaze on Bowers, too. Still watching over her baby brother.

When Slick returned with a spade, he began hacking at the ground next to the coop. After a few jabs, he swore.

"There's chicken wire underground."

Bowers, still watching Bryce, said, "It keeps the predators out."

"We're wasting time." Bryce told The Black Stallion trio to search the coop.

Once they were inside, I tracked their progress by the squawks until suddenly, I could see them from Lola's point of view. They were hulking shadows, clumsily shoving my fellow chickens.

When Scar yanked aside the privacy curtains one by one and dug through the nesting material, anger built in my chest, and the memory of Duane tossing me around put me on the offensive. I growled.

Bryce narrowed his eyes at me. "What's the matter with her?"

Bowers finally moved his gaze to me. So did Dymphna, but she looked interested instead of panicked. I caught their expressions before Lola took over again.

Scar reached out. A shot of rage made me stiffen all over. "Don't do it, don't do it, don't do it," I whispered.

The hen disconnected from me, and I winced at the squawk, followed by a man's scream and a lot of thuds. All three men raced out of the coop.

"That bird is out of its mind!"

I called to them. "She's broody."

Bryce stared at me. "You seem to know a lot about what goes on in that coop." He took a menacing step forward, and Bowers tensed.

"She attacked me, too." I held out my hands and showed him the scabs. "It's not her fault. She's hormonal. Or something like that."

Scar sucked the blood off the back of his hand where Lola had scratched him and then shook it. "There isn't enough room in there to hide a notebook." He motioned his gun hand at Smoking Guy. "I think Harold's right. Duane must have hidden them in the septic tank."

"I ain't going in there." Smoking Guy shook his head. "Not me. I made the suggestion. Someone else should have to break into it."

"You'll do what I tell you." Bryce jerked his head toward the exit, and we were about to leave the run, when the worst thing that could happen happened.

The back door opened, and June leaned out. "Is that you, Marty?"

Hero and Chauncey leapt over the stairs and charged, ready to defend the chickens.

The bad guys swiveled toward the oncoming attack, and Bowers made his move. He elbowed Scar in the face and relieved the man of his gun. Dymphna grabbed hold of me, tight, and being taller than me, when she wrapped her arms around me, they covered my head and blinded me to the surrounding chaos.

I heard a dog's snarl, a shot, and a whimper. I pushed

Dymphna aside and saw Chauncey's limp form on the ground. And then I lost it.

Rage filled me, and I launched myself at the most horrible person alive. Curled fingers jabbed at Bryce's eyes and pulled his hair. He shouted and covered his face with his hands, so I sunk my teeth into his shoulder and bit down until I drew blood.

Dymphna gaped. She should have made a run for it because Bryce grabbed us both by the hair and forced us to our knees. Everyone stopped moving, and that's when I noticed that Slick and The Painted Pony guys had disabled The Black Stallion Guys.

Only Bowers stood alone, his gun aimed at Bryce. I caught his horrified expression right before the cop face came down.

"That's going to cost you, detective. Who's it going to be?" He jabbed the tip of his gun into the back of my head. "Your girlfriend?" The gun left me, and I assume he jabbed it at Dymphna. "Or your sister?"

Dymphna and I answered for him. "Save her!"

"She's your sister, Bowers." My voice shook as I tried to sound reasonable. "You'd never forgive yourself if anything happened to her. June would never forgive you."

"Don't worry about me, Marty," Dymphna said. "With Duane gone, I'm not afraid of death."

"Isn't that sweet?" Bryce sneered. At least I assume he did. His voice sounded sneery. "Maybe I'll do them both."

"It ain't nice to shoot women," Mort the Mountain said from his position kneeling on the ground.

I wasn't sure what made the master criminal scream until I saw the white ball clamped onto his ankle. He shook his leg and bent to swipe at Windy, and Dymphna and I grabbed his gun arm and hung on, putting our combined weight into keeping him in a bent position. Bowers' sister wrestled the gun free and then planted her feet and aimed the weapon at him like she knew how to handle it.

"Touch my dog and the first shot gets you right between the eyes." The whispery fairy-girl had vanished, leaving Annie Oakley in her place. Without moving her gaze from her target, she said, "Come here, Sweetums."

Windy trotted to her and tried to climb her leg. It was cute, but I had my own dog worries.

I ran across the yard and dropped to my knees next to the lifeless form of Chauncey. Hero was licking his face but moved aside when I threw myself on my pet, sobbing.

Bowers crouched next to me. "Frankie," he said, gently. "You need to move so I can see where he's hurt."

I looked up, still clutching Chauncey. If I'd been more aware, I would have noticed my furry friend was still breathing. I scooted back on my knees and watched Bowers run his hands over the dog. He held up a bloody paw and cocked his head.

"Frankie, honey, I think Chauncey fainted."

Hero nudged me and wagged his tail.

"Fainted?"

Bowers patted my pup's haunches. "He's going to be fine."

I took several deep breaths, stood, and blinked at the surrounding scene. Nothing made sense. Slick's employees had handcuffed The Black Stallion trio, and Slick was doing the same to Bryce under Dymphna's supervision.

Men's voices shouted and Carl, Paul, Tom, Joe, Luther, and the local law came running.

"We heard shots," Carl said, and the men stopped and gaped. I gaped right back because they were all armed with rifles.

WHAT THE CLUCK? IT'S MURDER

June stood at the gate in a blue terry cloth bathrobe and a pair of work boots. She stepped aside to let the men pass.

Marshal Kipper approached Slick. Instead of pulling out his cuffs, he gave the Southwest version of hello. A brief nod. "Did you find 'em?"

"Harold suggested the septic tank. It's not a bad idea."

"I know where they are." It just came out, which was funny, because I didn't even know what *they* were, though I suspected.

Bryce swore, and Kipper and Slick raised their brows. Harold sighed with relief at his escape from the septic talk.

Bowers shifted uncomfortably in place. He didn't want to ask what I knew or how I knew it, so I just nodded and led him into the coop.

The chickens had settled back into place, but they made clucks of protests as we entered. I pointed at the raised platform the nesting boxes rested on.

"Does that open?"

"It shouldn't," Carl said.

Bowers crouched down and felt along the edges. When he reached the far side, he pulled out his trusty scouting knife and pried the board loose. I moved next to him and bent over as he turned on his flashlight.

Kipper snorted. "I'll be damned. Sorry, ma'am. Darned."

The beam made a slow path over a stockpile of guns. Lots and lots of guns.

THIRTY-FOUR

That night, June dropped her rule about no dogs on the couch.

Bowers lifted Chauncey in his arms and carried him inside. His eldest sister already had the bandages ready, and once she had cleaned his paw, she clucked like one of the hens.

"Poor thing. He lost a nail. That's going to hurt for a while."

Hero joined his friend and curled up next to his head. As June bandaged Chauncey up, he opened his eyes and whined. I stroked his head and cooed over him.

"See? Your new buddy is right here, and so am I. You'll be fine, my big protector." I looked up at June. "Hero never left Chauncey's side."

She nodded. "It's the training. Always stay be the injured animal. We wouldn't want coyotes to get to them before help came."

Hero licked my dog's face and Chauncey wagged his tail.

"Look," I joked, my voice unsteady. "It's a bromance."

June snipped the bandage and packed up her first aid kit.

"I thought you worked with animals. Hero's a bitch." She looked at Bowers. "So, is anyone going to tell me what in Hades just happened in my backyard?"

Since the room was crowded, and Chauncey and Hero took up half the couch, Dymphna and I sat on the floor and June moved in the dining room chairs for the guests.

Bowers cleared his throat and gestured to Slick. "I'd like to introduce Special Agent Troy with the ATF. He's part of a task force assigned to stop arms smuggling into Mexico. His employees at The Painted Pony are agents, too."

Dymphna nodded as if this wasn't news to her.

I narrowed my eyes at Bowers. "Then he's the one who told you about our encounter downtown? Not Susi?"

Agent Troy grinned. "Sorry about that. I didn't want you poking around and putting yourself at risk. I let Detective Bowers know about it in case you mentioned something."

Bowers returned my glare with the superior calm of a martyr. "Which you didn't."

Checkmate.

June raised a finger. "I don't understand. Then he," she motioned to Troy, "wasn't dealing in stolen cars?"

"Actually, I was, as part of my cover, in cooperation with local law enforcement. Kip and I go back a long way, and I trust him."

Marshal Kipper nodded agreement.

"I asked him to find someone on the inside who could help us locate the guns."

"Duane," Dymphna mumbled, her head resting on her knees.

Agatha huffed. "On the inside? I knew Duane was no good. Stealing cars."

Bowers held up his hand to stop Dymphna's rebuttal. "Duane fell in with the crowd Agent Troy wanted to penetrate, but he wasn't one of them. So, Troy set up Duane with a stolen car. After he was caught—"

"You mean framed," Dymphna said.

Bowers nodded. "True, but it gave him more credibility with Bryce's group. And then they gave him a choice between jail time and helping the good guys."

Dymphna barked out a harsh laugh. "He would have helped if you had asked. There wasn't any need to strong-arm him. No one ever gave him credit for being a good man."

While everyone else averted their eyes, Agent Troy addressed her directly. "I didn't know him then, Ms. Bowers. I gave him a tough task and had to make sure he'd do it. After introducing him to Bryce, I recommended him to the team, saying he had access to the perfect hiding place. The caves. But Duane's job was really to monitor the gang and let me know when the guns arrived."

He nodded to June. "We'll reimburse you for your Guinea Hens."

"Why didn't he?" June asked, exasperated. "I mean, why didn't he tell you when the guns arrived?"

"He did. But right after he confirmed they were in the caves, Duane heard they were moving the guns early. I arranged a diversion to get the guards off the cave so Duane could transfer them to a hiding place. He died before he could tell me where he put them."

I raised my hand. "Is that why Teri pretended to be Duane's girlfriend?"

Kipper nodded. "Mort sent her to check out Duane's

cabin for any clues. She's a bright girl. She recognized the drawing of the caves and thought the poem might be code."

"But it was just bad poetry." I sighed. "But why write a love poem about the caves?"

Dymphna sniffed. "We used to walk there for privacy. So we could talk about things without interruptions."

"And Duane's benders?" I looked to Agent Troy for an explanation.

"He needed a safe excuse to get away when we needed to meet up."

"Your meetings couldn't have taken that long," June said. "He'd disappear for a day or two."

"He stayed at my place," Dymphna mumbled. "To make the excuse seem real."

Agent Troy got up and stood before Dymphna. "I found your boyfriend to be resourceful and dedicated. He risked his life and lost it for a good cause. You should be proud of him, Ms. Bowers."

She lifted her chin. "I am."

I remembered how worried Dymphna looked in my vision. "Did Duane tell you what he was doing?"

"I tried to talk him out of it."

"You found him that night," I whispered.

When his sister nodded, Bowers groaned. "Oh, Dym."

There were gasps and murmurs from the sisters.

"But I couldn't do anything for him. He knew they might kill him if they figured out he was helping the law. When he didn't show up for our date, I got worried and came here. He was already gone, and I was afraid anything I did might mess up the scene and help those bastards get away with it."

As the rest of us gaped, she stood and walked out of the room, her tiny, white warrior on her heels.

When everyone had left or gone to bed, Bowers took my hand and said, "Come with me."

I still felt shaky on my legs, but the cool night air filled my lungs and braced me.

"Your sister Dymphna is incredibly strong. I can't believe she held it together this weekend."

"I told you not to underestimate her."

"I underestimated *you*. You knew all along about the guns. Yet you bravely kept that information to yourself. It was a heroic silence. Maybe we should build a statue in your honor."

"I asked if I could share the information with you."

"You did?"

"But the fewer people who knew about the operation, the better. You can understand Troy's point of view."

I shrugged one shoulder. "I guess that makes it alright."

We walked to the fence where we had met up with the horses, but Matilda and friends were inside the warm barn where The Painted Pony guys had declined to search and instead spent their time stroking noses and scratching ears.

Bowers took a deep breath. "I don't ever want to go through something like that again."

"Wolf Creek is a hotbed of crime," I kidded. "You have gunfights all the time at work, don't you?"

He pulled me close and wrapped his arms around my shoulders, resting his chin on my head. "Seeing you and my sister on your knees in front of that scumbag was my worst nightmare come true."

"Dymphna seems really comfortable around guns for such an airy-fairy type."

"Again, I told you not to let her fool you."

"That you did."

We stood in comfortable silence for a few minutes and then Bowers stepped back.

"This isn't how I imagined it—" He kicked at the ground, his hands on his hips, and let out an embarrassed laugh.

"Imagined what?"

He shrugged. "This whole weekend. I wish I'd never brought you here."

That felt like a punch in the gut, and tears stung behind my lashes. His sisters didn't like me, and Bowers couldn't get past that. I didn't want him to see how his words affected me. I still had one night to go. So, I made a joke to show it didn't bother me.

"I think I can safely assume your sister Joan won't be inviting me back soon."

He became still. "Why's that? You mean you wouldn't come if she did?"

I laughed. "Come on, Bowers. I don't think any of your sisters liked my company, though Cecelia did enjoy lecturing me on organs. Agatha punched or slapped me every chance she got, and I rolled around on the floor with Dymphna trying to open her locket. I lied to June by omission and endangered you by getting involved. A mortal sin. Dymphna gets to share blame for that, but at least she didn't embarrass your entire family at Mass." I sighed. "I guess I'm not good with people."

As I went down the list, my heart grew heavy in my chest. Maybe Bowers and I could continue dating without putting too much emphasis on a future together. That way, when he met someone his sisters would adore, it wouldn't hurt so much. "I hope you're not disappointed in me."

He cocked his head. "I'm confused. Why am I

disappointed?" He took in a breath and nodded as if he finally got it. "Frankie, if my sisters disliked you, they would have been super sweet all weekend."

They hadn't gone the sweetness route with me. "Seriously?"

"I wanted you to meet my family. To see where I come from. Who I am. This wasn't a test."

"It wasn't? I mean, I know it wasn't, but I thought you wanted to see if I fit in. You know," I said with an unsteady laugh. "To see if I was a keeper."

He closed his eyes and laughed softly. "You nut. I told you before, I'm not playing with you." He directed those serious, deep-blue eyes at me. "I love you."

My insides tingled. "You do?"

He hesitated, not sure if he should continue. "And I want to marry you."

My knees went weak, and I leaned back against the fence. "You do?"

He rubbed a hand across his mouth. "You don't have to say anything. I just wanted you to know where I stand."

I was on emotional overload. Bad guy threatening to kill me. My fear I would lose Chauncey. And now, Bowers loved me. I did what any self-respecting female would do. I started to cry, quietly at first, crescendoing into sobs.

He rubbed the sides of my shoulders. "What am I thinking? I'm an idiot. I shouldn't have sprung this on you. Not today. But almost losing you—it made me feel I shouldn't wait."

I inhaled deeply a few times, hiccuped once, and stood.

"That's a relief."

"My sisters say crying is a healthy release."

"I mean that you love me. Because I'd feel stupid if my feelings weren't reciprocated. Bowers, I love you, too."

He nodded a few times and cleared his throat. "That's good. That's very good." He leaned his head back to look at the stars, avoiding my soppy gaze. "What did you think about the rest of it? I mean, I know it's not a proper proposal, and I don't have a ring on me, but, well, is the idea repulsive?"

"I'm a little worried."

He looked at me. "About what?"

"You said you would never lie to me, and yet . . . ."

He smirked. "If you think back, everything I told you was the truth."

I huffed. "You said Susi saw me downtown when I ran into Agent Troy and his minions."

He put his hands on his hips and shook his head. "No. I said Susi called. And she did. June special ordered a magazine, and it had come in. You're the one who assumed she was a witness."

I frantically scanned my memory banks to find an example of his perfidy to throw in his face, but he spoke the truth. He'd skirted around direct lies.

"Wow. You're good. And I'm . . .not. I made you a promise, and I broke it."

"I've been thinking about that. Now, I'm not talking as a policeman, and I won't even mention the word fraud, but before you met Sandy the golden retriever," he said, mentioning the first dog to break through and communicate with me, "you went on appointments as a pet psychic because people had problems with their animals."

"That's why they called me." I laughed, nervous about the direction this conversation was headed. "And boy did they have problems."

"And you *did* help them. You weren't cheating them. You gave them expert advice."

"I did."

"But you had to get creative with how you presented your solutions."

That made me snicker. "I once told a lady with an overweight dog that her pup wanted to slim down so she'd look better in her doggie sweater."

His brow wrinkled. "Right. Like I said. Creative. I think it has just become a bad habit. And I might have a habit of holding back information when it suits me. We can break our bad habits. Together. If you think it's worth it."

I knew Bowers was worth it. I hoped he'd feel the same in three months.

"Would that make me one of the Bowers girls?"

"Is that a yes?"

"Yes."

I held out my hand. "Partners?"

He pulled me against him. "You're not getting off with a handshake."

And then he kissed me properly. We didn't get back inside for a long while.

THIRTY-FIVE

I dragged my luggage down the steps and left it by the back door. We'd finished breakfast an hour ago and were ready to take off for Wolf Creek.

Cecelia and Joe were seated at the table finishing coffee, and June was already started on her next baked delight.

I was going to miss June's cooking. "It's not fair!" Marc wailed from the den. "I miss everything fun!"

"Fun?" Agatha snapped. "You adjust your attitude, young man, or I'll show you fun."

Bowers walked in from the living room and grinned at me. My heart flipped, and I think I blushed. He took me in his arms and planted a good one on my lips right in front of June. She didn't even blink.

"So, when's the wedding?"

Bowers' head jerked in her direction so fast I would have laughed but my head was doing the same. Then Agatha walked in with her son and husband behind her.

"You better make me a bridesmaid." She punched my arm. "I look awful in green. Keep that in mind."

Marc looked up at his uncle with wide eyes. "You're getting married? Yuck!"

Carl came in through the back door. "What's this about getting married?"

Cecelia pulled a calendar out of her purse. "Fall's a busy season. You're thinking of a winter wedding I hope?"

Bowers held up a hand. "Hold on. Frankie and I haven't said a word." He looked down at me. "Have you?"

I made a zipping motion across my mouth.

June laughed. "It's so obvious. You both have the glow of two people who've taken the plunge. Half joy, half terror."

Handshakes and hugs were exchanged. I wasn't comfortable being the center of attention but melting into the walls wasn't an option.

Dymphna slipped into the room carrying Windy. "What's everyone so excited about?"

That ended the festivities. Everyone knew acutely that Dymphna has lost someone she loved. Someone she might have considered marrying. Someone who hadn't been treated fairly by the rest of the family.

June spoke up. "Your brother's getting married."

She gave us a sad smile. "Congratulations." She held Windy up and whispered in her ear. "Isn't that great, Sweetums?" She looked at me with a spark in her eyes. "But you already know she's happy for the two of you, don't you? She probably told you."

My breath caught in my throat. "Told me?"

June giggled nervously. "You're obsessive about that dog, Dym."

"Just like she told you about me and Duane."

"Dym," Bowers said, warning her off.

She rolled her eyes. "We all know."

"Know what?" My voice cracked.

Cecelia looked up from her calendar. "We did our research. Looked you up before you came. We had to know what kind of girl caught Marty's eye."

If they searched the internet, they must have seen the article Jeff's floozy wrote about me. The room swayed.

"And you kept wanting to see the chickens," Agatha added. "Which makes sense. But you never shared what they were thinking." She shook her head and frowned, disappointed.

"Aggie, leave her alone," June said. "The woman deserves her privacy." She pursed her lips. "I had an aunt who talked to her roses, but they never talked back."

I cleared my throat a few times. "You probably saw—"

Agatha interrupted. "That article instigated by your boneheaded ex-boyfriend? Little twerp. His loss, Marty's gain."

Bowers squeezed my shoulders.

"He was probably jealous," Cecelia put in. "And unemployed. The devil loves idle hands. And idle minds."

After a glance at his watch, Bowers said, "I'm on duty tonight. We better head out."

They streamed out the back door behind us. Chauncey and Hero wagged their tails, wondering if the loud cheery voices meant treats.

Chauncey.

I stared at my dog, hopping around with his wrapped paw. He seemed so happy, and I knew what I had to do.

"Bowers," I whispered.

He put his arm around me. "I think so, but it's up to you."

I took a step forward. "June," I said, trying to keep my voice steady. "Do you have room for a second dog?"

Her expression softened. "Honey, it would be our pleasure."

An ache welled up in my chest and my throat tightened. As Bowers put my luggage in the car, I knelt and held Chauncey's big face close.

"I think you're going to like it here with your girlfriend. You better miss me because I'm going to miss you."

I buried my face in his scruff and then kissed his nose. As I got in the car, he cocked his head, uncertain. Bowers backed the car up, and I kept my eyes on Chauncey's face.

Hero nudged him, and he wagged his tail. Chauncey's golden-brown eyes fixed on me, and then my dog, the one who always blocked my attempts to get into his head, said very clearly, *Thank you.*

Want to keep reading? The next Frankie Chandler adventure, *A Scaly Tail of Murder*, is available. Keep turning pages for a preview, book club questions, and more.

If you enjoyed this book, please consider leaving a review. Reviews help readers discover new books, and the author, who socializes mostly with dogs, appreciates the human feedback.

A NOTE FROM THE AUTHOR

Ah, chickens. An innocent comment by my cousin started this book. She said, "Chickens will eat anything!"

Anything? Hmm. I peppered her with a series of questions that made her rethink our phone call. Thanks, Susi!

A PREVIEW OF A SCALY TAIL OF MURDER

The woman who stared back at me from my bathroom mirror had nice eyes. Hazel, with more green than brown. They sat under natural brows somewhere between pencil thin and caterpillar. Auburn hair that hung past her shoulders curled inconveniently from an overabundance of cowlicks. Slightly full lips. Enough to notice she had lips. Not a classic beauty, but not an ogre.

Leaning forward, I studied the light creases edging my eyes. They couldn't be laugh lines. Not with my disposition. Now that I was in my thirties, I had to stop squinting. And frowning.

I fought off disappointment. Silly, I know, but I thought my recent engagement to Detective Martin Bowers would show on the outside. My face. Or my posture. I thought I'd look different. Peaceful. Glowing. Ready to break into song.

Straightening my shoulders, I let one drop in a relaxed pose. My left hand crept up to my cheek like a pale spider.

"Oh," I said, affecting surprise. "This?"

When I wiggled the fourth finger on my left hand, my engagement ring didn't sparkle because it was a pull tab from a can of soda. Bowers had taken the morning off to whisk me away on a quest for the perfect symbol of our love. Not having worn a ring since I'd won a plastic ruby at the fairgrounds—I was seven—I thought I should practice.

Lowering my voice to a sultry level, I puckered my lips. "Darling. You shouldn't have."

I sucked in my cheeks and ran my fingers through my hair. The tab caught, and it took five minutes to work it free. With a long, loud sigh, I moved back to my bedroom and hung up the clothes piled on my bed, all discards in my quest to look like the perfect fiancée. Or at least a grown up.

Bowers, dressed for work, would most likely wear a suit, or at least a sports jacket and tie. At six feet tall, with short hair a shade above black and deep-blue eyes, my fiancé could wear a gunny sack and still make pulses race. Not that he was metrosexual or obsessed with hair products. He was rugged enough to be manly without overdoing it. Not the kind of nut whose idea of a fun date included hiking Mount Everest or paddling the English Channel.

PE, or Pre-Engagement, my go-to outfit was sweatpants and a t-shirt. Maybe jeans. However, if we walked down the street holding hands, I wanted the people we passed to think *What a lovely couple*. Not *That's one seedy customer Detective Bowers is hauling to the station.*

For today's grand event, I'd settled on a short-sleeved royal blue blouse with white polka-dots, beige slacks, and leather sandals with low heels. Open-toed sandals. Should I have attempted to paint my nails? Did I own a bottle of nail polish? No need to go crazy.

I moved back to my home's combination living room/dining room for a quick assessment. After a sniff, I sprayed an evergreen aerosol to mask Emily's cat odors. Then I sprayed again. Once I'd straightened the mismatched pillows on the blue-and-white plaid couch donated to me by my parents, I tried to see my home through impartial eyes. Well, not impartial eyes. Bowers' eyes.

Would he be surprised by the watercolor of a Gambel's quail that now hung above the couch? I'd brought her home last night. Painted by a local Wolf Creek artist, the picture gave me a rush of joy every time I gazed at it.

I frowned. She might be lonely. The rest of my standard off-white walls were bare. Then the arrangement of dried flowers on the end table next to the lamp caught my eye. That counted as a decoration.

As I considered the rest of the room, my excitement died. What had one painting and a vase of crummy flowers accomplished? I'd created a glaring contrast to the rest of my home.

Boring off-white. Like the curtains covering the sliding

back door that led to my patio and my dingy old carpet. Pedestrian, like my second-hand furniture, which included a marred dinner table with a row of divots that made me think of a bear mauling. And the coffee table that reminded me of Grandma's house. Who was I kidding? My home's interior resembled an indifferent safehouse.

At least it was neat for once. Everything in its place. Except my bra. Right where I'd dropped it last night on the floor between the couch and the torchiere lamp. As I tossed it into my bedroom, I wondered if I'd have to give up comfortable habits like discarding my clothes on the floor after we were married. Closing the door behind me, I sniffed my armpits and ran my tongue over my minty-fresh teeth.

Ten minutes to go before Bowers arrived. Excitement and nervousness battled for control. Excitement over what engagement ring shopping meant. Nervous for the same reason. And I had little experience with jewelry. Not that I hated jewelry. It just wasn't on my list of priorities.

Nerves took the lead.

Stepping out my back door for a change of scenery, the heat immediately settled on me like a wool blanket worn at the beach. Tricky thing, the Arizona sun. While it allowed you to remain free of sticky sweat, luring the uninitiated into skipping sunscreen and loitering outdoors, it sucked the liquids from your body until even your eyeballs were thirsty.

The morning trills of a Lucy's warbler brought me to the stone wall that looked over the dry creek bed behind my house. Straining my ears, I waited for the comforting three-part call of the Gambel's quail that frequented the shrubby area near the bank.

When I set my hands on the wall, I heard a metal ping.

I'd forgotten the pseudo engagement ring. I twisted the pull tab off my finger. It left behind an indentation. Mortified, I rubbed the skin until it looked like I'd frolicked in ragweed. Better Bowers should think I had allergies than know I'd been prancing around the house pretending to show off my ring.

Finally, the quail called out. A good omen. If she could make her home in the overgrowth that had reclaimed the creek, surely, I could establish an inviting environment for Bowers and I to live in with my credit card and a few decorating magazines.

I stepped inside. After closing and locking the sliding door, I pulled the monotonous off-white curtains shut to keep out the heat.

Bowers would be here any minute.

Returning to the bathroom mirror for one last critical review, I forced out a reassuring nod. *Frankie Chandler, you've come a long way.* Since fleeing to Wolf Creek, Arizona, two years, eight months, and five days ago, I'd slowly rebuilt my confidence and carved out a new life.

I was engaged to the man I loved. A man who at one time feared touching me after I'd transmitted an image of an angry cat to him while we were holding hands.

My best friend lived a few miles away, and I saw her for breakfast at her bistro almost every morning. My pet psychic business, which I kept subtly tucked behind an animal behavior storefront called U-Behave, had grown to where I didn't have to buy my parents a tin of popcorn for Christmas.

When the doorbell rang, I straightened the collar on my blouse and ran a hand over my slacks. Bowers was just as lucky to have me as I was to have him. I'd have to repeat that mantra a few times, but it would stick. Eventually.

Especially after we married, and I discovered his faults. I walked to the front door and swung it open with a bright smile on my face. It wasn't Bowers.

The man on my front stoop stood over six feet tall, wore a tight-fitting white t-shirt over his muscled torso, and his smile showed off straight white teeth. In one hand, he held a dark-green gym bag. He ran the other hand over his short light-brown hair in a self-conscious move.

I couldn't remember how to breathe. I shouldn't need instructions, but the natural mechanics of pulling in air escaped me.

"Jeff?" I croaked.

And then the room swam.

BOOK CLUB QUESTIONS

What the Cluck? It's Murder

- Frankie is terrified of meeting Bowers' sisters. Have you had to meet the family or friends of someone you wanted to impress? Was it difficult? Did they turn out better than you expected?

- Dymphna was in love with Duane, much to the disapproval of her sisters. Have your family members ever disapproved of your friends? Did they turn out to be right? Or wrong?

- Do you think Dymphna was smart to keep her relationship with Duane a secret? Or do you think she should have been open about her feelings?

- Bowers didn't keep Frankie informed about the undercover operation. Do you think she had a right to know?

BOOK CLUB QUESTIONS

• June, realizing Frankie can't cook, gives her credit for the meal they cooked together even though June did most of the cooking. Do you think this was condescending? Or generous?

• When Frankie frees the squirrel at The Black Stallion, she does so without warning Bowers. Do you think she was wrong to put him in danger without telling him first? Or does this show she's confident he can handle anything?

• Frankie, falling back on habit from her days as a fake pet psychic, fibs a lot. (And omits the truth.) Do you think she can overcome this? Do you think it makes her unworthy of Bowers?

• Do you think Frankie and Bowers are ready for marriage? Explain your reasoning.

• Dympha has a habit of speaking in a whispery voice. What are some reasons she might do this?

• At the end of the story, Frankie leaves Chauncey with June. (And Hero.) Do you think she should have taken him home with her?

ABOUT THE AUTHOR

Jacqueline Vick writes the Frankie Chandler Pet Psychic Mystery Series about a woman who, after faking her psychic abilities for years, discovers animals *can* communicate with her. Her second series, the Harlow Brothers mysteries, features a former college linebacker turned etiquette author and his secretary brother. Her books are known for satirical humor and engaging characters who are reluctant to accept their greatest (and often embarrassing) gifts.

Visit the author at jacquelinevick.com.

ALSO BY JACQUELINE VICK

Frankie Chandler Mysteries

Barking Mad at Murder

A Bird's Eye View of Murder

An Almost Purrfect Murder

What the Cluck? It's Murder

A Scaly Tail of Murder

A Scape Goat for Murder

Some Like Murder Hot

Harlow Brother Mysteries

Civility Rules

Bad Behavior

Deadly Decorum

Standalone Novels

The Body Guy

An Unhealthy Attachment

Family Matters